EXPOSED

HOSTAGE RESCUE TEAM SERIES

KAYLEA CROSS

EXPOSED

Copyright © 2015
by Kaylea Cross

* * * * *

Cover Art & Formatting by
Sweet 'N Spicy Designs

* * * * *

ISBN: 978-1517062552

Dedication

To all the HRT fans out there. Thank you so much for loving this series and the cast of characters as much as I do!

Kaylea

Author's Note

Hope you enjoy watching Cruzie fall head over heels for the last person he ever would have expected. He took me by surprise a few times in this one, and I love him even more for that.

Vance is up next, and if the sparks are already flying for him in this story, you can just imagine the trouble he'll get into in his own book.

Happy reading!

Kaylea Cross

Chapter One

His victim didn't see him coming. They never did. Materializing from the shadows where he'd been waiting for the past hour, Bautista stepped out of the foliage behind his target. The man caught a glimpse of him in his peripheral, but too late. Always too late.

His victim started to whip around, one hand going for the weapon at the small of his back. Bautista caught his wrist in a crushing grip and wrenched his arm up behind his back. Bones snapped. The man jerked, drew breath to scream. Bautista locked his free arm around the man's throat and squeezed, cutting off the thin scream abruptly, the sound swallowed by the night.

"Screaming won't do you any good," he said close to the man's ear, his voice barely above a murmur. "There's no one around to hear you."

The guy struggled, his free hand coming up to claw at Bautista's forearm, locked tight around his throat. Having that element of surprise had given Bautista all the advantage he needed.

He held the blood choke, waited for the man to go

1

limp before dragging him into the rustic cabin. His victim would only be unconscious for a few moments. He wanted him alive for the rest. Wanted the man to feel everything he did to him. This bastard was going to pay for his crimes.

Insects hummed and frogs sang in the darkness, the air tinged with the damp, salty scent of the marsh. He dragged the tall, wiry body inside the shack and shut the door, placing him in the corner of the wood-paneled room before turning on the single light overhead. He'd already drawn the curtains over the two windows while he waited.

The man began to stir. Bautista knew the exact moment he regained awareness. He jerked and hissed in pain, cradling his broken wrist to his chest as he glanced around the room. When the man's wild-eyed gaze landed on him, Bautista smiled.

A cold, menacing smile that made the man's sweaty face turn paler.

"W-who are you?" he stuttered, his gaze locked on Bautista.

"Perez sent me."

The man's throat worked as he swallowed, the sound overly-pronounced in the taut silence. "I haven't done anything, man."

Liar. You know exactly what you did.

He really wanted to play it this way? Every time he went out on a hit, Bautista hoped one of his victims would show some balls. Stare back at him in defiance, give him a fair fight. Just one worthy opponent. That was all he asked.

Unfortunately, this man was like all the others. Weak and stupid. "No?"

He licked his lips, a nervous twitch of movement. "I've got bodyguards nearby."

"Not anymore." He'd taken both of them out with two shots from a silenced pistol.

A much kinder fate than what he would deliver to this piece of filth. He only tortured the true criminals and never killed the innocent. Some would call it a fucked-up code of honor, but it was the only code he had, and all that drove him.

The man shifted, bending one knee and leaning his weight to the side, his gaze raking toward the door. He thought he could run? There was no escape for this stupid fucking waste of skin.

"Look, I don't know what the hell you want," the man said with a show of bravado ruined by the grimace of pain at the end.

Bautista was in a sadistic mood tonight and decided to indulge him a little longer. He had all the time in the world to get what he needed out of the man. This far out into the Everglades there was no one around to hear his screams. And the gators would dispose of the body afterward. Once he torched this shack, come morning, there'd be no evidence left to find.

"Don't you?"

The man shook his head, the movement jerky, mechanical.

"You've been skimming funds from Perez for the past two months. Little bits would have been smarter, but you? Oh, no, you wanted to take a big chunk out of what wasn't yours and make a run for it."

He let that register for a moment, watched the man twitch before continuing. "Perez isn't a bad guy in most respects, but when it comes to business, he doesn't play. Those wire transfers you made last week?" He tisked. "Fucking stupid, man. Perez knows exactly where his money goes, and when some of it goes missing, he knows exactly how much. Down to the goddamn penny. And, funny thing, your wire transfers added up to the exact amount unspoken for."

A bead of sweat rolled down the side of the man's

face, dripped onto the white wife-beater he wore. "I was gonna pay him back. I didn't steal it, it was just a kind of advance to—"

Bautista threw his KA-BAR knife. The man screamed as the blade drove through his shoulder and buried into the wall behind him, pinning him to it.

Shrill shrieks rent the air, the pitch so high they grated on Bautista's ears. His victim thrashed around like a fish on a hook, a stream of blood already snaking down his useless arm, pooling on the floor around him.

Bautista didn't move from his position on the other side of the small room. He waited for the initial agony to fade, for the man to cease his useless thrashing, his broken wrist preventing him from grabbing the hilt of the knife to pull it free. Eventually he stopped struggling and sagged there, his breathing rapid and shallow, his face bathed in sweat, those hollow blue eyes locked on him.

"No one robs Perez and gets away with it," Bautista said in a flat voice.

Perez was the only man who'd earned Bautista's loyalty. His lieutenant had given him direction when he'd had none. Provided him the means to exact his revenge from the neighborhood thugs who had caved in his grandmother's skull and left her little better than a vegetable, sentencing them both to a life of hell.

The man before him now was just like those thugs. A spineless waste of space, an opportunistic parasite out to make himself rich off the backs of others, not caring who he stepped on along the way.

Bautista had researched his target carefully before coming on this op. This man had killed dozens of people to get where he was, including an innocent woman and child during a hit on another drug dealer. For that alone he deserved to die a slow, painful death.

"Who the fuck are you," the man panted between gritted teeth.

The trail of blood had nearly reached the toe of Bautista's boot now. Rather than answer, he hunkered down and drew a gloved fingertip through the glossy crimson liquid staining the weathered wood floorboards. He drew a thin oval, then stood.

A harsh intake of air came from his victim. The man's gaze flew from the symbol to Bautista's face, and the abject terror there filled him with fierce satisfaction. "*El Santo*," he breathed, his voice full of horror.

Bautista smiled again. A cold, hard smile. "You've heard of me."

His panicked expression was answer enough, but the man shook his head vigorously, his choppy breathing growing more labored. "Look, man, I'll give you whatever you want," he gasped out. "Whatever he's paying you, I'll double it."

His disgust for the man quadrupled. "I'm not interested in your money. Most of it belongs to Perez anyhow."

"No, man, I got my own. I'll triple your fee. Just let me go."

"Not gonna happen," he said in a flat tone.

The man shook his head, the movement jerky, his eyes wide. "Wait. Don't kill me. Please—"

Bautista withdrew another knife from the inside of his jacket. A slender switchblade he'd had custom made to fit his grip perfectly.

The man fell silent, his stare locked on the flashing silver blade.

Better. Pleas never worked on him. He preferred it when his victims showed some spine, some sort of fire at least before they died.

Not this one though. The man cringed as Bautista approached, his rubber-soled boots almost silent on the wood floor. He was still cradling his broken wrist in his lap.

Bautista lashed out with one foot, stomped on it. The answering scream turned blood curdling when he immediately sliced through one strap of the wife-beater and carved his symbol into the left side of the man's bare chest.

A halo. Marking him as a victim of *el Santo*.

"No! Fuck you, no! Lemme go," he cried, writhing against the wall.

He should have saved his breath, because his pleas fell on deaf ears. In a few minutes when Bautista was finished with him, he'd go straight to hell where he belonged.

Before he left he'd take pictures for proof of death, which Perez would circulate to send a message to the others. Then he'd dump the body for the gators and leave, head back to Miami and collect his ridiculous paycheck his lieutenant always gave him for a hit. Money Bautista funneled carefully into an offshore account in the Caymans and managed with the knowledge he'd accumulated while earning his degree in finance years ago.

After that, he'd likely have at least a few days off before another job came in. And another one *would* come in. Because in his world, there were always more victims for him to hunt.

Raising the switchblade high, letting the light glint off the blade and the blood dripping from it, he set about cutting his victim's blackened soul free in the most painful way possible.

****

"Man, I'm looking forward to having some home cookin' tonight."

Special Agent Ethan Cruz glanced sideways at his best friend Vance, seated beside him in the front passenger seat of the rental truck they'd picked up at the airport last night. "You wish. We're not going there for dinner, we're just stopping in to say hi and for you and my mom to get a fix of each other before we head to the hotel to meet the rest of the guys. You'll get your fill of her cooking on Saturday anyway."

"But that's two whole days from now," he complained.

Ethan grinned and reached for the knob on the dash, turning it to a country music station. "Here, focus on this instead. And don't say I never do anything for you. You know I hate this Hee Haw shit."

Vance's expression brightened and he began nodding in time to the male singer's voice. "It's 'cuz you have no taste in real music, my brother. No taste at all."

Now he laughed and just for fun, rolled down the windows before blasting it. They made for a comical picture in this neighborhood. "Look at us, two homies cruising through my old neighborhood, cranking out the country tunes."

This area of Miami Gardens wasn't as rough as some, but it was still a long way from the safer, middle-class neighborhoods to the south of the city. Rap and hip-hop were the soundtrack here, not country.

Hard-edged, tatted guys from their teens through their thirties stood around smoking on street corners even though it was early afternoon on a Thursday. Here it was mostly Cuban or Puerto Rican families like his own, blue-collar workers or dealers struggling to make ends meet, living from paycheck to paycheck. A lot of those were issued from the welfare department.

Everyone stopped and stared at them as they drove by, unfamiliar tunes pulsing through the open windows.

"Think they got a hate-on for my music or something?" Vance asked dryly.

"They've never seen anything like you before,

Vance, I guaran-damn-tee it."

His teammate grinned, showing even, white teeth against his dark skin as he tipped the brim of his black felt cowboy hat. "Can't help it that I'm a redneck."

Right down to the shitkickers he wore, Ethan thought with a fond grin. "You're one of a kind, my friend. I'll give you that."

Vance settled back against his seat, that amused grin still in place. "Sticks and stones, man. Sticks and stones."

They pulled through an intersection and crossed into a slightly nicer area, but there were still plenty of dealers and junkies around on the corners looking to either sell or score a fix. "Wonder how many of these guys are selling or using product from Fuentes?" Vance mused.

"All of them, probably," Ethan muttered, ignoring the strange looks they got.

"Bet it sure makes you glad you made the right decision in getting outta here when you did, huh?"

"No shit," he answered. He could easily have wound up being one of the guys standing around on a street corner here in the middle of the day, selling drugs. "But my mama didn't raise no fools."

Vance leveled a sideways look at him. "You mean she beat the fear of God into you whenever you stepped outta line."

"Yeah, and that too." He'd run with a rough crowd through high school, none of whom he kept in touch with. Low-level gang member wannabes, looking to gain street cred and make a fast buck. Last he'd heard, most of them either had been or were currently in jail, and more than a handful were dead.

Luckily his mom hadn't been willing to allow her boy to go down that road. She and his father had ridden his ass through eleventh and twelfth grades, making sure he stayed out of trouble and graduated. And when he did, the next day they marched him down to the closest Marine recruiting office.

He'd been itching for the chance to leave home and see some of the world beyond Miami, and knew if he continued along the same path he was on he'd wind up in jail or dead. He'd been only too happy to sign the contract.

Goodbye Miami, hello Parris Island. Not an easy transition to make, but the best thing that had ever happened to him.

"Whatever, it's not like you were such an angel either," Ethan muttered.

"Sure as hell was, compared to you, anyway. My daddy woulda worn out his belt on me if I'd pulled half the shit you did." Vance had been raised in Oklahoma by a hard-working, single dad farmer who subscribed to the *spare the rod, spoil the child* philosophy. And Vance sure as hell hadn't been spoiled. Probably why he'd developed such a soft spot for Ethan's mom right off the bat, since she loved to spoil the people close to her. They adored each other and she considered Vance her adopted son.

"Well, my dad tried that a few times too. Didn't take." And besides, seeing disappointment in his mother's eyes after he'd done something stupid was way worse than any whupping his father could dish out with his belt.

He shook his head and continued. "When I think of what I put my mom through all those years, I thank my lucky stars she didn't give up on me. No idea how she put up with me back then."

"I don't know how we put up with you *now*," Vance remarked, jabbing him in the right shoulder with a meaty fist. Right where he'd taken two rubber bullets earlier that morning while working in the shoot house with the DEA's FAST team.

Ethan winced and gritted his teeth. "You suck," he grumbled.

Vance's grin was unrepentant. "Yup. So tell me more about that girl you mentioned before."

Ethan's mind went blank for a second. "What girl?" He hadn't dated anyone for a couple months. Things had been crazy at work lately, ever since the terrorist attacks at the Qureshi trial back in April. It was hard enough to date, let alone have a relationship with someone when he couldn't tell the woman what he really did or explain why he had to suddenly cancel or even leave partway through a date.

That never went over too well with the ladies, and so far in his time with the FBI's Hostage Rescue Team, none of them had stuck around long enough to find out the truth. Which was fine for now, since he was happy with keeping things casual.

Vance shot him an annoyed frown. "You know, the one who lived near you growing up. You told me her parents' place is across from your mom's, and that she's an Assistant U.S. Attorney down here linked to the Fuentes case."

Oh. *That* girl. "Marisol Lorenzo."

"Her family Puerto Rican too?"

"No, Cuban." He hadn't seen her in four years, when she'd been partway through her law degree and he'd been getting ready to try out for the HRT. He'd been shocked to find the little-girl-next-door was all grown up, and not only that, but *hot*. The attraction he'd felt toward her had made him damned uncomfortable.

Since then he'd gotten periodic updates about her from his mother, who was still friends with Marisol's mom, but that was all. "Yeah, when I checked a couple weeks back I found out she landed a job with their High Intensity Drug Trafficking Area office in West Miami."

Vance nodded. "That's cool. Good for her."

"No, *not* good for her," Ethan said in a flat tone. "She's smart and always was driven, but she's only been on the job for a few months and has never dealt with anyone like Fuentes before. With this turf war going on between all his lieutenants, they'll be looking into who's involved with the case at the U.S. Attorney's office. She'll be at risk. You know exactly what kind of risk I'm talking about."

Together with the FAST team they'd been going over detailed intel compiled on the known lieutenants and their enforcers. One enforcer in particular had a reputation for making hardened criminals shit their pants when he showed up. Word on the street was, his victims begged for death before he ended their misery.

Ethan didn't want Marisol or anyone else he cared about within a hundred miles of someone like *el Santo*, let alone to wind up on his radar. "I'm going to talk to her while I'm in town, just to make sure she understands what she's dealing with and that she's taking the right precautions."

When Vance stared at him, eyebrows raised, Ethan scowled. "What?"

"That's pretty overbearing, considering you haven't seen her in four years, don't ya think?"

Ethan shrugged, the motion slightly belligerent. "She's been a friend of my family forever. I used to look out for her when we were growing up. It's no different now." If he felt she might be in danger, he was damn sure going to say something. He had elite training and she didn't. It was his responsibility to ensure she knew the stakes, so she could take appropriate precautions.

"If she's an Assistant U.S. Attorney, then she's smart enough to know the threat she's facing by working on this case," Vance pointed out in that maddeningly calm, practical way that irritated the shit out of Ethan when it pertained to something in his personal life. This time was no different.

"She's smart, but she's not street smart, even though she grew up here." She wasn't clueless about danger, not by any means, but he still didn't like it.

From the moment his mother had first mentioned it to him a few weeks ago, the thought of her being in the crosshairs of any one of Fuentes's men made all his hackles go up. The U.S. Attorney's office was trying to get the asshole to agree to a deal wherein he turned over some of his more ruthless lieutenants in exchange for a reduced sentence.

Because there was no way he wouldn't be convicted on multiple federal offenses once his case went to trial. Until his arrest the man had controlled a vast empire that stretched along the entire Gulf Coast and up the eastern seaboard.

Drugs, weapons, money laundering. And women. All bought, sold and traded on a private black market that had made Fuentes into a billionaire by age thirty. And those charges didn't even count the insane number of murders he was purported to have ordered. Thankfully he'd been caught while trying to flee to a non-extradition country.

Ethan turned the corner onto the street where he'd grown up. His parents' place was the second from the end of the block, on the right. A tidy one-story ranch-style house done up on a cheery yellow stucco with a bright red front door.

On the sidewalk thirty yards up from the house, a small crowd had gathered around one of the old trees along the side of the street.

"Looks like something exciting's going on," Vance remarked, ducking his head to get a better view. "Someone's halfway up that big-ass tree."

The huge live oak halfway up the block that Ethan and the other neighborhood kids had climbed thousands of times while growing up on this street. He slowed and turned down the music as everyone turned their heads to look at the SUV.

Pulling up to the curb, he closed the windows, put

the SUV in park and ducked a little to peer through the windshield. Whoever was up the tree looked like they were having trouble getting down.

Moments later, a shapely rear end clad in what looked like black yoga pants appeared in a gap between the foliage.

"Well, look at that. A bona fide damsel in distress, and it turns out I haven't done my good deed for the day yet," Vance said with a grin and reached for his door handle.

Ethan popped his own door open and stepped out into the humid Miami heat. The figure in the tree shifted, scooted down a sturdy branch and seemed to cling there, frozen. She had long, dark hair secured into a ponytail that ran down between her shoulder blades.

The crowd had turned away from Ethan and Vance and stood watching the woman again. Nobody seemed to be offering assistance.

Then the woman in the tree turned her head and recognition slammed into Ethan.

"Speak of the devil," he murmured with a smile, and hurried past Vance to get to her first.

Chapter Two

O kay, this wasn't how she'd planned to spend her afternoon off.

Marisol blew a stray strand of hair out of her mouth and tightened her grip on the branch of the live oak. It was ninety-two freaking degrees out and humid enough to coat her skin in a fine sheen of sweat that wasn't improving her grip any.

Tamping down her annoyance at the small crowd gathered around the base of the tree, she considered her next move. The onlookers were mostly elderly residents who lived on the street, a few mothers and their children. They'd been watching her so far futile efforts for the past ten minutes, occasionally offering up oh-so-helpful advice like, "try grabbing that branch to your left," "be careful" or, her favorite, "you should have called the fire department instead."

Really nice when she was already halfway up the freaking tree.

Mrs. Fernandez stood directly below her, wringing her hands in distress, her gray hair full of purple Velcro rollers. "He's climbing higher, Soli, quick."

Marisol glanced up and aimed a glare at the long-haired black-and-white cat peering down at her from another branch fifteen feet above her head, its green eyes curious.

"You little bugger," she muttered under her breath. She knew he was doing this on purpose, probably enjoyed seeing her make a spectacle of herself. Cats were like that.

"Careful—don't scare him! Hugo, come on, baby, come to mama." She crooned it again in Spanish for good measure.

Marisol was searching for the next good foothold when someone drove up behind her with country music blasting from their sound system. The music was so out of place in this neighborhood that she glanced back to look at the black SUV with tinted windows parking at the curb. Then the music shut off and Hugo let out a pathetic-sounding mewl that made Mrs. Fernandez frantic.

"Oh, my baby, he's so scared! Quick, Soli. Just a little farther. You can do it."

If I break my neck because I volunteered to go after this stupid cat, I'm gonna be pissed.

Setting her jaw, she carefully shifted her weight so she could reach for the next branch up. The sole of her sneaker slipped on the rough bark. She let out a squeak and grabbed hold of the closest branch, swaying precariously, sending leaves scattering to the ground. The small crowd let out a collective gasp.

Heart pounding, she didn't dare move. The closest branch above her was too far away to grab, and the one below was just as far. Going up from here was as impossible as getting back down again.

Crap. Now she was stuck halfway up the freaking tree, same as the cat. *I should have called the fire department instead.*

"Looks like you could use a hand up there."

She whipped her head around at the sound of that

masculine voice coming from beneath her. Her heart stuttered when she found herself staring down at none other than Ethan Cruz, former neighborhood bad boy-turned-Marine, and the object of all her teenage fantasies.

As well as plenty of her X-rated adult ones.

Those arresting golden brown eyes locked on hers, glinting with humor. He wore a gray T-shirt that hugged his muscular chest and left his sexy, ripped arms bare, exposing the tats on the back of each forearm. "Hey," she blurted out, surprised to see him, embarrassed that he'd see her like this.

"You stuck?" He was standing next to a heavily muscled black guy wearing cowboy boots and a cowboy hat. That explained the country music, then. Both men were watching her intently, along with everyone else. With her attention on the cat, she hadn't realized just how many people had come out to see what was going on.

Her face heated as blood rushed to her cheeks. There was no point denying it. She wasn't getting any higher or lower on her own and she was woman enough to admit it. "Yeah. Trying to get the cat down." She pointed to Hugo, still peering down at her.

Ethan nodded once, his eyes twinkling in that devilish way of his. "Hang on."

Before she could say anything he jumped up and caught hold of the lowest branch. In a show of controlled strength that made her insides flutter he pushed up with his arms to boost himself up, the cut muscles in his chest and shoulders straining against the gray T-shirt that fit him like a second skin, his biceps and forearms bulging. She blinked to clear the image from her brain but she was pretty sure it was burned there permanently now.

He grabbed the branch beside her and swung up onto it, landing on his feet with a catlike grace less than two feet away.

Face to face with him for the first time in four years,

she was surprised at how hard her heart pounded. He looked even better than she remembered, and she remembered plenty. "Hi." At the moment she couldn't come up with anything more intelligent to say.

"Hi." His gaze drifted over her once before coming back to her eyes. "You hurt?"

"Not yet, but I'm headed that way. Guess I'm not as good at climbing trees as I used to be," she offered with a sheepish smile.

He smiled back at her, a dimple appearing in his lean cheek beneath the few days' worth of dark stubble on his face. Way too gorgeous for his—or any woman's—own good. "Don't worry, I'll get you down." Tilting his head back, he searched through the branches. "So, Hugo, huh?"

"Yes. When I got halfway to him he bolted even higher up." Ungrateful little bastard.

"You stay put. I'll get him." He gripped the next branch up and proceeded to climb the tree like he was some kind of jungle animal. Fluid, powerful. It was amazing to watch, really. And if her gaze kept sliding down the taut muscles of his spine to the jeans that clung so perfectly to his equally hard butt, well, she was only human.

"Oh! Be careful—don't scare him any higher," Mrs. Fernandez called out from below.

Ethan didn't answer, just climbed up to the cat, grabbed it by the scruff and started climbing back down, ignoring its indignant yowls and hisses. When he reached her level he paused and tucked the animal in the curve of one thick bicep. Hugo's ears were flat against his head, eyes wide, fluffy tail twitching like a metronome. Just waiting to sink his fangs into Ethan, wherever he could reach.

"He's a biter," Marisol warned.

"Better not, after I just rescued him," Ethan muttered, sending the cat a threatening glare before turning his attention back to her. "You good here for a minute?"

She blew out a breath. "Yeah." Mostly she was just embarrassed and wanted to get home. She'd already endured a hot yoga class before coming here to visit her mother and happening upon Mrs. Fernandez calling to her cat in the damn tree. This is what being a Good Samaritan got a person. Public humiliation.

Ethan nodded. "'Kay. Hang tight."

It's not like I'm going anywhere.

He climbed to the ground and handed the cat to Mrs. Fernandez. She was crying now, hugging Hugo to her as he squalled and tried frantically to squirm away from her, ears pinned back and his eyes big and round.

"You can all go home now," Ethan announced to the onlookers, taking charge of the situation just like he always had. "I'll get Soli down."

She closed her eyes and sighed, shaking her head at herself. Once again Ethan was the hero riding to her rescue, making her feel like an awkward fifteen-year-old kid all over again. Except instead of scaring off her pushy date that wouldn't stop at a goodnight kiss, this time he was somehow going to get her out of this tree. At least he'd sent the gawkers away first.

"Can you get back down to the branch below you?" he called up.

She angled around to see which one he was talking about. "Yeah, think so." With some maneuvering and careful movements she managed to lower herself down and get her feet planted on it.

Her fingers dug into the rough bark as she leaned her weight against the solid trunk. When they were kids she'd climbed this tree like a monkey more times than she could count, even dangling upside down from her bent knees. Humbling to know how much her flexibility and upper body strength had diminished since then.

Ethan moved around below her. "Okay, I'm right beneath you. Sit down on the branch and push off toward me. I'll catch you."

He'd *catch* her? From this height? "Uh, I don't know if that's a good idea." She'd flatten him. They'd both wind up with broken bones.

"Come on." He lifted both muscular arms toward her, beckoned with his hands impatiently. "Drop down and jump."

God, she just wanted to go home. "Fine."

She lowered herself into a sitting position on the branch and peered down at him, ignoring his friend, who stood watching all this without saying a word. It was at least twelve feet down. She'd just seen a reminder of how strong Ethan was, but what if he missed her? She was working on the biggest case of her career so far, and a busted leg or pelvis would put a serious hitch in her plans.

His friend stood watch, his hands shoved in his front jeans pockets, face shadowed by the wide brim of his black cowboy hat. Ethan waved a hand again, signaling for her to hurry up. "What, you don't trust me all of a sudden? Come on, jump."

Oh, she trusted him. Her issues with him had never been about trusting him with her safety.

Still, her heart beat fast and her palms grew damp. With as much dignity as she could muster she leaned forward and pushed off the branch. She held in a yelp as she fell toward him.

Strong arms caught her a heartbeat later. Automatically she grabbed hold of his broad shoulders, a moment's shock zinging through her at the feel of those corded muscles beneath her hands. She'd fantasized about touching Ethan's muscles for years in something other than a platonic hug, but never imagined it would happen like this.

He bent his knees as he caught her, absorbing her

weight and slowing her descent. She had only another moment to be conscious of the hard length of him pressed against her front, for the warmth of his body to register before he released her. And he smelled good too, like soap and a hint of clean aftershave. "There," he said. "You okay?"

"Yes. Thanks." Her voice sounded a little breathless, which she blamed on the receding tide of adrenaline and not the feel of Ethan's body. Growing up, he'd always seen her as naïve and helpless, in need of protection. Throughout her teen years she'd wanted him to see her as more than that, and definitely not as a little sister of sorts. Because for many years now, her thoughts about him had been anything but sisterly.

Even four years ago he still hadn't seemed to notice that she was all grown up. She'd dreamed of turning his image of her on its head the next time they saw each other. Her dressed in a sleek skirt suit, hair and makeup done just so, having landed a kickass legal position. The image of polished, sophisticated corporate grace.

She'd managed the career part, but now she stood before him with salt stains showing on her yoga outfit.

So much for that fantasy.

"No worries." He gestured to the man next to him. "This is my buddy, Sawyer Vance. Vance, this is Marisol."

She shook his hand. His hand was huge around hers, but gentle. "Nice to meet you."

His dark eyes seemed to twinkle at her. "Likewise."

She tucked a strand of hair that had escaped her ponytail back behind her ear, acutely conscious of how good Ethan looked and how gross she was. "So, what are you doing here?"

"We're in Miami for a work thing. Wanted to stop by and see my mom for a bit."

She nodded. She knew he worked for the FBI now.

Their mothers talked to each other all the time. They were both widows, Marisol's dad having died of a heart attack and Ethan's dying in a car wreck years ago. They knew everything about each other's kids. Marisol eyed Ethan. Considering the shape he and Vance were both in though, she guessed they didn't have desk jobs with the Bureau.

"Heard you're with the U.S. Attorney's office down here," he said.

Her mother would have been sure to pass that onto Mama Cruz as soon as it happened. "Yeah, just started there a few months ago as an assistant attorney."

He nodded once. "Glad to see you made your dream come true."

She smiled. "Thanks." It had taken a lot of hard work and sacrifice and even some blind good luck to land this job, but now that it was hers she planned to work her ass off even more, make a name for herself. The Fuentes case was going to be her launch pad.

"You'll be working some big cases."

"Working on one now," she said without elaborating.

He nodded, something like concern in his eyes. "Listen, I wanted to talk to you about—"

"Oh, it *is* you!"

They all turned to see Mama Cruz up the street, running down her front steps then come jogging up the sidewalk toward them. Ethan's friend broke into a big smile and met her halfway, picking the petite woman up in a big bear hug. They were both laughing as he set her back down, the happy sound carrying to where Marisol stood with Ethan.

"Wow, she seems really happy to see him," she said in surprise.

Ethan snorted, but his grin was full of fondness as he watched them. "Those two are ridiculous. When he's around I definitely come in second."

He didn't seem too upset by that, however, and

hugged his mother tight when she reached them. "Oh, I'm so glad you got to see each other," Mama Cruz said, giving them a delighted smile as she looked between her and Ethan. "You were able to get Hugo down then?" she asked Marisol.

"No, Ethan did. And then he got me out of the tree after."

Mama Cruz beamed up at her son and patted his cheek. "That's my boy." She linked arms with both men and started back toward her house, glancing at Marisol. "Soli, you'll join us for lunch?"

"Thanks, but I can't. Have to go home and clean up before I head into the office for a while." Most of the night, probably.

She stopped and looked back at her. "Oh."

"Sorry." She aimed another smile at Ethan. "Thanks for the help."

"Anytime. But hey, I still want to talk to you about something."

She couldn't imagine what, after all this time without any contact. "Your mom's got my number. Nice to meet you, Sawyer."

The other man tipped the brim of his hat in a show of manners so unusual she couldn't help but be delighted. "You too."

Without waiting for a response from Ethan she crossed the street and headed for her car, feeling his stare on her the entire time. She shut the door and let out a heavy sigh before starting the ignition, refusing to look back.

Well, damn. Better luck with that impression thing next time.

Chapter Three

E than tugged a fresh T-shirt over his head and pulled his phone from his pocket when it buzzed. But it wasn't Marisol finally texting him, it was his sister. He was surprised by the amount of disappointment filtering through him as he slid it back into his pocket. He'd call Carmela back later.

"Wow, that's a long face. Not who you were hoping for, huh?" Jake Evers said to him as he stored his equipment into a locker beside Ethan's in the DEA facility they'd been training in all day.

He grunted in response.

Evers stopped and gave him a sharp look, lifted an eyebrow. "For you that reaction's damn near testy, which can only mean one thing: you're waiting on a woman to call you back. Who is she, this girl who hasn't succumbed to the infamous Cruzie charm yet? I wanna meet her."

"Yeah," Nate "Doc" Schroder drawled to Evers's right, watching Ethan with interest. "Anyone we know?" It had taken some getting used to, calling him plain Doc rather than Dr. Feelgood, the nickname everyone had used for the past several months. Schroder had made it clear

23

anyone calling him the latter ever again would get a throat punch, now that he was with Taya. Since Ethan respected the former PJ, he'd abided by his wishes.

For the most part.

"Nope," Ethan said. And he didn't *want* them to know Marisol. Even though she had to be what, twenty-five by now, she was still way too innocent for the likes of him and his teammates. She'd always been like that, the serious middle child of the three Lorenzo girls.

Studious and hard working, she'd stayed home on Saturday night instead of partying it up with the local guys the way all her friends had. The virtuous air she'd had back then had been obvious and Ethan had made sure to look out for her. Innocence like that was to be protected and cherished, especially in their tough neighborhood.

Schroder shut his locker and leaned against it, arms folded across his chest. "Now that's not gonna cut it with me. You were all over me about the scoop with Taya not even a month ago. Fair's fair, dude. Spill."

Ethan stowed his tactical vest in his locker and set some extra magazines on the top shelf, then shut the metal door. "It's nothing, just an old friend I'm trying to help out."

If she'd ever return his damn text or actually call him back. He knew she was busy working on the case, but damn. He'd gotten her number from his mom before leaving yesterday afternoon. Marisol was an educated adult and capable of taking care of herself, but he knew for a fact she'd never dealt with anyone like Fuentes and his crew. Even though Ethan hadn't had contact with her over the past few years and they weren't really friends anymore, he still cared and wanted her safe.

"What about you?" Schroder said to Vance, who'd just walked in the room a few seconds ago. "You know this girl he's hung up on?"

"I'm not hung up on her," Ethan argued. "She's just

an old friend. Like a sister."

Okay, not at all, and she sure as hell looked nothing like the girl he'd grown up with anymore. The body on her was impossible to ignore.

He remembered exactly what those trim curves had felt like up against him yesterday, and how his body had reacted. In an extremely un-brotherly manner he hoped she hadn't noticed because he'd been quick to set her away from him.

Vance put on that shuttered expression he used whenever he was hiding something. "Dunno."

Evers and Schroder exchanged knowing glances before looking back at Vance. "Dude, even a stranger would know you're holding out on us with that look."

Vance shook his head, his face totally blank now. "Nope. Don't know anything."

"Bullshit," Schroder said with a grin.

Ethan sighed. "She's working with the U.S. Attorney's office on the Fuentes case, all right? I've known her since she was five and want to make sure she knows what the hell she's up against, check that she's taking steps to protect herself. All right? Happy?" Yeah, he knew she was smart and all grown up, but he still needed to know she was being cautious. Marisol held a special place in his heart, always had.

Schroder lost the grin. They all knew about *el Santo* and the other enforcers out there hunting each other in the turf war raging while Fuentes was trapped behind bars. "Oh." He slanted a look at Vance. "Like Cruz's sister, huh?"

Vance's face went even stiffer, a sure sign he was covering something. He was the worst poker player on the team, which was why Ethan and the others loved playing him.

Schroder pounced, pointing at Vance. "Right there. Right there that tells me what I need to know." He snickered to himself. "Is she hot?"

Vance dropped the I-don't-know-anything act and grinned. "She's not hard to look at." His gaze shot to Ethan. "Not his usual type, though."

"I have a type?" he demanded in annoyance. First he'd heard of it.

Now all three of his teammates looked at each other. "Yeah," Vance said with a shrug.

"Really? And what type is that?" He raised an eyebrow and folded his arms across his chest.

"Young, hot and a bit uh...shallow."

"Whatever," he scoffed. It wasn't like he had a wide variety of women to choose from with his work schedule, not outside of one-night stands or a weekend fling. The good women weren't interested in light and casual for very long and he couldn't blame them. He was tired of it too. "Anyway, it's not like that with her, so you guys can find something else to hypothesize about."

"What's really got his panties in a twist," Vance added, apparently done with holding back now, "is that she's more interested in her work than in him. Barely gave him a second glance when we saw her yesterday. His ego's smarting. Fun to watch, actually."

Ethan rolled his eyes. "You three feel free to stay here and gossip some more. I'm getting some coffee."

It'd been three long days of pre-dawn wakeups and not hitting their hotel until almost midnight. They still had another meeting to get through tonight before he could head to their hotel and crash, and the moment they got a lock on their current target's location, they'd be heading out with the DEA boys to grab him. Here Ethan was trying to help watch out for Marisol, and she couldn't be bothered to give him the time of day.

He strode out to the kitchen area where his other three teammates were chowing down on cold pizza from last night. The coffee pot was almost empty. "How old is this?"

"Just made it ten minutes ago," Bauer answered between bites. His plate held no less than half a dozen crusts and he didn't look like he'd be slowing down any time soon. Biggest guy on the team meant one of the biggest appetites, too.

As he poured the little coffee that was left into a mug and started a fresh pot, Ethan frowned. If he was honest with himself, Marisol brushing him off wasn't all that was bugging him. Bumping into her yesterday had been a shock, and not an altogether pleasant one.

Seeing her in that skin-tight yoga outfit and looking into those sea green eyes, a shock of male awareness had shot through him. Then when he'd caught her, the feel of her lithe curves pressed to him had made it impossible to see her as anything but a woman rather than the-girl-next-door he'd grown up with. He'd worked hard at reminding himself she was the latter the past few times he'd come home to visit, purposely maintaining that mental barrier between them. Safer that way.

He knew when a woman was interested in him, and knew Marisol had had a crush on him off and on over the years. Even up until he'd left the Corps he'd sometimes caught her looking at him with that quiet yearning he didn't want to encourage.

The ironic thing was, now that she was all grown up, she'd looked at him with friendly recognition and nothing more. She'd been composed, a little remote. Why did that bother him? Hell, maybe his ego *was* smarting that she was ignoring him.

With the dregs of the coffee in hand, he left the room and stepped outside into the parking lot for some privacy and fresh air. He texted Marisol again, the early evening air was warm and muggy against his skin.

Really need to talk to you. When's a good time?

Not expecting a response any time soon, he started

to slip the phone back into his pocket and was surprised when it buzzed. He whipped it back out, read the text.

Busy at work. Will try to call you tonight if not too late.

He responded immediately. *Call me no matter when.*

She answered a moment later. *Okay.*

Putting his phone away, he wasn't convinced she'd actually follow through. But this was too important for him to let go. So if she didn't call, he'd have to take matters into his own hands.

****

The smell of the place still made him feel ill. Stale air, old people and an underlying scent of sickness that pervaded everything, combined with a heaviness to the air that came with being in what amounted to a warehouse that held people waiting to die. Souls and minds trapped in shells of bodies, forced to linger until their hearts finally gave out.

Bautista entered the care home and took the elevator to the third floor. The nurses at the desk there smiled at him but he didn't acknowledge them, just continued on to the last room in the corridor that looked out over the park across the street.

Not that his *abuela* had ever been able to enjoy the view.

He'd still insisted she have this room though, in the most state-of-the-art facility in southern Florida. It was the least he could do for her while she waited to die. And God knew he could afford it.

They'd propped the head of her bed up a little, had the foot elevated slightly so her knees were bent. The IV and gastro tubes were taped to her face and arm, braced with towels and special pillows to keep her muscles from seizing completely. Her deep blue eyes were partially open, staring sightlessly across the room while soft Latin music played from the top-of-the-line sound system he'd bought for her a year ago.

"Hi, *abuelita*," he murmured, bending to kiss her forehead, right where one of her surgical scars bisected the skin between her eyebrows.

Her eyelids flickered and eyes moved slightly, settling in his direction before wandering again.

Bautista set about adjusting her pillows and spent a few minutes manipulating her contractured limbs. She had only a few inches of movement at her elbows and wrists and they had to ensure she maintained that small range of motion. Her mattress was specially designed to reduce pressure points and help avoid bedsores.

The physical therapists worked hard to keep what little motion she had left. He knew, because he checked the room often, without them knowing. Remotely, using the hidden surveillance cameras he'd installed on three sides of the room. He watched the staff carefully to ensure they were doing their jobs and not abusing his grandmother, and he paid them well for it. If anyone dared abuse her here, they'd suffer dearly.

And he'd kill anyone who harmed her.

Even after all these years he hated coming here, hated seeing her like this. For twenty-two years she'd lain like this, a vegetable. At least in the past few years he'd made enough money to ensure she had what comforts he could give.

He lowered his weight into the leather easy chair beside her bed, forced himself to talk to her. About nothing, really. The weather. About the view of the park she would never see.

He didn't know if any of his words registered but he knew the pitch of his voice did. His grandmother still recognized his voice, knew when he visited. Her pulse rate would quicken when he spoke to her, then settle, and her eye movement would slow. He liked to think his presence relaxed her. That was why he came twice a week when he was home in Miami. Well, that and guilt.

He still felt responsible for what had happened to her. If he'd been home that day instead of off looking to escape from his own troubles, he might have been able to stop them. Would have shot those cowardly fuckers that had broken into his sweet *abuelita's* house looking for cash and jewelry they could turn over fast to buy their next fix of drugs.

His brave grandmother hadn't cowered from them though. Oh no, she'd stood her ground and told them off. The neighbors had heard her shouting right before one of them had taken a baseball bat to her head and caved her skull in.

That day he'd lost what little he had. A relative who'd given a lonely, bullied little boy a safe place to stay, and showed him the miracle of unconditional love.

He'd walked in to see the paramedics carrying his grandmother out of the kitchen on a stretcher, her head wrapped in bandages. Her blood had stained the linoleum floor, had splattered the cheerful yellow rose wallpaper near the table where he'd sat and done his homework and eaten home cooked meals. They'd taken him away and he'd bounced from foster home to foster home until he wished he'd died defending her that day.

Bautista blinked, clearing away the images imprinted in his mind, consciously uncurled his fists on the armrests of the leather chair. His time in the Army had saved him.

It had also made him into what he was today: a trained killer. He'd gained and perfected the skills he used to take lives. Then he'd met Perez, and the man had given him the one thing he'd craved most in the last twenty-two years.

Revenge.

Perez had given him his first job as a contract killer.

Not a calling that Bautista had been looking for, but one that had come to him. And it suited him perfectly. He'd known it from the moment he'd first realized why Perez had approached him.

He'd listened to the intel on the two targets; two low-level drug runners that were causing Perez trouble in Miami, both who had recently been paroled from prison for another murder they'd committed. He'd recognized their faces instantly as his *abuelita's* attackers. Perez had done his homework. Somehow he'd known Bautista would jump at the chance to take them out.

From that moment on, they'd been dead men walking.

Bautista had hunted them down relentlessly, paid them back for what they'd done. Tortured them for hours before finally caving in one of their skulls with a bat while the other one cried and sniveled in the corner, begging futilely to be spared the same fate.

Since then he'd dispatched many others to hell with those first victims, and he slept just fine at night.

His gaze slid over to his grandmother, past her to the medical equipment and monitors she was hooked up to, her treasured framed icons of the Virgin at her bedside, passed down from her Spanish ancestors. Her pulse and heart rate were calm, her respiration rate relaxed. Because he was near.

So many times he'd wanted to tell her what he'd done, but he hadn't. He knew she would have hated what he'd become, that she wouldn't have condoned his idea of justice and he never knew who might be listening anyway. The only reason he was still alive, still free, was because he was always so careful. Careful enough that no one ever found out who he really was.

A tap at the door made him look up. His heart lurched when *her* face appeared in the opening. He rose from his chair automatically, all his muscles locked.

Julia gave him a warm smile from the doorway, her expression soft. "Had a feeling I might see you this week," she said. "Want some company?"

"Sure," he said, a strange sense of relief filling him as she stepped inside and shut the door. She'd been volunteering twice a week at the nursing home for almost three months now. He'd gotten to know her pretty well, both from their conversations and the background check he'd done on her.

That flow of information only went one way though.

She was the only person he'd ever really talked with here, aside from the doctor in charge of his grandmother's care. He didn't care for company, but with her he didn't mind. In fact, he found himself hoping he'd see her every time he came here.

Julia crossed over to his grandmother's bed and perched on the foot of it, glanced at the monitors. Another smile lit her face, her mink brown hair shining in the sunlight streaming through the windows. "She loves it when you come to see her."

Bautista sat again, hating the sudden awkwardness he felt. He knew all about her, some of it by underhanded means, and she knew next to nothing about him. It felt like a violation of sorts. "I'm glad to come." He owed his grandmother that much at least.

"I wish all the patients here were as lucky to have such a devoted family member. Most of them lie in their beds day in and day out without anyone but the staff visiting them."

"She was good to me." Better than anyone ever had been, or ever would be.

She'd taken him in immediately, no questions asked, when his addict mother had died of an overdose, and done everything in her power to steer him away from the lifestyle that had killed her only child. Walking him to and from school each day, helping him with his homework.

Consoling him with hugs and homemade cookies when he broke down in tears when the bullying became too much. Keeping him on the straight and narrow.

Sometimes he thought it might be kinder to tell her the truth about the things he'd done, which would surely kill her. She wouldn't have wanted to waste away like this. But he couldn't let her go. Couldn't bear the thought of losing the only human connection he had left in this world.

Julia regarded him for a long moment, her clear, sky blue eyes so beautiful he couldn't look away. "Haven't seen you in a while."

"Been busy with work." So many scumbags to kill, so little time.

She nodded. "Well, it's good to see you." Without another word she got up and began gently manipulating the joints in his grandmother's gnarled fingers, her hands and wrists.

Bautista watched her, drinking in the sight of her, fit and graceful. He loved watching her move, with total surety. It alarmed him a little, how much he liked being around her. He'd thought he was dead inside, that he'd long since lost the ability to care about someone other than his grandmother. Over the past few months, Julia had proven him wrong.

"So," she finally said, casting him a sidelong glance with a little smile that made his heart kick. "Are you ever going to ask me out?"

He stared at her for a moment, at a loss for words. He'd known they were working their way to this point for a while now, but he didn't date. Ever. Had no interest in it.

He never let a woman in, except for a fast round of sex. He gave the whole wham-bam-thank you-ma'am thing new meaning. On the rare times he wanted to get laid he found a willing woman and fucked her, then walked away. They never knew his name, never knew anything about him.

And neither does Julia.

A tendril of shame curled inside him, shocking him. He'd learned long ago how to ignore the occasional twinges from his conscience, something that rarely happened anymore. But now his conscience pricked at him like sharp needles.

Julia didn't know about the blood staining his hands, his soul. She thought he was a devoted grandson and an upstanding, successful businessman who drove a Lexus and traveled frequently on business trips.

She didn't realize what he was capable of or what he did to earn the small fortune he was sitting on. That his victims usually begged for death before he gave it to them. That he *enjoyed* the release of it. And for some reason knowing he was lying to her made him feel…rotten inside.

Looking at her now, for just a moment he let himself imagine what it would be like to have a normal life. To get out of this game, start over somewhere and be able to do simple things like date if he wanted to.

The thought was far more appealing than he'd imagined it would be. As was the image of Julia sitting in a chair next to him on a white sand beach in the Caymans, where all his money was safely accumulated in accounts listed under various shell companies.

Virtually untraceable, at least to him, unless someone knew about him and exactly what they were looking for. He had enough to live ten lifetimes on and keep his grandmother here with the best care he could offer for the rest of her days. The trust he'd set up ensured she'd be taken care of if anything happened to him. A likely scenario, given his line of work.

Money didn't drive him anymore. Maintaining his reputation, and power, did.

"Well?" she prompted, raising one eyebrow as a smile tugged at her lips. "Unless…wait, is that my foot I taste in my mouth? If so, just forget I said anything."

He shook his head, not wanting her to feel embarrassed. She was wonderful with his grandmother and he liked her. Enjoyed being around her. She made him feel alive inside when he'd been ice cold for so long. "You don't want to go out with me." She deserved better than a liar and a killer.

She blinked, her smile fading. "I don't? Why's that?"

"I'm not good enough for you." Not even close.

Her eyes stayed on his, steady and eerily knowing somehow. As though she could see past his polished exterior to the darkness inside him. There was no way she could know, yet every once in a while something about the way she looked at him roused his suspicion.

Which was crazy. He'd checked her out thoroughly in the beginning. She was a twenty-six year old accountant who'd recently relocated to Miami from Tampa, and now volunteered here in her spare time. Not even a parking ticket to her name.

"I think that's up to me to decide," she said softly.

For the life of him he didn't know how to respond. He knew he should get up and leave, or say something abrupt to take the warmth from her eyes.

But he couldn't do it. Him, the trained assassin, unable to hurt this woman's feelings. It made him want to laugh at himself.

"So. Dinner? Whenever you can squeeze me in," she added.

He couldn't help the involuntary twitch of his lips. As close to a smile as he'd given in memory. It felt weird as hell. "I can't," he heard himself say.

Rather than pout or get angry, Julia merely measured him with that direct stare for a long moment. "Then how about I give you my number in case you change your mind?"

He already knew where she lived, but didn't say anything as she recited her number. Her persistence, her confidence even in the face of his rejection, made him like her all the more.

Still maintaining eye contact, Julia rounded the foot of his grandmother's bed and started toward him. He stiffened as she approached but didn't move as she reached for his hand. Her fingers curled around his, cool and soft. So fucking soft.

"I hope you'll change your mind," she murmured, then withdrew her hand and headed for the door. She paused there to shoot him a smile over her shoulder before disappearing into the hallway.

Heart pounding, he glanced over at his grandmother, felt the smile spread across his face.

Guess I'm not dead inside after all, abuelita. *Maybe there's hope for me yet.*

Chapter Four

Wow, this guy was a real prince.

Just when she thought she knew all the ugly things involved with this case, something worse surfaced. Marisol shook her head as she read through the latest information she'd compiled on Diego Fuentes. Men like him were the reason she'd wanted a job with the U.S. Attorney's office in the first place, so she could help put them away forever.

She'd known he was the worst of the worst in the drug trade, but uncovering all his dark deeds was a constant eye-opener. In addition to his drug trafficking empire, she'd found at least some evidence that he'd also been involved with weapons smuggling, and two witnesses willing to testify claimed to have info on possible human trafficking as well. Selling women into sexual slavery in South America and the Caribbean.

That part turned her stomach more than anything.

As the biggest kingpin of the drug scene in the Gulf region, with his empire stretching south even into Mexico and parts of the Caribbean, Fuentes was also responsible for the murders of at least twenty-three people over the past four years.

Those were just the cases they could confirm. Marisol and her team had some evidence of dozens more. Fuentes never did the dirty work himself, of course, always having subordinates carry out the hits instead. Still made him guilty as shit.

She blew out a breath and pushed away the legal pad she'd been scribbling notes on, preferring to write things out longhand before typing them into a proper document in her computer. They definitely had enough evidence to have a jury reach a guilty verdict on the racketeering and trafficking charges. Finding people willing to testify against Fuentes in court was proving far more difficult.

She had three meetings with potential witnesses lined up next week, including one down in Key West. And now that Fuentes was behind bars, his so-called "lieutenants" were having a full-out turf war. Willing to kill each other and anyone else who stood in their way from taking over Fuentes's role.

They all knew the U.S. Attorney's office was trying to cut a deal with Fuentes, trying to get him to roll over on his lieutenants in exchange for a reduced sentence. Now all the lieutenants were scrambling for more territory, more power.

More murder victims were turning up every day across Miami and south Florida, the sudden increase in body count courtesy of the cartel's lethal enforcers. Dangerous men who lived in the shadows and didn't think twice about taking out a rival.

She looked up at a soft knock at her door. Her assistant, Emma, stood there, her caramel-brown hair wound into a sleek bun at the back of her head. "You about ready for a break yet? I ordered us some lunch," she said, pushing her black-framed glasses up higher on the bridge of her nose.

"Yeah, that sounds good. I'm starving." With this

kind of workload she'd been pulling ridiculously long hours over the past few weeks, and it was only going to get worse leading up to the trial itself. "Did you confirm the meeting with Clancy next week?" The key witness had insider knowledge about Fuentes's financial activities, and hopefully, some evidence on the human trafficking so they could bring charges.

If that happened, they'd want to put him on the stand to nail Fuentes on those counts. Whether or not they could make it happen remained to be seen.

"I talked to him again this morning. We're still on for Monday at nine."

"Great. Just let me finish up this last file and I'll join you in the staff room."

"Okay."

Marisol typed up her hand-written notes into the document she'd prepared, then saved it and shut down her computer. Grabbing her purse, she took out her phone to check for messages. Emma was under strict instructions not to forward any phone calls to her desk unless it was urgent and directly involved in the Fuentes case, and Marisol always silenced her phone when she was working. Too many distractions otherwise.

And speaking of distractions, there was Ethan's number on her display, along with several texts asking her to call him. She'd been too tired to talk to him last night after she'd dragged herself home from the office just before midnight, and too busy today.

She had a voicemail too. Punching in her code, she waited for it to play back.

But it wasn't Ethan's smooth, deep voice on the other end. An electronic, synthesized voice spoke instead.

Marisol Lorenzo, you are in serious danger. Stop working on the Fuentes case now, before you and people you care about get hurt. You're being watched. This is your only warning.

The message ended abruptly.

She disconnected, a wave of cold suffusing her. Barely anyone had her cell number outside of her close friends, family and coworkers. Had someone involved with Fuentes's network tracked down her cell number? It wouldn't be that hard to get her number and given her job she'd known something like this might happen with one of her cases.

Concerned, she left her office and went straight to her boss's. Frank Escobar sat behind his massive, antique walnut desk, poring over a thick stack of files before him.

He glanced up at her when she shut the door behind her, and frowned. "You okay?"

She nodded. "You got a second?"

"Sure." He leaned back and indicated one of the leather chairs in front of the desk.

She sat, crossing her legs at the ankle and slid her phone onto the desk. "I just found this when I checked my messages and thought you should hear it." She played it for him.

His dark eyebrows crashed together at the end of the first sentence, and the frown became a full-on scowl by the time the message ended. He looked up from the phone, his deep brown eyes intense. "Who sent that?"

"I don't recognize the number. But it's a Miami area code." And if someone had taken the time to digitize their voice, then they had to be using a burner phone.

Frank picked up the phone to examine it himself. Still staring at the screen, he reached for the landline on his desk and dialed out, holding the receiver to his ear with his shoulder. "Agent Lammers, it's Frank Escobar. Something's just come up and I want you to look into it personally."

Marisol stayed put while he outlined the message, gave a brief overview about the case they were working on. Not much needed to be explained, because the detective would know all about Fuentes and they'd worked with him quite a bit on the case already.

While listening to him, she ran through a list of possible suspects in her head. People they'd contacted about the case, witnesses they were trying to secure for testifying. Dangerous people with even more dangerous connections.

And they'd singled her out personally. Maybe because she was a woman and new to the job? Did they see her as the weak link on this case? The thought made her feel even colder.

"Great. See you in twenty." Frank hung up, settled his gaze on her. "He's heading over now with a couple other guys. They'll take your statement, start looking into who it might be."

She let out a relieved breath. "Good." Although her line of work didn't gain her a lot of friends in the criminal underworld.

Frank grunted. "It's probably nothing. Not the first time we've gotten threats around here," he added with a smile. "Rarely leads to anything worse."

Well it was the first time she'd ever been threatened directly, and she didn't like it. Being mentally prepared for this possibility and facing it for real were two very different things. "I'll feel better once it's been investigated."

"Of course, of course," he said. "Come on. Let's go eat while we're waiting. Don't say anything to the others."

"I won't." No sense upsetting everyone until they knew for sure if the threat was credible or not. She didn't have much of an appetite but followed him to the staff room where the other assistant attorneys and staff were gathered. Today it was Mexican, picked up from a place just down the street. Marisol forced herself to eat half her chicken burrito but barely tasted it.

Special Agent Lammers and his team arrived right

on time. Emma glanced at her with wide eyes when she saw them but Marisol didn't say anything as she headed back into Frank's office with them.

The FBI agent was a solidly-built man somewhere in his mid-forties. He listened to the message on her phone, gathered some more background information from her, then started asking more pointed questions.

"Have you noticed anything suspicious recently?"

She blinked at him. "Nothing other than this message."

"No one's followed you, you haven't noticed anyone hanging around your place or anything like that?"

She knew he was just being thorough, but his questions chilled her nonetheless. "No, not that I know of." God, had someone been watching her and she simply hadn't noticed? Growing up in the neighborhood she had, she'd developed a pretty good internal radar.

"Any jealous ex-boyfriends, problems with co-workers or anyone else like that?"

"None." The last time she'd gone out with a man was seven months ago, and only for one dinner. Two hours in a restaurant with him was more than enough time to remind her why she'd decided to stop dating.

"Okay, I'm already familiar with a lot of this case, but tell me more about the contacts you've been working with recently."

And there went her work schedule for the afternoon, because this was going to take a while. Still, better safe than sorry. "Sure."

"In the meantime I'd like to have my people take your phone for a little bit, see if we can find out where the call originated, maybe find out where the phone was purchased and see if we can ID the buyer via security footage of some kind at or around the store."

"Go ahead." Leaving her phone with him, she went to her office to gather her files, sending Emma a reassuring smile on her way past. Back in Frank's office she laid out everyone she'd talked to or had communication with about the case and began reviewing the list.

When she mentioned some of the more recently contacted key players they were hoping to get to testify against Fuentes, Lammers frowned. It was obvious from his expression that he knew the men, knew of their criminal histories. No doubt many of them had had run-ins with Lammers and his people at some point at least over the years.

He made notes, asked questions from time to time, then reviewed Frank's list of contacts. An hour later Marisol was no closer to figuring out who might have called her.

Lammers's cell rang. He listened to the caller for a few moments, then his hazel gaze shot to her and stayed locked on her face. "Understood. Keep digging." He hung up, his expression grave. "Our techs said the software needed to generate that kind of voice in the first place is highly sophisticated. They were also unable to figure out where the call originated from. Not only was it a burner phone, it had enough encryption on it to scramble the usual signal and stump my guys. And my guys don't stump easy."

Marisol clenched her fingers together in her lap, kept her expression calm despite the dread unfurling deep inside. "So you're saying I should definitely be worried?" *Because after hearing that, I'm already there.*

"I'm saying we need to take this seriously since you were singled out specifically. And given the nature of the case and the list of suspects you just gave me, for your safety we need to fast track this investigation."

Oh, shit. "Okay." There was nothing else she could say at the moment. Whoever had sent the message knew what the hell they were doing, and knew how to cover their tracks. If this threat against her was legitimate and not just a scare tactic, then she was all for working with the Feds or anyone else who could help. But she was absolutely not letting some asshole scare her off this case.

Lammers nodded and got back on the phone. From the way he spoke she guessed he was talking to a contact he had at the Miami FBI office. She shared a long look with Frank over the top of his desk. From the crease between his eyebrows, she knew he was as worried as her.

Lammers ended the call and spoke to her. "More agents are coming out now. They're going to take your phone to analyze it further, make sure the caller didn't somehow plant tracking software or anything like that on it, and then go over all of this with us again."

"Should we let the other staff know?" she asked. Everyone in the office already knew something was up, and if they were in danger too, even indirectly, they had a right to know what was going on.

"Not just yet," Lammers said. "Anyone you need to call before they get here?"

She briefly thought about contacting Ethan, then dismissed it. Until she'd heard the other FBI agents' opinion, there was no point letting him know. She didn't want to come off as weak or scared to him, especially over a phone message that might turn out to be nothing. He'd always been borderline overbearing in his protectiveness toward her.

No, she needed to handle this on her own. If he found out about the threat from someone at the agency later, at least she'd have demonstrated she was fully capable of taking care of herself in the meantime.

****

Ethan's phone rang for the second time in the past minute. Same blocked number as the first time, and he didn't feel like talking to anyone he didn't know right now so he didn't pick up. After another long day of joint training with the DEA team he was bagged, not to mention really fucking annoyed that Marisol still hadn't bothered to call him back yet.

"Not gonna answer that?" Vance asked from across the booth in the diner they were eating at, ketchup bottle poised in one big hand, tilted over his mound of fries.

"Nah. If it was important they'd either text or leave a message." He set it back down on the table and dug into his bacon cheeseburger, savoring every bite.

For the most part he ate really well but oh, God, it had been weeks since he'd eaten a meal like this. An entire plate full of fat-laden, empty calories, but they tasted so damn good he didn't even feel guilty. And with the amount of training they were doing right now, he'd burn it off and then some tomorrow anyhow.

Vance moaned around a bite of his double bacon BBQ cheeseburger, nodded at Ethan in agreement. "Heaven on a bun. Texas beef is almost as good as the stuff we raised back home."

"Oh yeah," Ethan said, and took another bite of his. His phone rang again. Annoyed, he glanced at it, then saw it was Tuck calling. Immediately he dropped the burger, wiped his hands and answered. "Hey."

"Celida's been trying to reach you," his team leader said without preamble.

That had been Celida calling? "Oh." Why the blocked number? And why not leave a message then? "What about?"

"She just said something's come up and she wanted to talk to you about it."

"But she didn't tell you what?"

"No."

That was weird. Maybe it had to do with her and Tuck's upcoming wedding in a couple months. It was the only thing he could think of, but didn't explain the urgency or the blocked number. "Okay, I'll call her back."

"Sounded important," Tuck added.

Ethan had no clue what she wanted. "Yeah, okay, I'll call her right now. Thanks." He disconnected and dialed the previous number.

Celida answered on the first ring, her tone full of annoyance. "Screening your calls, I see?"

"Something like that. You should have just texted me. I thought you were a telemarketer," he joked.

She snorted. She knew as well as he did that the encryption on his phone blocked that kind of shit. "So, anything interesting going on down there today?" she asked, her tone casual.

Uh... He looked across the table at Vance, who continued to watch him as he stuffed his face. "No, just the usual." Lots of training, plenty of meetings, hardly any sleep and all the regular aches and pains that went with that. He was just shy of thirty but his body sure didn't recover as quickly as it had a decade ago. "Why, what's up?"

"Heard through the grapevine that there's been a development in the Fuentes case, involving someone you might know."

Ethan frowned, not liking the sound of that. "Who?"

"Assistant U.S. Attorney named Marisol Lorenzo."

His spine went rigid. "What about her?"

"Agents from the Miami office just went to talk to her and her boss about a threat she received this morning."

His hand tightened around the phone. "Someone threatened her? Her, specifically?"

"That's what it sounds like. How well do you know her?"

"Pretty well. I used to, anyway. We grew up together." But it was obvious he didn't know her the way he used to. The Marisol he'd known before wouldn't ignore him like this. He glanced at his watch. "What time did they head over, do you know?"

"About an hour ago. Probably still there now."

"Thanks. I'll talk to her." One way or another, he was absolutely talking to her about this. Tonight.

"No problem. Thought you'd want to know."

Oh, he definitely wanted to know if Marisol was being threatened. Because the thought of anyone hurting her triggered a deep, primal instinct he couldn't shut off. He felt compelled to protect her, then find out who'd dared to threaten her and pound the shit out of them.

Why the hell hadn't she called him for help? She knew he worked for the FBI. Not that he was with the HRT, but that he was an agent at least. It baffled and frustrated him.

"Trouble?" Vance asked, his burger paused halfway to his mouth.

"Someone involved in the Fuentes case just threatened Marisol. Local agents are talking to her and her boss now."

At that Vance's eyes widened and he set down his burger. "You serious?"

Did he look like he was joking? "Celida just told me."

Now Vance frowned. "What kind of threat?"

Any threat against her personally was reason enough to be concerned, especially if it had to do with the Fuentes case. "Dunno. But I'm gonna find out." He found her number in his contacts and dialed.

Of course it went straight to voicemail.

He didn't bother texting, because he knew damn well she'd just ignore that too, same as she'd ignored all his other messages. Jesus, that aggravated him. She'd be working regularly with other law enforcement and had her own contacts, but it still made him nuts that she refused to come to him for help when she clearly could use it.

Ethan stood, pulled two twenties from his wallet and dropped them on the table. "Come on," he said to Vance. "We're heading to her office." If she wouldn't come to him, then he'd go to her.

Vance grabbed his burger and followed him out to the rental truck.

Chapter Five

B y the time Ethan walked into the third floor of the
High Intensity Drug Trafficking Area office in
West Miami, he was good and pissed off. Several
FBI agents had been leaving as he and Vance had come
in the front entrance. Ethan hadn't bothered to ask the lead
investigator any questions, knowing he'd get nowhere.
And he wanted to hear it from Marisol anyway.

Vance headed to the right when they stepped off the
elevator. "Think I'll sit this one out, champ," he said in a
wry voice, helping himself to a sports magazine laid out
on the table in the waiting area. He sank onto one of the
leather couches and immediately began reading, ignoring
Ethan. Probably just as well. He didn't want an audience
for this conversation anyway.

He stalked to the reception desk. A young woman
with light brown hair and dark-rimmed glasses looked up
at him with wide blue eyes. "Can I help you, sir?"

He pulled out his ID. "Special Agent Ethan Cruz,
here to see Marisol Lorenzo." He was going to find out
what the hell was going on, and exactly what her problem
with him was.

The brunette nodded and got to her feet. "I'll tell her you're here."

"You do that," he said with a tight smile. He was beyond the ability to be pleasant at the moment.

She reappeared a few moments later, gave him a hesitant smile. "Right this way."

Ethan followed her down a hallway lined with offices, where she stopped at the last one on the left. "Go right in," she murmured.

He walked through the door and stopped. Marisol sat behind a wide, polished desk housing a computer and neatly stacked files. Her long, dark hair was pulled into some sort of clip at the back of her head, and what he could see of her body was concealed by a pale gray suit jacket and cream-colored blouse.

She was on the phone with someone, furiously writing notes on a yellow pad of paper in front of her. She cast him a fleeting glance then dismissed him as she kept on with her conversation.

Ethan folded his arms across his chest and stood there while the door clicked shut behind him, his annoyance growing with each passing second. He didn't budge from his spot directly in front of her desk, didn't take his eyes off her as she spoke to the caller. If she thought she could ignore him for long, she'd better think again.

Finally she hung up and lifted that sea green gaze to his, the look in her eyes cool. "I guess this means you heard about the message?" she asked.

A muscle bunched in his jaw. "Yeah." When she didn't say anything else, just kept looking at him with that closed expression, his temper snapped. "Dammit, Soli, why didn't you call me?"

She set down her pen and leaned back in her seat with a sigh. "Because there was no need to involve you. I've handled it. The police and FBI are looking into it. You're busy, I'm busy and I didn't want to bother you. I'm sorry you felt the need to interrupt your day and come over here. But there's nothing you can do for me."

Ethan stared at her. She thought she could dismiss him so easily? Not freaking likely. And he was thoroughly sick of this whole too-polite, distant thing she was pulling. As if they were barely acquaintances. "You're not a bother. You should have called me."

She shook her head. "I'm not your responsibility, Ethan," she said, her tone firm and edged with a hint of incredulity. "You don't have to play the white knight anymore just because you're in town."

More than the words, something in her tone bothered him. "You've got a problem with me looking out for you?"

She rolled her eyes. "This is exactly why I didn't call you. Because I knew you'd react like this—that you'd take it as a personal insult if I didn't."

Damn right he was insulted. "You used to trust me. I know we haven't kept in touch lately, but what's happened to keep you from turning to me for help with something like this?"

"I still trust you, that's not the point."

"Then what *is* the point? Because from where I'm standing it feels like you're doing everything possible to shut me out." It was making him nuts.

He missed the way she used to look at him. With her heart in her eyes. As if he was her hero.

And okay, it didn't make any sense considering they hadn't seen each other in years, but if he was honest, it hurt that she was rejecting him as a friend, as a man, when she was all he'd been able to think about for the past two days.

That cool façade finally cracked. A spark of anger lit her eyes. She pushed to her feet and braced her hands on her desk, leaning toward him. "I'm not a helpless teenager anymore. In case you haven't noticed, I'm all grown up and able to take care of myself. I appreciate your concern, but I don't need you to run interference for me."

What? Where the hell had all that come from? He'd have to be dead not to notice that she was definitely all grown up. He was having a hard time keeping his eyes off her chest, where her blouse was pulled taut over her breasts. And for some unknown reason that show of temper from her lit his blood up. "I never saw you as helpless, and that's not why I'm here. I'm worried about you, okay?"

She cocked her head, gave him a *get-real* look that said she didn't believe him. "You and my entire family always saw me that way. That's why I've worked long and hard to earn my independence. I'm not stupid, Ethan, I've done all the right things since I got the message this morning. The Fuentes case has the potential to set up the rest of my career and my reputation is riding on my performance. I was given a golden opportunity when I landed this job in the first place and I'm taking it seriously. I'm not backing away or stepping down just because some asshole wants to scare me."

He held up a hand, stunned by her words. "Whoa, hold it. Nobody's disputing your dedication to the job, and sure as hell nobody's calling you stupid." She was defensive, damn near hostile with him and he didn't understand why. He needed to diffuse the situation in a hurry, before she closed up on him again. "And I'm sorry I ever made you feel that way. I didn't know. I always saw it as me looking out for you, not that I was interfering."

Her expression softened instantly, the anger draining from her eyes as her shoulders relaxed. "No, it's…" She pushed out a sigh. "I'm the one who's sorry. I know you're just trying to help." She sat back down and leaned her head against the chair. After a moment her gaze lifted to him once more. "I really did appreciate you looking out for me back then. It's just, I hated that you seemed to see me as weak and helpless all the time."

She made it sound like he'd pitied her or something, which he hadn't. The truth was he'd respected the hell out of her and the example she set for those around her. "Not helpless. More like innocent, I guess, at least compared to everyone else in our neighborhood. I didn't want to see you get taken advantage of."

Her lips twitched in the barest hint of a smile and her eyes were full of warmth as she looked at him. "Yeah, and you did a damn good job of protecting me. Especially that one night. I didn't get asked out for months after word got around about that."

The night when her dipshit of a date had pushed her for more than she'd wanted to give. Ethan remembered it clearly. He'd been twenty-one, full of himself home on leave from the Corps, and Marisol had been just sixteen.

After a date of his own he'd come up the sidewalk to his parents' driveway and noticed her across the street in the front seat of a car with the guy. Instinct had warned him something was wrong. He'd seen her push the guy away and tried to get out of the car before her date had grabbed her, manhandled her.

Ethan had seen red. He'd run across the street, ripped open the driver's door and dragged the asshole out of the car by the scruff of his neck. Ethan had ordered Marisol into her house, waited until she'd fled up the front steps before leaning into the guy's face and telling him through gritted teeth exactly what would happen to him if he ever laid a hand on Marisol again. "My only regret is that I didn't break at least one bone in his face."

Marisol grinned, shaking her head a little. "Your white knight complex is showing again."

Ethan shrugged, not about to apologize for it. "Can't help it." Not where she was concerned, anyway. He realized she was going to be exposed to a certain amount of ugly shit in her job. She was just so sweet and good; he didn't want any of the evil in this world to touch her. But as of that phone call, it had tried to. And that was unacceptable.

"Now, will you tell me about the call?" he asked.

"The agents have my phone to check to see if the caller tampered with it at all, but I'll tell you what the message said. My assistant's setting up a replacement phone for me right now."

He listened carefully, watching her expression. She seemed calm, unafraid, but he was betting it was a front. Anyone with half a brain would have the sense to be scared if someone in Fuentes's network threatened them. Marisol was far smarter than most.

The implicit threat, made in a computerized voice no less, made his hackles rise. He was glad she'd immediately gone to the authorities, and relieved the FBI was involved. That still didn't make him feel any less uneasy about her personal security. "Do they have any leads yet?" he asked.

"No, they couldn't even trace the signal due to encryption on the other phone but they're already working on it and said they'd let me know if they found anything."

Whoever had sent the message had access to sophisticated equipment. At this point it could either have been someone trying to look out for her and offer a warning, or an enemy threatening her. Ethan was more worried about the latter.

Uncrossing his arms, he lowered his weight into one of the leather wing-back chairs opposite her desk. "What about personal security? Did the agents talk to you about that?"

"They did. They told me to be aware of my surroundings, avoid being out late at night by myself, basic common sense things like that. They said there's no need to change my lifestyle for now though."

"Are you...seeing anyone? Living with someone?" God, he didn't even know that about her.

"No and no."

Something inside him breathed easier at her answer. So she was still unattached. The borderline territorial feeling he had toward her might not make sense but he couldn't deny it was there. "Have you got an alarm system in your place?"

"Of course."

"Surveillance cameras?"

"No."

"I can have some installed." He pulled his phone out. "Let me make a call—"

"Ethan."

He looked up to find her watching him with a mixed expression of exasperation and fondness on her face. "What?"

"Look, I really appreciate you trying to help, but for right now I'm going to leave things as they are. This office gets threats from time to time, as you can imagine, and ninety-nine-point-nine percent of the time they're just that. Threats and intimidation. Just words, used to try and scare us into stopping our work or dropping a case." She snorted as though the idea was ludicrous. "For the time being we're going to keep operating as normal. This case goes to trial in ten days and we've got to be ready. I can't afford to back off my workload and I'm not going to let someone intimidate me with a phone call, no matter what the circumstances."

Ethan searched her eyes, admiring her conviction and work ethic, but concerned about what she might be getting herself into. "How much do you know about Fuentes?"

She indicated a thick folder on the corner of her desk with a nod. "Enough to know I never want him seeing the outside of a jail cell ever again. That's my job, to keep him there for the rest of his natural life, or to end it with the death penalty. Either or, but nothing less."

He rubbed his hands on his thighs, his palms brushing against the soft denim. "What about his lieutenants and enforcers?"

"I've got files on seventeen people right now, and my coworkers are compiling more. Law enforcement gave us all their files some time ago on people related to the case."

Ethan shook his head. Again, that was investigative information. Not the same as seeing it firsthand or knowing the intricate details of their work. Ethan had seen more than enough of it over the past week, and the thought of any one of those bastards setting their sights on Marisol twisted his gut into knots. "These men, Soli, they're bad news."

"I know."

No, she didn't. Not to the extent he did. He shook his head. "Most of the enforcers are former military. Not all are American, but they've all got training. Serious training." He waited, unable to divulge too much because of the sensitive nature of the intel. She didn't have security clearance. The upcoming operation to nab Alvarez, one of Fuentes's higher-ranking lieutenants, hinged on everyone maintaining secrecy, including the informants the agency had paid off.

"I realize that." She narrowed her eyes slightly. "What are you trying to say, Ethan?"

"That you can't just put your head down and hope this will all go away on its own. If that call came from one of the enforcers or someone in their network, then you need to be careful. Real careful. Promise me you'll be on the alert." He couldn't stand the thought of anything happening to her, especially not at the hands of an enforcer like the ones Fuentes's lieutenants used. The idea made him feel sick.

She nodded. "I will be, I promise." Then she folded

her arms across her chest, the motion pushing her breasts together. He could just see the top of her cleavage in the open neckline of her blouse, the edge of those tempting mounds teasing his gaze. He jerked his attention back to her face, fighting the guilty flush trying to creep up his neck. "And, by the way, what is it you do for the FBI, exactly? Are you involved in the Fuentes case as well?"

"In a way, yeah," he allowed with a nod.

She raised her brows questioningly, waited.

He leaned back in his chair, released a breath. Normally he wouldn't tell anyone what he did, but he trusted Marisol, and if he wanted that trust to extend both ways, then he had to be honest with her now. They'd lost more ground than he'd realized over the past several years. He wanted to bridge that gap. "I'm with the HRT."

Her eyes widened. "As in, the Hostage Rescue Team?"

He nodded.

She shook her head, a rueful smile curving her mouth. Her eyes traveled over his chest and shoulders, down his arms, a hint of female appreciation in her gaze that he liked way more than he should have. She'd never looked at him like that before, at least not so overtly that she'd let him see. Rivulets of heat rippled along his skin. Yeah, he liked how this new Marisol had just looked at him.

"Of course," she murmured. "Should have figured that out on my own."

He shrugged, trying and failing to ignore the effect that long look had on his body. He worked damn hard to stay in this kind of shape and he couldn't deny he liked Marisol's eyes on him that way. In fact, he wanted more. Wanted to see desire in her eyes when she looked at him, some of that quiet yearning he used to see there. "It's not something I like getting around."

"I won't say anything to anyone."

"Thanks." She'd always been someone he could count on to keep her word.

"So what you're in town for, it pertains to Fuentes?" she guessed.

He nodded. "Someone involved in his organization." Several people, actually, if the right intel came in.

"You're working in conjunction with the DEA?"

He hid a grin. She was quick, but that didn't surprise him. "Maybe."

She considered him for a long moment, her eyes locked on his. "Are you going after *el Santo*?"

Ethan's hands contracted into fists at the mention of the name. "You know about him?"

"I know no one knows who he really is, or where to find him. He's come up multiple times during our investigation. I've got a meeting scheduled Monday morning with an informant willing to share information pertaining to him. The DEA's involved as well."

Christ, he didn't want her within a hundred miles of anyone affiliated with *el Santo*, yet here she was questioning people about him. His concern for her doubled. "He's a person of interest to us," he said carefully.

She nodded, apparently accepting his evasive response. "I'll bet he is."

"What do you know about him?"

"Stories, mostly. Rumors. And I've seen the odd photographic evidence of some of his kills. Nothing to pin him with. So far there's never been any DNA or other hard evidence to put him at the scene of any of the murders I've read about. He's very good at what he does."

Ethan held her gaze, wanting to get his point across without scaring her to death. "He's like a ghost. Likely Spec Ops trained."

"He's no ghost," she scoffed. "And sooner or later, he'll either be caught, or killed by a rival. No one can escape justice forever."

He opened his mouth to argue that a man like *el Santo* might be able to do exactly that, but stopped when a brisk knock interrupted him. A middle-aged man appeared in the doorway. He glanced at Ethan, then Marisol. "Is this a bad time?"

"No," she said. "We were just finishing up."

Ethan shot her an annoyed look. In other words, this meeting was over? If she thought she could just up and dismiss him again after this, she thought wrong. He realized she had an important job, but so did he, and he refused to let her treat him like he was insignificant to her. Not given their history, and not after the way she'd just looked at him a minute ago. No way.

"What do you need?" she asked the man, who Ethan assumed was her boss.

"Just got the affidavit we were waiting on. Come to my office when you're done."

"Be right there."

When they were alone again Marisol shifted her gaze back to him. "Duty calls." She pushed back from the desk and stood.

"Yeah." Ethan stood too, feeling strangely off-center as he rubbed a hand over the back of his neck. He wasn't ready to say goodbye, not until she gave him her word that she'd come to him if she needed help, and he didn't want to walk away.

His instincts were screaming at him not to. They warned that if he left now, she'd just retreat back behind the professional armor she'd enclosed herself in and she'd disappear from his life just when they'd been reconnected again.

He took a step toward her. "Look, I need you to promise you'll call me if you need me. That's all, okay?" he continued when it looked like she would argue. "If you need me, I'll be there."

She surprised him by reaching out to take his free hand. Her fingers were slender and soft in his, and he felt that simple touch all the way up his arm.

"Thank you, I appreciate it. I'm going to be careful," she told him with a soft smile that lit a spark of desire in his gut.

Even in her heels the top of her head only came to his chin. He let his gaze wander over her. She was wearing a snug pencil skirt that matched her jacket, and it hugged the trim curve of her hips to perfection. The very image of corporate sophistication. Class, brains and a quiet confidence that he found insanely sexy. Sophisticated and composed. Looking at her now, he couldn't even recall the sweet girl-next-door she'd always been to him.

And she wasn't off limits to him anymore.

He had the sudden urge to plunge his hands into her hair, pull it free of the clip, wrap his hands in the long strands as he kissed and tasted that pink-glossed mouth until she moaned and melted against him. He wanted to muss her up in the worst way. Shatter that cool exterior, watch her skin go all rosy as he stripped that elegant suit off her and melted the remote shell she'd cloaked herself in.

Unable to quell the urge to touch her, Ethan cupped the side of her face with one hand. She drew in a small breath and automatically reached up to grip his wrist, her body stilling. The space between them suddenly turned heavy with anticipation.

Her skin was so damn soft against his palm, the pad of his thumb as he stroked it across her cheek. Her pupils expanded as she gazed up at him, then her eyes dipped down to his mouth. Ethan barely resisted the urge to lean down and kiss her, nip at that tempting, plump lower lip. Desire roared through him, sudden and intense, catching him off guard.

Fighting back the instinct to taste, to take, he held her

gaze in the taut silence, feeling a little drunk on the triumph of knowing she wanted him too. "I don't want to see you get hurt," he murmured, letting his gaze roam downward, over her throat.

The pulse in the side of her neck beat hard against her skin. He wanted to taste that fragile skin. Rub his nose up the column of her neck, taste that soft spot and feel her shiver in his arms. When his gaze trailed lower over her chest, he saw that her nipples were hard points against her bra beneath the cream blouse where the jacket gaped open.

Marisol snatched her hand back from his wrist and cleared her throat almost guiltily as she took a step back and drew that regal air about her like a cloak. She gave him a stiff smile, a soft blush staining her cheeks. "It was good to see you. I'll definitely call you if anything happens. Now I've got to get back to work." She walked past him out of her office without another word.

Ethan watched her go without trying to stop her. She could try to pretend nothing had just happened between them but they both knew better. And she hadn't seen the last of him. Not by a long shot.

He wanted to see her again, soon, so she wouldn't have time to distance herself from him again. Because there was something more between them now than just a shared history and two decades of friendship. That spark had been real and he wasn't going to let her pretend it hadn't happened.

Next time he saw her, he intended to pick up where they'd just left off.

Chapter Six

*G**ood lord.**

In her mother's kitchen, Marisol shifted her grip on the overfull, still-warm casserole she'd just pulled out of the oven. "Think you made enough *tostones?*" she called out in a dry tone.

"But Ethan loves them," Vero, her nine year-old niece said from the kitchen table where she was studying for the last spelling test of the year.

"Yes, I'm well aware," she murmured, fishing in the drawer for a piece of aluminum foil to cover the fried plantains with. "You can come over and say hello with me if you want."

Mama Cruz had invited them all over for the barbecue. After another long day at work, Marisol needed a break. Spending time at the Cruz house wasn't exactly a hardship, even if she felt a little awkward around Ethan now, especially after that almost-kiss yesterday in her office.

She'd gone back and forth about it several times since then, alternately congratulating herself for keeping from making a disastrous mistake by kissing him, and wishing she'd gone for it. She wasn't interested in a fling or a one-night stand, and as far as she remembered, that's all Ethan had ever wanted from a woman.

Vero shook her head and sighed dramatically. "I can't. It's gonna take me *hours* to learn these words."

Hours to a nine year-old roughly translated to about fifteen minutes, in Marisol's experience. "Well if you change your mind, I'm sure *abuela* will take you across the street later once you're done."

"Can't," her mother called down from upstairs. "We're going to meet Paulina at the park with her granddaughter in a little while."

"More plantains for me, I guess," Marisol said, coming around the table to wrap her arms around Vero from behind and kiss the top of her head.

The little girl tipped her head back to look at her. "You'll say hi to Ethan for me?"

"Yes. I think he'll be in town for a few days yet, maybe more, so you might get to see him still." Vero had only met Ethan a couple of times over the past few years when he'd come home to visit, yet that hadn't prevented her from developing some sort of crush on him. Marisol empathized. The man had a way about him that made it impossible for a woman to forget him.

"Good." Vero's face lit up with a big smile. "Will I see you later too?"

"Probably not tonight, but maybe tomorrow night if I don't have to work late. I'll try my best, okay?"

"Okay." Apparently satisfied, Vero turned back to her spelling.

Marisol slipped on some oven mitts and picked up the casserole dish. At the kitchen doorway she stopped and looked back at her niece. Vero was bent over her books, a tiny frown of concentration creasing her eyebrows.

Marisol smiled. That little girl had her auntie Soli

wrapped so hard around her little finger it wasn't even funny. She might not have come into this world under the best circumstances, being born to a single mother struggling to make ends meet, but she was loved by all four of the Lorenzo women.

Her eldest sister Ynez had shocked the family by getting pregnant in her junior year of high school, then dropped out of school and nearly ruined her life. Finishing high school while taking care of a newborn hadn't been easy, but Marisol and the others had refused to let Ynez give up.

Their mother had taken care of Vero while Ynez worked and finished her schooling, and Marisol and their other sister, Bianca, had helped out where needed. Ynez had gone to college part time for years until Vero was old enough to be in school full time. Now she was a hard-working single mom with an accounting degree, a shining example of perseverance for her daughter.

But it hadn't been easy. Marisol had learned an important lesson from that cautionary tale. It was why she'd decided not to have sex until she was out of law school. She just hadn't gotten around to doing anything about it yet.

"I'll call you about dinner tomorrow when I get a better sense of my workload tomorrow," she called out to her mother.

"That's fine, dear. Say hello to Ethan for us."

"I will." The late afternoon sun was warm against her skin as she shut the front door behind her. She had on a sleeveless white-and-turquoise print summer dress that skimmed just below her knees, and a pair of white strappy sandals. The outfit made her feel feminine and pretty and the soft cotton material breathed well in this humid heat.

She started down the concrete steps, past her mother's potted collection of zinnias and Gerbera daisies lining the edges. The big black truck Ethan had driven the other day was parked at the curb in front of his parents' house. Nervous butterflies took flight in her tummy at the thought of seeing him.

For a split second in her office she'd been seriously thinking about kissing him, wondering what he would do if she tried. Thankfully she'd come to her senses and put distance between them instead. Ethan wasn't the kind of man for someone as inexperienced as her to experiment with. He had a reputation for loving and leaving, at least back in the day, and that's not what she wanted for her first lover.

"Marisol."

She whipped her head around to look behind her. A well-built man stood twenty feet away on the sidewalk. She squinted to see him better. He was tall, dark-haired, wearing a ball cap and sunglasses.

He started toward her. An instant of fear grabbed her. He was a stranger, knew her name. The FBI didn't know who'd sent her the message. She'd been so careful on her way here, making sure no one was following, but what if…

Instinctively she took a step back. The heel of her right shoe caught in a crack in the sidewalk. She bit back a gasp as she stumbled, tried to keep hold of the dish as she tipped over.

Strong hands grabbed her by the shoulders, stopping her fall. God, he moved fast.

Heart thudding, she straightened and whipped her head up to look at him. And stilled. She couldn't see his eyes but the shape of the face, the set of the mouth was familiar.

Recognition hit her an instant later and she berated herself for ever being afraid of him. "Miguel," she said with a startled smile. He was three years older than her but they'd gone to school together.

He nodded and stepped back, giving her space.

"Been a long time."

"A really long time," she agreed, letting her eyes run over the length of him. She hadn't seen him in years and years. "Wow, you've changed." He'd filled out big time, his thin physique now hard with muscle.

A wry smile curved his mouth. "Yeah, guess I have since you last saw me." He stuck his hands into his pockets.

"What are you doing here?" Last she'd heard through the neighborhood grapevine he'd been in the military, mostly overseas.

He shrugged, looked down the street at the place he used to live. "Feeling nostalgic, I guess. Thought I'd come see the old neighborhood again." He focused back on her, his eyes hidden by the sunglasses. "Just visiting your mom?"

She lifted the casserole dish a little. "Picking up some plantains she cooked. I'm just heading over to Mama Cruz's place for a barbecue. Ethan's there. Want to come over and say hello?"

For just an instant his face tightened but then he shook his head. "Thanks, but I can't. Working."

She groaned. "What are you doing now?"

"Security."

He looked it. It'd been nearly a decade since she'd last seen him around and looked so different now. "Working on a Saturday night. Man, do I know how that goes. I should be there right now too. I feel guilty for taking a night off."

"So I'm betting you became a lawyer after all, am I right?"

She grinned. "I did."

"No surprise there."

"No, guess not." Everyone had known that's what she'd dreamed of becoming.

"What kind of law do you practice?"

"Criminal."

He nodded. "Got your own practice?"

She shook her head. "I'm actually with the U.S. Attorney's Office."

His eyebrows went up. "That's pretty good for someone as young as you, isn't it?"

"Well, I got lucky."

"Doubt that. They get some pretty big cases. High profile ones too."

"They do. But I love it."

His expression was neutral, but she recognized that was his default expression, one he'd learned at a young age to mask his emotions. "Lots of bad people involved with that kind of thing. Be careful."

Man, he sounded just like Ethan. "I will be." The next pause was just long enough to be awkward, so she put on a smile and took a step toward the edge of the sidewalk. "Well, better get these to the party before they get cold. It was great seeing you again, take care of yourself."

"Yeah, you too." He turned and started up the sidewalk.

"Miguel."

He stopped, looked back at her over his broad shoulder.

"How's your grandmother?"

She couldn't be sure but he seemed surprised by her question. "Still alive. She's one strong lady."

Marisol smiled softly. "Always was. Well, bye."

She crossed the street and paused to look back just in time to see him climbing behind the wheel of a newer-model Lexus. Whatever security job he was working, it paid well. Had to be a private contractor of some kind.

At the top of the Cruz's steps she took a deep breath and rang the doorbell, prepared to face Ethan again. She'd just pretend nothing had happened yesterday.

She waited a few seconds and rang it again. When still no one answered, she balanced the casserole dish on one oven-mitted hand before trying the knob and found it unlocked as usual when Mama Cruz was expecting guests. But when she opened the door the sound of multiple male voices registered.

Frowning, she headed through the entryway and into the kitchen, her heels clicking on the tile floor. She peered out the sliding glass doors that led to the back deck and internally groaned as she took in the scene. The tiny backyard was filled with big, fit men.

Her gaze found Ethan standing beside the grill, a beer in one hand as he flipped the burgers and talked to two guys who were built like linebackers. And that Sawyer guy was in a lawn chair talking to Mama Cruz, his black Stetson shading his face.

Not just a simple family barbecue, then, as she'd assumed. She withheld a groan. She should have just stayed at work because she didn't feel like socializing with a bunch of strangers right now.

"Hey, Soli," a bright female voice said from behind her.

Marisol turned to face Carmela, Ethan's sister. "Hi." She set the casserole dish on the counter and hugged her. "I uh, didn't realize there'd be so many people here."

Carmela waved a dismissive hand. "Mom invited Ethan's teammates a few weeks back when she heard they might be coming to Miami. They're all nice guys, don't worry."

She wasn't worried about them, she was worried about Ethan.

Carmela lifted the foil on the dish, made a hungry sound. "Mmm, *tostones*." She grabbed Marisol's hand and towed her toward the sliding glass doors. "Come on, I'll introduce you to the guys."

With no choice but to follow, Marisol trailed after

her.

****

Ethan shuffled some burgers around on the grill and listened half-heartedly to the questions his mom was throwing Tuck's way. His team leader didn't seem the least bit fazed by the not-so-subtle interrogation.

"Heard you're getting married," his mom said.

"I am, yeah."

"So when's the big day?"

"Sometime this fall. We haven't nailed down a date yet. Our work schedules are still up in the air, makes it hard to plan anything."

His mother snorted. "I would think that getting married would take top priority. Surely the FBI can spare you for a couple of weeks, let you tie the knot and go on a proper honeymoon."

Ethan smirked at the outrage in her voice. "Don't hold back, Ma," he said to her. "Tell him how you really feel."

"Well I can't help it," his mother protested. "You young people these days, always too busy with work to settle down." She shot Ethan a pointed look he was all too accustomed to receiving.

"Oh, I'm settled," Tuck drawled, his Alabama accent easy on the ears. "Settled as I've ever been. As soon as we can pin down a date, it's on."

His mother beamed. "Will it be a church wedding?"

"No. More than likely we'll just elope. Easier that way."

His mother started to make a face, then stopped herself. "Do you have a picture of her?"

"Sure do." Grinning, Tuck pulled out his phone and started shuffling through his photos.

Her face lit up. "Is she Puerto Rican? She looks

Puerto Rican."

"Cuban."

"That still earns you major points with my mom," Ethan told him. "You about done nosing around in Tuck's personal life, Ma?"

She shot Ethan a mock glare. "Showing interest isn't nosing around. God knows you've got no romantic life to tell me about, so I'm getting my fix elsewhere."

Ethan shook his head good-naturedly and put more burgers on the grill. His mom meant well, but he was happy to avoid the hot seat for once.

She couldn't help herself and tended to mother everyone, including his and Carmela's friends. Nothing would make her happier than having both her children get married and having half a dozen kids each so she could spoil them all rotten. Unfortunately for her, he and Carmela were busy with their careers and weren't looking to settle down anytime soon.

"Anyway, Brad, you were saying?" she prompted Tuck.

Ethan kept part of his attention on her conversation with Tuck as he manned the grill. She already knew better than to bug Vance about his personal life, since he was pretty tight-lipped about his split from his former fiancée just over a year ago. Ethan had also warned her beforehand not to pry into Blackwell's business, no matter how well-meaning she might be.

He wasn't sure what the deal was since Blackwell was private about stuff like that, but from what Ethan gathered, his teammate's marriage was on its last legs. Their high-tempo workload and schedule, the constant training and traveling sure took a toll on their personal relationships. It took a really special woman—strong and independent, but supportive—to make things work with one of them long term. Ethan hadn't dated a woman yet that could handle it.

Marisol seemed just as career-oriented though, he mused as he moved the nearly cooked burgers to a cooler part of the grill. He'd bet she could handle it.

As soon as that thought took shape in his mind, he deleted it. The attraction between them couldn't go anywhere. He'd decided that last night, had kept reminding himself of that throughout the day today.

Over in the corner of the yard, Schroder stepped away from where he'd been talking with Evers and Vance and headed toward him, eyeing the grill with interest. "Any bacon going on these babies?"

Their medic was a total bacon whore and everyone knew it. "Yup, it's inside. Got you covered, man."

"Awesome."

"What about you, Nathan?" Ethan's mom asked, shading her eyes with one hand as she peered up at him. "Have you got a young lady in your life?"

A wide smile broke over Schroder's face. "Do I ever." The former PJ shooed Tuck out of the lawn chair beside her and sat down to show her his phone. "Her name's Taya."

"That's a pretty name."

Ethan smirked. Oh, his mom was going to love this one. He busied himself with placing a slice of cheese on the cooked patties. "It's a great story, Ma. Go ahead, tell her, Doc," Ethan told him.

"Well now I definitely want to hear it," his mom said, her expression full of interest.

While Schroder began the tale of how he and Taya had met in Afghanistan five years ago, Ethan basted the chicken breasts with a final coat of barbecue sauce. He picked up his non-alcoholic beer—technically they were still on the clock and if the call came in about Alvarez, they'd have to rush back to headquarters, so no drinking for any of them. As he set down the bottle the sliding glass door off the kitchen opened up.

Everything inside him stilled when Marisol stepped out onto the deck with his sister. Her long, dark hair was loose, spilling past her shoulders in soft, dark-chocolate waves. The white and blue dress she wore showed off the shapely curve of her breasts and left her bronzed, sexy calves bare to his gaze.

She walked across the patio with Carmela, stopping to meet the guys sitting there. Ethan suppressed the instinct to go over and stand between her and the others, because it was ridiculous. All his teammates were spoken for except for Vance, and if his best buddy so much as looked at her wrong, Ethan would set him straight real fast. Soli was off limits.

The intensity of the possessive thought surprised him. He wasn't normally like that around women. For some reason Marisol revved the caveman part of his brain.

She was smiling at Blackwell as she shook his hand. Ethan set down his metal spatula and closed the lid on the grill before heading her way. She glanced over at him, her body stiffening slightly as he approached. Almost as if she was gearing up to face him.

He didn't like knowing that she felt the need to do that.

"Glad you could make it," he said.

Her skin practically glowed under the light from the setting sun. This close to her he could smell the fresh, clean mix of light perfume and soap that clung to her. It made him want to lean in and press his nose to the side of her neck, breathe her in. Would she shove him away? Or would she grab his shoulders and gasp, go still as she waited to see what he'd do next?

Her cheeks flushed a little at the way he was staring at her but she met his gaze squarely. "Me too. Carmela was just introducing me to your teammates."

"I'll do it," he said to his sister, and took Marisol's hand. She didn't resist as he led her down the two wooden steps and introduced her to everyone she hadn't met yet. Tuck, Bauer, Evers, Blackwell and finally Schroder. Their medic stopped talking to Ethan's mom and stood to shake Marisol's hand, then offered her his lawn chair.

"Had enough of the hot seat, huh?" Marisol teased as she sat down and crossed her gorgeous legs at the ankles.

Schroder grinned at her. Ethan's mom gasped and playfully batted her on the shoulder. "I'm just getting to know them. I want to know about the men who my son entrusts his life to on a daily basis, is that such a crime?"

Ethan handed Marisol a chilled bottle of sweet tea, her favorite. "Food's just about ready. You hungry? I'll get you a plate."

She peered up at him, gave a little smile that did strange things to his insides. "I'd like that, thank you."

He nodded, trying like hell not to stare at the way the dress pulled taut across her breasts, or how smooth and toned her legs were. The hem rode a few inches above her knees, exposing a hint of thigh. He had a sudden image of his hand on her bare knee, slowly inching it up beneath the soft fabric. He could almost feel her skin against his palm, warm and silky smooth.

Off limits, remember? Now feed her.

Jerking himself back to reality, he stepped up to the grill and grabbed a plate. He set a chicken breast and a heaping mound of salad on it. She'd never liked beef that much.

"Here," Carmela said, placing a casserole dish and the plate of cooked bacon down on the table beside him. "Soli's mom cooked *tostones*."

"Great." Ethan dished up a few more sides onto Marisol's plate and carried it to her. She accepted it with another smile and a murmured thanks, then turned back to Schroder.

That warm smile made him question why he'd decided she was off limits.

"Taya's still in North Carolina with her dad but I'm hoping she'll come to Virginia soon," Schroder was saying.

Tuck sauntered up and helped himself to a plate, held it out to Ethan with a grin. "You serving?"

"Just this once, so don't get used to it," he teased, and dished out food while all the guys lined up. When everyone was served he made himself a plate. His mother got up to go inside and Ethan seized his chance to sit beside Marisol.

She glanced at him out of the corner of her eye as she cut into her chicken. "This is really good, thanks."

"Welcome." Everyone else was either busy or involved in their own conversations, giving him and Marisol a semblance of privacy. "So," he began. "How are you doing? Any new developments at work?"

"You mean about the phone call?"

He nodded.

She shook her head. "I talked to the head FBI agent again this afternoon. Still no leads as to who the caller was. And before you ask, yes, I've been careful. I got myself a rental car and I'm staying at a friend's place for the time being. I circled the block a couple times before parking down the street, just to make sure no one had been following me."

He barely kept from asking whether it was a guy friend or a girl friend's place she was staying at. "That's good."

"What about you? Things okay at work today?"

"Yeah, they're good." Word was the Bureau's contact was closing in on a location for Alvarez. And from what Ethan had heard, Fuentes seemed close to agreeing to take a deal.

His mom came back a moment later and though Ethan didn't want to move from Marisol's side, he got up anyway and gave her his seat. By way of thanks she snagged the back of his neck with one hand to pull him down and plant a smacking kiss on his cheek.

"See this?" he called out to Vance, who looked over at him from where he was seated on the deck. "This is the treatment you get when you're her blood—and favorite, I might add—son."

Vance's mouth twitched. "Whatever. I already got my kiss before dinner."

Ethan's mom laughed and pushed at his shoulder. "Don't be jealous, Ethan. You know my heart's big enough to fit all of you in it."

"It's okay, I know you love me best," he murmured, sharing a smile with her and giving her a smacking kiss on the cheek. Before he'd even straightened, she'd launched into a conversation with Marisol, giving her an easy out.

He stood beside her and ate his dinner. When she showed no sign of letting up in her conversation with his mom, he wandered over and shot the shit with Blackwell for a few minutes, then Bauer. No surprise, the former SEAL's plate was piled high with two burgers, two chicken breasts and all the sides.

Out of the corner of his eye, he noticed Marisol get up and follow his mother toward the deck. Ethan tossed his empty plate into the garbage can next to the grill and scraped the grill clean. He eyed Marisol as she made her way into the kitchen with some empty platters, appreciating the sexy sway of her hips as she moved.

"Wow, so subtle," Carmela said sarcastically as she came up beside him.

"What?" he demanded.

"You're damn near stripping her with your eyes from all the way over here." Carm shook her head. "Since when have you been interested in her that way?"

Since she jumped out of a tree into my arms. "I'm not."

His sister threw him a bland look. "Whatever. Listen," she said as she spooned the leftover Greek salad into a container she'd brought from the kitchen, "just a friendly heads up then, because I love you. You might want to rethink your strategy here."

Ethan turned to face her. "Meaning?" Carm rarely stuck her nose in his business, and the few times she had, he'd learned to listen to what she had to say. He raised his drink, took a big swig.

"If you're looking for a hookup, think again."

He scowled as he swallowed the mouthful. "Whoa, that's—"

"Oh, please. That's *exactly* how you were just looking at her, and don't deny it."

He felt a flush creep up the back of his neck. "I'm not looking to hook up with her."

Okay, so he'd fantasized about it. Didn't mean he'd act on it, and even if he did, he sure as hell wouldn't make her feel cheap. He knew how to treat a woman right, and with Marisol he'd make damn sure he saw to her every need.

She was too important to him to just fuck and walk away, even if she was interested. They had too much history together and he didn't want to ruin a twenty-year friendship over a one-night stand.

So what do you want then?

Fuck if he knew. He just knew the attraction he felt wasn't going away, and that he couldn't touch her if he couldn't offer her more than a fling while he was in town.

"Well, good," his sister said. "She deserves better."

Ethan drew his head back, taken aback by his sister's comment. "What the hell, Carm?"

"I'm just saying, I'm glad you're not going to try anything. She's not anywhere near as, ah, experienced as you."

He raised one eyebrow. "Meaning?" He took another

pull from the bottle.

"Oh, for God's sake." Carm rolled her eyes at his apparent stupidity and leaned in close so that no one else would overhear her. "I mean she's a virgin, dumbass," she murmured.

He nearly choked on his fake beer. Quickly swallowing, he fought back a cough and gaped at his sister, wiping the back of one hand across his mouth. "Are you fucking serious?"

She nodded. "Dead serious."

It couldn't be true. There was no way. It just wasn't possible. "How the hell do you know that?" he blurted. There was no way Marisol would just go around telling people that, not even Carmela.

Carm gave him a pitying look and sighed. "I'm best friends with her older sister, that's how."

Yeah, he guessed that would do it. But seriously, Marisol was still a virgin? *How*? It made no sense.

"All I'm saying is, if I read that look you gave her right, just don't play with her. She deserves better. That's all I meant."

Ethan didn't answer, just shifted his gaze to the house as Carm walked away, carrying the container. He could see Marisol in the kitchen with his mom, laughing as they stood doing something at the kitchen counter together.

It felt like he was looking at her with brand new eyes. She was in her mid-twenties. How could a woman as smart and hot as her make it to that age without having sex? Obviously she hadn't wanted to, but why?

As he stared at her from afar, that dark sense of possessiveness she brought out in him surged to the surface. She'd never had sex, had never slept with a man before. And if she'd stayed a virgin this long, it meant she had strong reasons for doing so. The man she chose for her first lover would have to earn that right. Be worthy of it.

I could be her first.

The thought was loud in his head, and undeniable. Hell, at that moment all he could think about was how much he *wanted* to be her first.

He had a sudden, vivid image of him stretched out on top of her naked body, his hips wedged between her open thighs, his hands fisting her hair as he surged inside her, watching her face the entire time. It was so freaking hot he could barely drag air into his lungs.

She trusted him, she'd even said so. She knew he would never hurt her. He could show her how good sex could be with the right partner, how good he could make her feel.

A warning tingle started up in his gut, cautioning him to be careful. She'd already gotten under his skin, without even trying. He had the feeling that if things ever went that far between them, he'd never be able to get her out of his system. A real problem when she was rooted so deeply here and he was leaving Miami soon.

A set of keys suddenly appeared in front of his eyes, dangling from a dark fist. He looked over his shoulder to find Vance standing behind him, a half smirk on his face. "What?" Ethan demanded.

"I said your name twice and you didn't hear me. I'm gonna catch a ride back to the hotel with Evers and Bauer," he said. "You go do whatcha gotta do, brother. See her home safe."

Ethan took the keys with a nod, glad Vance understood and that he didn't have to explain anything. Because he was absolutely seeing Marisol home safely tonight.

Vance smacked him on his sore shoulder on the way past and Ethan couldn't even drum up enough annoyance to glare at him. He was too focused on the mysterious and tantalizing woman somewhere in his mom's house.

He hurried over to the deck and stepped inside the kitchen. Marisol stood over beside the sink. She paused in the midst of drying her hands on a kitchen towel, her sea green gaze finding his.

Her purse lay in front of her on the counter, her keys set next to it. He knew in his gut she'd totally planned on bailing without a word to him. Because he made her uncomfortable? Unless it was because she was unsure of how to handle the attraction between them, he wasn't okay with that.

He slid his hands into his front pockets. "You weren't gonna leave without saying goodbye, were you?"

"No, but I didn't want to interrupt you and your friends. I was just going to wave at you from the deck and then go."

Like hell he'd have allowed her to brush him off that way. "I'll follow you back to your friend's place, make sure you get there safe."

"It's not necessary—"

"Soli. I'm following you." He put just enough steel into his voice to make it clear there was no room for argument.

She sighed, nodded. "All right." She went out onto the deck to hug his mother and Carm goodbye. When she headed for the front door without looking at him, Ethan was right behind her.

Chapter Seven

⸺⸺⸺⸺⸺

"**I**'m so not letting him live this down next time I see him."

Special Agent Sawyer Vance grinned at Schroder, who'd just taken the empty deck chair beside him a minute ago to watch Ethan leave with Marisol. "Payback?"

"Kind of. Mostly I just like to give you guys a hard time whenever I get the chance." Schroder took a bite of a thick wedge of brownie Mama Cruz had set out for them on a platter. Sawyer had already devoured three of them.

In addition to being a sweet but albeit nosy lady, his adopted mother was one helluva cook. He'd already eaten the better part of her famous flan and a serving of bread pudding, which she'd made especially for him because she knew they were his favorites.

"So I overheard you say Taya might be moving to Virginia soon?"

"Yeah, we hope in the next few weeks. Her dad's better now and it sucks being apart from her when I'm back in Quantico. It'd be way easier if she moved in with me. We're both looking forward to spending more time together, instead of the odd day here and there when I can get time off to go see her down in Raleigh."

"That's great, man. Glad to hear it." That lady had been through hell and back and she'd done wonders for Schroder's headspace already. They deserved to be together, deserved every bit of happiness they could wring out of this life.

Schroder smiled and took a sip of his drink. "Thanks. You seeing anybody?" he asked casually.

"Nah." He'd gone on a handful of dates over the past few months, but nothing had ever come from them. It was probably too soon for him to date anyway. The raw wounds he'd been carrying around inside had only recently begun to heal.

"Hard to put yourself out there with our line of work."

"I guess." Normally this kind of conversation with one of the guys would make him uncomfortable as hell, but with Schroder he didn't mind. The guy had a way about him that made him easy to talk to. "Not easy to find someone worthwhile, you know?" Even when he thought he'd found The One, he'd been proven dead wrong about that, as he'd learned a little over a year ago. While he wasn't bitter about the split anymore, he no longer trusted his instincts where women were concerned.

And speaking of the opposite sex, there was one woman he was trying desperately not to notice in that way.

"No, it's not," Schroder agreed with a shake of his head before chomping down on the brownie. Sawyer knew they were still warm from the oven. He could totally go for another one. Or three.

A whiff of something fruity and delicious was his only warning an instant before a warm weight settled on his knee.

"Hey, you." Carmela leaned in to push up the brim

of his Stetson with one finger, a teasing smile on her face.

And just that fast, he went rigid.

All over.

"Hey," he answered, automatically grabbing her hips to keep her from shifting any closer to his groin. That was a mistake too, though, since all it did was draw attention to how soft yet firm her hips were. The woman had curves that wouldn't quit, no matter how hard he tried not to notice. It was torture.

"If I didn't know better, I'd think you've been trying to avoid me all night." She tilted her head, her light brown eyes delving into his. Refusing to let him worm his way out of this. "Hope that's not true."

"Ah, no. No, of course not." Out of the corner of his eye he caught Schroder staring at them with obvious interest, paused mid-chew with his mouth full of brownie. His teammate raised both eyebrows at him before getting up and sauntering off, but not before Sawyer saw the little smirk on the guy's face. Oh yeah, he hadn't heard the last on this.

Seeming not to notice his teammate, Carmela drew a gentle fingertip down the side of his cheek. "The goatee's new. I like it."

The gesture could be construed as merely affectionate, but he didn't think so, not anymore. And his body thought otherwise as well. Her seemingly intimate touch sizzled across the nerve endings in his face, making his jeans even tighter at the crotch.

Shit, shit, shit.

He shifted slightly, his fingers digging into the swell of her hips and it was impossible to ignore the sudden image that popped into his head. Her, naked straddling him, her long, chocolate-brown hair spilling down her back, him holding her this same way as he guided her up and down his erection.

It made him feel guilty as fuck, because she was

Ethan's freaking *sister*. What was wrong with him?

"Um, thanks," he muttered. Seemed like the right response even as he banished the erotic images from his head. He was glad Ethan wasn't here because if he even suspected something was up between them, he'd kill him.

Or maybe cut Sawyer's balls off with a rusty knife while he slept.

Ethan was his best friend and had been for the past two years, but Sawyer adored both Carmela and their mother too. They'd accepted him as part of their family and that meant the world to him. He wouldn't let anything jeopardize that, not even his new and not-so-brotherly feelings for Carmela.

No matter how much he'd fantasized about stripping the woman on his lap and pinning her to the nearest flat surface while he made her writhe and sob in pleasure until she came, calling his name.

He relaxed his grip on her, made himself let go. Shit, he had to stop this dangerous train of thought, but he didn't know how. He'd been so careful to hide his growing feelings for her over the past few months. Ever since she'd started giving subtle signals that she was attracted to him when she'd come up to Quantico to visit Ethan in February.

She'd always teased him a little, a light and borderline flirtation he hadn't thought much of before, but lately when they talked occasionally on the phone or via e-mail, she'd been less subtle. Her flirting had become more obvious, her tone more suggestive. Again, he hadn't worried because of the thousand miles between them. He'd always thought she was sexy but he'd ruthlessly squelched those thoughts around her.

Tonight there was zero distance, and no question that she'd just upped the ante. It was dangerous. It felt like he and Carmela were on a collision course to disaster and he was helpless to stop it from happening.

Sawyer cleared his throat, glanced away as he forced his body to relax. Nobody else was paying any attention to them except for Schroder, who was grinning at him from over in the corner of the yard while stuffing his face with yet another brownie where he stood with Blackwell and Evers.

He struggled to think of something safe to say to Carmela. He sensed that if he showed her even a hint of interest, it would be game over. She wouldn't do anything too overt here in front of her mother and the guys, but he had to be very careful to avoid being alone with her.

Because God help him, he didn't think he had the strength to stop her, let alone turn her down if she made a move, consequences or not. He could easily shut her down now and be nice about it, sure, but he just couldn't do it. Didn't *want* to.

"So Ethan seems to be pretty into Marisol, huh?" he said to change the subject. Throwing his buddy under the bus while he wasn't here to defend himself might be kinda low, but at least it took the heat off Sawyer's predicament for the moment.

Carmela was still way too close. Smelled way too good. "I saw that. I already warned him to keep his hands off. Soli doesn't play around like that."

Sawyer shifted his gaze back to her. "I don't think he's aiming to play with her." He'd seen the way Ethan had looked at Marisol tonight and he'd looked like a man with anything but playing on his mind, which was why he'd handed over the keys to the vehicle. His buddy seemed to have some things to straighten out with her.

She grinned. "I love it when your accent comes through like that."

"I don't have an accent." Not anymore.

"Sure you do. It's subtle, but it comes out every now and again. Like now, when you said 'aiming to play with her'. It sounded very Oklahoma."

EXPOSED

"Well, I guess you can take the boy out of Oklahoma, but you can't take Oklahoma out of the boy."

"Trust me, there's nothing boyish about you. Except maybe your grin, and when I make you blush," she added in a near whisper, leaning a little closer.

It felt like she was challenging him. He should have leaned away but his stubborn streak wouldn't let him. He didn't back down. Wouldn't, even if he knew what would happen if he let things go too far.

He could feel the heat creeping up the back of his neck as she stared at him. "So, how did your brother take that news about Marisol?" he asked to change the subject again.

Carmela snorted. "You just saw for yourself how he marched out the door to follow her home." She shook her head. "I know he's a decent guy and that he'd never hurt her on purpose. It's him hurting her by accident that worries me. It'd be awkward, you know? If anything bad happened between them it would wreck everything."

"Yeah." *Just like it would wreck everything with you and me.* Not to mention his relationship with her family. Sawyer couldn't handle those consequences. Not again.

Carmela shifted on his knee, settling more of her weight onto his thigh, then stopped, searching his eyes. "Am I hurting your leg?"

He nearly snorted at the question. "No." He was a big guy and she was maybe a hundred and forty pounds, soaking wet.

Mmmm, Carmela, naked and soaking wet...

No, her weight felt way too fucking good. And man, her scent was making his mouth water. Coconut and something tart, like lime or something. A fresh mix of sweet and tart, just like her. He'd bet she tasted just as good as she smelled, too.

He mentally slapped the thought away. It may have been months since he'd last been with a woman, but his current erection had nothing to do with sexual frustration and everything to do with the woman perched on his knee. Carmela was hot and smart and sweet. And way too freaking sexy for his own good.

He wasn't even sure when his feelings for her had started to change. A couple months after he'd broken up with Trina, maybe. All he knew was, they were getting stronger and he couldn't shut them off. And he wasn't a saint.

But none of that mattered because as tempting as Carmela was, she was absolutely forbidden to him. Guys didn't do their best friend's sister. Said so right there in the first rule of the best friend handbook. A rule he wished he'd paid attention to earlier.

Mama Cruz stepped out onto the deck from the kitchen. Her gaze landed on him and Carmela, a flash of surprise flitting across her face when she saw her daughter perched atop his lap before she masked it and smiled at him. "Sawyer, did you get enough of my brownies?"

"I was thinking of having one more," he said, trying and failing to ignore how close Carmela still was. Mama Cruz was sharp as hell, but thankfully she didn't seem to pick up on the undercurrent simmering between him and Carmela. At least, not that he could tell. He hoped. "They're awesome."

"I thought you might. Here." She handed him a foil-wrapped package and gave him a wink. "I made you an extra batch to take with you, and wrapped up the leftover bread pudding." Then she aimed a hard look at her daughter. "Carmela, stop monopolizing him and let him unwind with his friends. I need a hand with the cleanup."

"I'll help," he blurted, glad for an excuse to get up and put some space between them.

Mama Cruz smiled at him. "Thanks, sweetie."

Man, he loved it when she called him that. Maybe it was because his mom had taken off when he was three and left him and his dad behind for greener pastures—but he just adored the woman, would do anything for her.

Including never acting on his feelings for her daughter.

Carmela huffed out a laugh. "All right, all right," she grumbled. When Mama Cruz headed down the steps with another plate of brownies for the others, Carmela met his gaze once more. "So, are you going to have any more free time while you're down here?"

Yep. Trouble with a capital T. "Not sure. Just depends how things go." As in, if they got the intel they needed to go execute the standing warrant for Alvarez or any one of Fuentes's cronies.

"You still owe me that two-stepping lesson you promised," she reminded him.

Shit, he had promised her, hadn't he? Maybe he was a closet masochist and just hadn't realized it before. "Right."

She set a hand on his shoulder and pushed herself up. His muscles automatically tensed and he shot out a hand to steady her, his fingers wrapping around the curve of her waist. He bit back a groan at the feel of her, her flesh warm and resilient through the material of the dress she wore.

"Hey, man. You ready to go?"

Sawyer swung his head around as Blackwell came up the wooden steps onto the deck, Evers and Bauer right behind him. "Sure." He stood, put a foot or two of distance between him and Carmela as he faced her once more. "Was good to see you."

She gave him a soft smile, all traces of innuendo gone. "You too. If you have some time while you're here, call me."

"I will." He wouldn't though. And if he was smart, he'd avoid her at all costs until he was safely back in Quantico.

****

Bautista watched from the end of the street as Marisol exited the Cruz's house. He'd left for a while after she'd gone to the barbecue and come back after his phone call to Perez was done. The next target was confirmed. Bautista was going in tomorrow night to take care of it.

He'd been waiting here for the past hour, waiting for Marisol to come out because he liked to study the people on his list. He'd been thinking a lot about Julia, and what she'd said, had made up his mind to ask her out, when Marisol walked out.

And then Ethan Cruz appeared and followed her out onto the sidewalk.

He mentally cursed and tugged the brim of his ball cap lower on his forehead. He was parked at the far end of the street in the shade of a big palm tree, so neither of them could see his face from that distance.

Marisol didn't glance his way but Ethan did, his gaze stopping on the Lexus before scanning the rest of the street. It only confirmed what he already knew about the guy, that he'd served in the Corps with MARSOC and now worked for the FBI.

As a kid and teenager, Ethan had run with a rough crowd. Back then it had been all about street cred and reputation in their neighborhood. They hadn't hung around together or anything, and Bautista sure as hell hadn't been popular enough to run with Ethan's crowd. Marisol had always been kind to him though. It was *still* about reputation, but the stakes for both him and Ethan had changed. Now it was a matter of life and death.

Seeing them together put him in a uniquely sticky situation. A warning tingle in his gut told him a confrontation was inevitable. Only Bautista didn't have to play by the same rules as Ethan did.

He knew Marisol was working on the Fuentes case. She'd been right that he'd changed a lot since she'd last seen him. In more ways than she could possibly imagine. He wasn't the same person she'd known back then, not in name or in spirit.

He also knew Ethan was no ordinary Fed. Upon doing some research, he'd learned that the HRT was in town on a joint-training exercise with the DEA. Which was just a cover story for what was really going on.

The truth was the HRT was in town working with the FAST team, waiting to take down Alvarez. While Bautista wouldn't mind the help in eliminating that particular target, it put him in direct conflict with Ethan. And now maybe Marisol too, because of him.

Bautista watched them walk up the sidewalk to the big black Ford pickup parked at the curb. Ethan stopped as he let her in to scan the road again, ever vigilant. Not an easy man to sneak up on.

This was a complication he hadn't planned on, but one he needed to plan for. The time may come when he was forced into the position of having to kill one or both of them.

He wouldn't enjoy doing it, especially in Marisol's case, but he'd do whatever was necessary to protect himself. He'd never killed a woman before, let alone someone he knew and liked, so he would only do it as a last resort.

The conflict and frustration brewing inside him continued to grow by the second.

She didn't deserve to die. Did she have any idea what she'd gotten herself into in this case? What she was setting herself up for?

He'd warned her once already to stay out of it and he hoped she was smart enough to heed it. She wasn't irreplaceable to the U.S. Attorney's Office or the case. Her death would merely be a hindrance, slow the trial down a little. It wouldn't stop anything, except maybe to scare away some key witnesses willing to testify. If someone like Marisol wasn't safe, then the criminals being brought to testify would be spooked about their own security.

Not that Bautista gave a rat's ass about Fuentes or the case in general. He had to watch Marisol carefully from here on out though. Because she was fucking smart, and had a reputation of being a bulldog when it came to following up a lead. If she kept digging long enough and somehow was able to figure out who he really was…

He'd have no choice.

Don't force my hand, Marisol.

He waited until the truck turned the corner at the far end of the block. Then he stayed another few minutes to make sure Ethan didn't double back. When he didn't, Bautista turned the ignition and drove away in the opposite direction. He had more investigative work to do in the coming hours and another, more severe warning to deliver tomorrow night.

Chapter Eight

T he sun had almost set by the time Ethan pulled up to the curb a half block away from Marisol's friend's house in a quiet Coral Gables neighborhood. He'd driven her to where she'd parked her rental a block from her mom's place, then followed her here.

He watched while she pulled into the garage and closed the door without exiting her vehicle, as he'd told her to before leaving. He'd been vigilant on his way over and hadn't noticed anyone tailing them. It was still possible someone could have though, and he wasn't taking chances with her safety.

Shutting the truck door, he rounded the hood and started up the sidewalk, casting a covert look around. A few people were out walking their dog and a couple of kids were playing in a sprinkler on the front lawn of their house across from where Marisol was staying.

She opened the side garage door for him, her expression composed, a little remote. It annoyed him that she kept putting up that barrier between them.

Her purse strap was draped over one shoulder, the keys dangling from her hand. "I assume no one followed us?" Her tone was even, but he sensed a slight sarcastic edge to it. She was the very definition of forbidden temptation standing there in that sexy dress and heels.

It made him want to slide a hand into her hair and twist her face up to his so he could kiss her. Tease her, taste her until she melted and trembled against him.

He ignored the tone, not wanting to get into an argument with her. Right now his priority was making sure she was settled and safe. "As far as I can tell, no."

She let out a deep breath. "You don't think this is overkill? I'm already staying here as a precaution while Lindsay's away and I've agreed to keep a low profile from here on out."

"Nope, not even a little." He strode past her toward the door that led inside. A whiff of her warm, clean scent reached him. "Did you already disable the alarm?"

"Yes." She followed him, her high heels clicking on the concrete floor.

Since they made her legs look insanely sexy, it was probably better that he couldn't see them right now. Because when he did, all he could think about was sliding his hands up their bare length, pushing that dress up to see what she had on beneath it. And then imagine those gorgeous legs wrapped around his shoulders as he teased the soft flesh between them with his mouth.

"Wait here a minute." He said it gently but she still folded her arms and raised an eyebrow. "Just until I can check everything out."

She relented with a nod. "Be my guest."

He entered into the kitchen and swept the downstairs. It consisted of the living room, a small den and a powder room near the front door. All the blinds were closed and the air conditioning was on. Upstairs he checked the master suite, guest room and guest bath before coming back down.

Marisol was waiting for him where he'd left her in

the garage. She looked a bit tired now, her guard dropping slightly to reveal the sweet, soft woman beneath it. It made the urge to kiss her even stronger.

"All clear?" she murmured.

His fingers itched to wind into the thick fall of her hair, tilt her head back as he leaned in to kiss her. "Yep. Do you keep the blinds closed all the time and the windows locked?"

"Since I got here yesterday, yes."

Her cool expression told him she was placating him but he didn't care. "I'll go check the yard." He also wanted to get the lay of the land, make note of any blatant security lapses he could correct while here.

"Go ahead." She set her purse down on the kitchen island and headed for the fridge, her hips swaying in an enticing way and the muscles in her calves defined by the high heels.

God.

Ethan let himself out the sliding glass door onto the back patio. Immediately two security lights attached to the side of the house came on. All the windows were closed. The small yard was surrounded by an eight-foot tall privacy fence. He checked around both sides of the house too, for good measure. Everything looked secure.

He let himself back into the kitchen, locked the sliders and pulled the blinds. Marisol was seated at a bar stool at the island, sipping a sparkling water. "Looks good," he told her, trying to ignore the way her full lower lip shone with moisture as she lowered the bottle. He wanted to lick it away, steal inside to taste her.

"I'm glad." She held up her bottle, raised an eyebrow. "Want one?"

It would give him an excuse to stay for a little while longer. "Sure, thanks."

She got up and brought him one, sitting back on the bar stool while he stood and leaned a forearm on the opposite side of the island.

"How's the case going?"

"Good. Lots of research to do still and plenty of people to interview. I see Fuentes tomorrow."

Shit, he hated the thought of her being in the same room as that twisted fuck, but he kept that to himself and nodded as he took a sip of the water he didn't really want. He hated sparkling water. Water should be flat, not fizzy. It was wrong. If he wanted something carbonated he'd drink either beer or soda. He made himself take another sip.

"Still trying to set up a deal he'll bite at. If we sweeten it enough, he might give us information on his lieutenants. Provided he even knows where they are, and who their enforcers are."

He made a sound of agreement, congratulating himself on how calm he appeared when in reality he rebelled at the very idea of her working with Fuentes. He respected the hell out of what she did though. She was smart and capable, apparently a damn good lawyer if she'd already made Assistant U.S. Attorney.

Didn't mean he had to like her taking the risks that came with the territory, however.

She cast him a look from beneath her lashes, then smiled a little. "Your mom really seemed to enjoy having your teammates there tonight."

"Yeah, she's been wanting to meet them all for a long time."

"It's sweet how she dotes on your friend Sawyer. She's definitely got a soft spot for him."

Ethan grunted. "I think she'd like to trade him for me sometimes," he said wryly. "But nah, it's all good. He grew up with a single dad, so he loves it that my mom makes a fuss over him."

Her smile widened. "That's nice to hear. And if he sticks around long enough, sooner or later he'll start getting the little digs she always gives you and Carm about settling down and giving her nineteen grandkids."

Ethan made a face. "God, I hope so. She's relentless."

Marisol laughed softly, the husky sound revving his already overactive hormones. "Yeah, I know how that works." She fiddled with the bottle for a moment, her fingers stroking the glass, and he imagined them stroking over a certain portion of his anatomy that was currently making his jeans uncomfortably tight. "You still try to convince her to move every now and again?"

"Yeah, little good it does. She won't leave, period." Their neighborhood had improved a lot since he was a kid, but there were still plenty of nicer, safer places for his mother to live in Miami. But she was stubborn as a freaking ox.

"Mine either." She sighed. "She's too attached to the people there, won't leave no matter what my sisters and I say. She just tells us we're ridiculous that we worry about her safety there."

"How are your sisters, anyway?"

"Good. Ynez is an accountant for a company downtown and Bianca teaches at an elementary school in Coconut Grove."

"And your niece? How's she?" A real cutie pie who kept all the Lorenzo women hopping.

Marisol gave a soft smile, her expression a mix of pride and tenderness. Ethan had always thought she'd had a strong maternal streak. She was a fantastic aunt and he had no doubt she'd be a great mother one day to some lucky kid. He knew she'd always wanted that. Marriage and a family of her own.

Another reason why he should keep his distance.

"Vero's nine already, if you can believe it. She said to say hi to you."

The years went by pretty quick. "Say hi back."

"I think she's got a serious hero worship complex when it comes to you."

Ethan smiled. "Yeah?"

She nodded. "She doesn't have a lot of men in her life."

He set down his water. This was the perfect opening to broach the subject he was dying to ask her about. But he had to go slowly, be subtle about it. Not exactly his strong suit, but for her he'd make the effort. "Both your sisters still single?"

"Ynez is. She's super protective with her daughter and won't date anyone for very long if they don't measure up to be a good role model for Vero. Bianca's been dating a guy for the past year or so. We all like him. Ynez and I have a bet going about when he'll propose."

"And what about you?"

Her gaze shifted up to his for a second, then lowered her eyes. "Haven't dated anyone for a while. You?"

"No. Too busy with work."

She nodded. "Yeah, me too. This case has me working crazy hours. And I'll bet it's tough for you to date anyone long term given your job and security clearance and whatnot."

"That too, yeah." *How can you still be a virgin?* he wanted to blurt out.

It defied logic. The longer he was around her, the more beautiful she became. Her brains and drive were sexy as hell. And though she'd earned the reputation of Ice Princess back in the day by coming across as standoffish and unattainable to the guys in the neighborhood, once you got to know her and she let down her guard a little, her charm and kindness were impossible to ignore.

Right now, he was having a hard time staying where he was instead of rounding the island and kissing her until she was breathless.

A heavy silence spread between them, spiked with a heavy undercurrent of desire. Marisol was the first to glance away, her gaze shifting to the bottle between her hands on the island top.

Her cheeks turned pink in the most adorable way and Ethan couldn't help but wonder if she'd turn pink all over if she knew the things he wanted to do with her. With his hands and mouth, and other parts.

"Well," she said, pushing up from the stool. "I appreciate you seeing me here and checking everything out, but I should probably call it a night. Have some work to do before I can hit the hay and then I've got to be at the office early."

"Sure." A little disappointed even though he understood and could use some sleep himself, he carried his half empty water to the sink and emptied it.

She came up beside him to do the same. Once again his senses heightened. She was small but not too small, and definitely not fragile, especially in disposition. Her sweet scent teased him, made him want to lean in and run his nose up the side of her neck where her pulse throbbed visibly beneath her lightly bronzed skin.

Marisol seemed to still next to him, avoiding eye contact as she stood there with her hand wrapped around the bottle.

He couldn't fight the need to touch her for a moment longer. Ethan allowed himself to slide a hand into those dark-chocolate waves. Her gaze darted up to his, held. Her hair was silky soft, cool to the touch. And though he read a little hesitation in her eyes, they also held growing desire.

He wouldn't push her for more tonight. "Lock up tight and set the alarm after I leave," he murmured. Her eyes were so gorgeous. He could get lost in them if he let himself.

Part of him wanted that. To lean down and kiss her,

sink into her. See if she'd want what he could offer, the pleasure he wanted to give her, even if it was only short term. He'd give her so much more than he'd take.

But he had no right to make a move if he had no intention of giving her more than a few days at most. Even if he wanted to, he couldn't. He'd be leaving Miami and heading back to Quantico as soon as this op was done. "And if anything happens that makes you nervous, call me," he added.

She nodded and whispered, "I will."

The seconds stretched out, the pause growing taut with anticipation. His hand tightened briefly in her hair, the strands thick and soft against his skin. Though he wanted to wrap both his hands in it and turn her mouth up to his, instead he bent and pressed a kiss to the middle of her forehead, aching to give her so much more. "Sleep tight."

She swallowed, seemed surprised that he hadn't pushed for more. "Thanks. You too."

Releasing her, he stepped back and headed for the door, aware of her following behind him. Tantalizingly close, but still so far away.

****

Seated across a sleek metal table from the defendant the next morning, Marisol kept her hands loosely clasped in her lap and refused to shrink away from the hard stare aimed at her. It's what Fuentes wanted. To intimidate her. The sole female in the room, an easy target. The weak link.

Or so he thought.

She held that cold black gaze out of pure defiance as her boss continued to outline the terms of the deal they were prepared to offer him.

"If you want to avoid a needle at the end of your

sentencing, then you need to give us enough to get Alvarez or Perez, preferably both, and their enforcers. Most importantly, *el Santo*," Frank told him.

Fuentes's full lips twisted into a condescending sneer as he shifted his gaze to Frank. "You think I'm afraid of dying?"

Frank didn't miss a beat. "I don't care one way or the other. I'm just saying that if you want to live past the age of forty-two, then you'd better seriously consider taking this deal."

Fuentes leaned back in his seat, the plastic creaking under his weight. Even in an orange prison jumpsuit with his hands and feet chained, he still radiated danger. And power. The kind that came from holding men's lives in his hands. "You think I have a fucking clue where *el Santo* is? Or even *who* he is?"

"I think you know a lot more than you've admitted to previously, yeah," Frank said, his tone just as hard.

Fuentes's answering smile was a hard slash in the midst of his neatly-trimmed goatee. "You might be disappointed."

Marisol barely resisted the urge to roll her eyes. This asshole was playing them, still, even though the trial was less than a month away. She shot Frank a look that said it was time to leave. They wouldn't get anything else out of the man. They'd made their offer, now it was up to him to decide whether his life was worth taking the deal.

"And what about her?" Fuentes added in a silky voice. He nodded at Marisol, his eyes still on Frank.

"Her? She's only the best assistant attorney in my office."

Fuentes shook his head, a soft chuckle escaping that raised the hair on the back of Marisol's neck. "Wrong. She's the sacrificial lamb in this little game." Now his black gaze settled on her, chilling her from the inside out.

She suppressed a shiver, refusing to let him see how

much he repulsed her.

"I knew as soon as you walked in here with her that you're not nearly as smart as you like to think you are. She's fresh meat. Any one of my lieutenants will have her in their crosshairs, and I hear someone's already got her in their sights."

She barely refrained from shooting a questioning look at Frank. Had Fuentes ordered someone to target her? Or was this merely another scare tactic?

Had to be. This facility was secure. They'd moved him here immediately after the attacks in D.C. during the Qureshi trial, to prevent a similar attack from happening. Dozens of militants had stormed the courthouse back in April, killing scores of people and injuring countless others.

"You think you can protect her, Escobar?" Fuentes continued in a taunting voice. "From someone like *el Santo* if his boss gives the order to take her out?" He let out a flat laugh. "Right. She's hot, I'll give you that, and I'm sure she gives good head under your desk while you're pushing paper around, but the truth is, she's a liability."

Marisol's gut clenched and she barely withheld a gasp. She'd dealt with some asshole defendants and witnesses before, but none as disgusting as him. Frank tensed beside her, his expression tight.

She struggled to bite her tongue. Just because she was quiet didn't mean she was a doormat. Every word of this was being recorded and there was a team of FBI agents on the other side of the two-way mirrored wall behind her. She still wanted to spit in his face. But she shouldn't be surprised. He was a disgusting human being who peddled drugs, weapons and human beings for profit.

"They'll make an example out of her," Fuentes went on, the gleam in his eyes telling her he was enjoying himself now. "Killing her will slow down the trial, maybe even kill your case if the witnesses you say you've got lined up suddenly decide to split town rather than testify against me." He smirked at them both. "What then? You brought her on board for this, her first big case. Can you live with that if anything happens to her, Frank?"

Enough.

She leveled a cutting glare across the table and held her ground. "You don't scare me, Fuentes."

His gaze shot back to her, a hint of surprise showing in his oily black eyes.

"You're the one in chains. And frankly, if I'm not getting a death threat on a weekly basis, then it means I'm not doing my job. But you know what? I am doing my job." She threw him a smug smile, just to make her words burn a little more. "That's why you're never going to see the outside of a jail cell once the trial is over." *You pathetic, scum-sucking waste of skin*, she added to herself.

Fuentes narrowed his eyes at her and opened his mouth to respond but Frank snatched the folder from the desk with an angry swipe. He pushed his chair back, the metal legs scraping over the concrete floor with a grating sound that put Marisol's nerves further on edge. "This is the federal government's final offer, Fuentes," he said, waving the file. "Take it or leave it, I don't give a shit." He threw it down in front of him with a thwap that was surprisingly loud in the austere room.

Fuentes didn't answer, merely stared up at Frank with an insolent expression until her boss turned away and started for the door. "We're done here."

Marisol stood, refusing to show how much he'd angered her as she got to her feet. Her heart was knocking against her sternum as she followed Frank.

"Sweetheart."

She didn't stop, didn't acknowledge the blatant disrespect in Fuentes's tone with even a single glance as she reached the doorway.

"You've got balls, I'll give you that, but think about what I said," he called after her. "It's not too late to get out. Take my advice, quit while you still can."

The steel door shut behind them with a resounding clang. Marisol took a steadying breath there in the hallway, kept a rapid pace as she put distance between herself and that room. Agent Lammers was there, along with two others.

"You get all that?" Frank asked him.

"Yeah. We'll keep digging into it, see if there's any indication that call to Marisol came on his orders, but my gut says it was orchestrated by someone on the outside. I'll be in touch."

It absolutely could have come from Fuentes himself, but Marisol kept her mouth shut. He could have paid off any number of guards or officials, let alone inmates, even from this high security prison.

Frank nodded and indicated for her to follow him toward the exit. She fell in step with him and headed for the front doors, still fuming inside. *Let it go. He's not escaping justice this time.*

"Hey."

She stopped and looked up at her boss with a carefully composed expression, paused before the exit. His face was a study in concern. "He's boxed into a corner and he knows it. He's just trying to mess with you, screw with your head because he hates that he's powerless now. Don't let him get to you. Trust me, you're the furthest thing from a weak link in this case."

"I won't." She raised her chin, pretended she wasn't rattled in the least. At the moment all she wanted was to get out of there and get back to work. "I'm hungry. Want to grab a bite on the way back to the office?"

His lips twitched in a half-smile. "Yeah, sure." Then he sobered. "There's no way he could have orchestrated anything from in here."

Frank was only trying to make her feel better, so she pasted on a smile. "Personally, I hope he rejects the deal and opts for the needle."

Frank huffed out a laugh and patted her once on the back. "Damn, I wish I could clone you, Lorenzo. If I had a dozen assistant attorneys like you, we'd win the drug war down here within a year."

She held onto those words for the rest of the afternoon and into the evening. Every time Fuentes's face crept into her mind or that oily smile flitted through her concentration, she thought about what Frank had said. Diego Fuentes was a sore loser and a misogynistic asshole, plain and simple. She refused to let him shake her confidence or make her afraid.

By the time she finished up a file she'd been working on in preparation for the coming interview down in Key West on Monday morning, it was almost midnight. After shutting down her computer and grabbing all her stuff she headed for the elevator.

Manny, one of the other assistant attorneys on the case was there. He was a couple years older than her and though he'd hinted at being interested in her she'd made it clear early on that she only wanted to be friendly colleagues and nothing more.

Noting how tired he looked, she smiled at him. "Long day, huh?"

"Oh yeah," he agreed, shifting his grip on a couple of banker's boxes holding files. "I love burning the candle at both ends. Reminds me of law school."

She chuckled. "Doesn't it though? Ah, memories…"

Together they rode to the lobby. It was dark out and even though the building was well lit and had security on site, she still felt a spike of unease as they approached the front doors.

"Hey, would you mind walking me to my car?" she asked Manny. "I'm parked around the far side."

"Sure, no problem."

She was glad he didn't make a big deal out of her security situation. Everyone in the office now knew she'd received a threat involving the Fuentes case.

Manny kept up some friendly chatter as he walked her to her car. It made everything seem less ominous. At the far end of the east side of the building they turned toward the overflow parking lot.

"Which one's yours?" Manny asked her.

"Silver Buick, parked over by—"

He suddenly stopped and dropped the boxes he carried, grabbing her wrist to pull her back.

Alarm punched through her. "What?" she demanded, her heart rate shooting up.

"Look," he said, staring toward the parking lot.

She followed his gaze. Her silver rental sat at the far end of a pool of light cast by one of the overhead lamps. Someone had painted a large black oval on the hood.

Her belly constricted. *Oh my God, that's—*

"It's *el Santo's* mark," Manny said grimly. "Come on." He gripped her hand and began rushing her back toward the building entrance.

Marisol hurried after him, fear detonating in her chest. She'd just been marked for death by the most lethal enforcer in the U.S.'s drug trade.

Chapter Nine

E than got out of his rental truck just as a team of men escorted Marisol out of her office building into the parking lot. Police and other unmarked vehicles were parked out front of the law firm and the increased security presence told him something big had happened.

He jogged over to the entrance, held up his ID for the cops out front and headed straight for Marisol. She looked unhurt but tired, and her features were tight with strain.

While he was relieved she was okay, he wanted to know what the hell had happened. He'd come out of a meeting to find a message from Celida on his phone, telling him she wasn't sure of the details but that Marisol had been threatened again, this time by *el Santo*. He'd jumped into his rental truck and broken half a dozen traffic laws getting here. He was still in his fatigues, hadn't even taken the time to change before heading here.

"What's going on?" he asked her, ignoring the other agents around her.

"Not here," one of them said. A middle-aged man who seemed to be in charge. "I'm Special Agent In

Charge Lammers. U.S. Marshals are moving her to a safe location. One of my agents is already picking up her things and will drop them off at the safe house later on."

A safe house? Jesus. "I'll follow you there," he said, falling in step with them. He just wanted Marisol away from here and somewhere safe.

Lammers eyed his uniform for a moment as they walked. "You're HRT?"

"Yes."

"How do you two know each other?" He nodded between him and Marisol.

"We grew up together," Marisol said from the middle of the pack of agents escorting her. She had her arms wrapped around her waist, her spine rigid.

One of the marshals' phone rang. He checked the screen, frowned before answering. "Travnik." His gaze strayed to Ethan as he listened. "Yeah, he's here now." A pause. "All right. Appreciate it." He disconnected and said to Ethan, "That was my boss. Apparently someone named DeLuca got you approval to accompany Miss Lorenzo to the safe house. If it's okay with her."

Ethan owed that man a beer.

"You comfortable with him following us?" the marshal asked Marisol.

Marisol looked at Ethan and nodded, and he plainly saw the relief in her eyes. "Yes, it's fine."

"All right then." Travnik doled out instructions to the other agents before addressing Ethan again. "You can follow me there. My agents will take her to the house by a different route."

Sounded good to Ethan. He shifted his gaze to Marisol. "I'll be there right after you arrive."

"Okay. Thanks."

"You don't need to thank me for that." He just wanted to ensure she was being taken care of properly and find out what the hell had happened to cause this sudden leap in security measures.

The team escorting Marisol headed west after leaving the parking lot, while Travnik headed south. Ethan followed him to a quiet Coral Gables neighborhood.

They circled around the area a few times before Travnik entered a gated community and pulled into the driveway of a two-story Spanish-style house at the end of a cul-de-sac. Ethan parked at the curb a few houses down and waited a few minutes before walking to the front door, where Travnik let him in.

"We've checked the perimeter and all's clear," the man said after shutting and locking the door. Ethan could see two others talking to Marisol in the kitchen down the hall. "She's all set up here and my agent already brought her things over. We'll have another marshal posted outside, down the street. Will you be staying with her? Protocol dictates at least two of us stay with her at all times, but we can keep watch outside if you're going to stay."

"Not sure. Depends on what happens." They could get the call to execute the op on Alvarez at any time. And despite his commander getting approval for him to be here, Ethan wasn't sure what DeLuca would think of him crashing here instead of with the others when they might be called in at any moment. He was about twenty minutes from headquarters here. Too far away if he needed to go operational.

"Here's my personal cell number," he said, handing Ethan a card. "I told her to call me if anything comes up. You do the same."

The other agents left with Travnik. Ethan locked the door behind them just as Marisol walked up behind him. He swept his gaze over her.

"Let's talk in the living room," she said, gesturing for him to follow her. He sat at the end of the same couch she sank onto. Drawing her feet up beneath her in a ladylike pose, she tucked a lock of hair behind her ear before speaking. "*El Santo* or someone working for him spray painted his symbol on the hood of my rental sometime between nine-thirty and nine-forty, while I was still inside working."

Holy shit. "Did they find anything?"

She sighed. "There was an explosive device attached to the undercarriage, but it wasn't hooked up. Because of the symbol on the hood, we know that last part wasn't an accident. And when they reviewed the security footage there's a blackout of those ten minutes. The security officer on patrol in the parking lot was on the far side when it happened and didn't notice anything. They're still trying to look at other cameras and city CCTV footage to see if they can figure out who might have done it, but if it was *el Santo*, then they're likely not going to see him. He didn't gain his reputation by being sloppy."

No, he hadn't. And no wonder the FBI had immediately moved her to a safe house. The symbol alone was enough reason to take extra precautions, but that he'd left an inactivated bomb strapped to her undercarriage made Ethan's blood turn cold. "I'm glad they're taking this seriously."

"Me too. The weird thing is, Fuentes hinted that he knew about the threat I'd received. Or maybe he knew that this was coming, I don't know. It would be hard for him to orchestrate anything from where he is, but not impossible. He said I'm the sacrificial lamb on this case."

A warning buzz started up in Ethan's stomach. "He threatened you during an interview?"

She nodded. "He knew damn well every word he said was being recorded, and he had to know there were others watching from the other side of the two-way mirror. He was either talking out of his ass to make himself feel less helpless, or he knows what's going on. Anyway, the FBI are looking into it now."

On the outside she seemed to be handling it all fine. It was the inside he was concerned about. "When's the last time you ate something?"

Marisol blinked at him. "I don't know. Lunch maybe. Why?"

"You look done in."

She rubbed a hand over her face and rolled her head from side to side. "Just been a long day. A long week, actually."

He got up and headed into the kitchen. "I didn't get dinner either. Let's see what they left you in the fridge."

She followed and started looking in the cupboards. "There's bread and pasta, a couple of cans of soup."

He studied the contents of the fridge. "They've got some salad greens and cheddar cheese in here." He looked at her over his shoulder. "Grilled cheese and salad?"

A grin tugged at her mouth. "Sure."

It took them a few minutes to find the equipment they needed. Ethan made the sandwiches while Marisol cut up some veggies and tossed the salad. They ate together on the couch, settling into a companionable silence. Ethan paused in the midst of chewing a bite of salad when his phone chimed with a text.

He pulled it out, expecting to find a message from DeLuca calling him in, but instead saw Schroder's number along with a picture of a massive double bacon cheeseburger in his teammate's hand. Another picture appeared a second later, the same kind of burger in Vance's big hand, his cheeks bulging with a massive mouthful of beef and bacon. Beneath them were the words *Wish you were here*.

Grinning, he typed back, *No you don't*.

You're right, Schroder answered a moment later. *More bacon for me this way*.

Ethan snorted then said to Marisol, "Hold up your

plate for a second." She threw him a questioning glance but did as he said. He took a picture of her grilled cheese and texted it back. *Gourmet grilled cheese sammies. And the company's better here anyhow.*

Schroder responded a moment later. *That hurts, man. Seriously, ow.*

Ethan chuckled and put his phone back into his pocket. Marisol swallowed the mouthful she'd been chewing and quirked a brow. "Gonna share?"

"Oh. It's just Schroder."

"You said he's the team medic?"

He nodded. "We're all trained in combat first aid, but he's way advanced compared to the rest of us. He was a former PJ."

She frowned. "What's that?"

"Pararescue Jumper. Air Force Special Ops. There aren't very many of them. Anyway, he's kind of the team shit disturber. In a good way," he added. Hard not to like the guy.

She smiled at him. "I think it's neat that you guys seem so close."

"That's by design. We get a big say in who makes the team, so we only pick guys we know we'll like and be able to work with. Our team's awesome. I love working with them, they're the best." It was hard, physically demanding work and the pace was damn near frenetic, but he wouldn't have it any other way and knew the others would agree.

He noticed Marisol's plate was empty now. "Here." He took it from her, stayed her protest as he headed for the kitchen. After loading the plates into the dishwasher and giving the countertop a wipe he sat down next to her, closer this time.

She gave a contented sigh. "That hit the spot, thanks. I feel better."

"Good. Can I do anything else to help? Want me to

stay while you take a shower or whatever?"

"That's sweet, but no, I'm good for now. Just want to unwind for a bit." She laid her head back on the couch cushion.

Unwinding for a little while sounded good to him, especially if it meant spending more time alone with her. He leaned back into the couch, put an arm along the backrest, his hand just inches from her shoulder. Marisol had her legs tucked beneath her, her lower legs bare from the knee down, her toenails painted a soft coral pink.

He dragged his eyes from the length of her sleek, sexy legs and back up to her face. "Are you still going to Key West to interview that witness this coming week?"

"Of course," she said, sounding surprised that he'd asked.

"Did Lammers or Travnik tell you there'll be a security detail with you?"

"We didn't talk about it, but I assume we'll have some kind of security with us. Travnik is already having someone escort me to and from the office, and increasing security there. I'll be talking to him in the morning. I'll talk to Frank about the Key West trip and then check with both Lammers and Travnik."

Ethan frowned. "You're still planning to work out of the office after this?"

She shrugged. "I have to. Trial's coming up fast. I'll have an armed escort to and from the building. And besides, I won't let some thug intimidate me."

Ethan set his jaw. "*El Santo's* not just any thug, Marisol. That's why you've got three federal marshals staying with you at all times."

She shot him an annoyed look. "I know that."

"So you're not scared after what happened tonight? What would have happened if he hadn't warned you with that symbol spray painted on the hood then hooked up the device and you'd climbed inside and started the engine?"

Because the thought was enough to give him fucking nightmares.

She shifted a little, glanced away. "It shook me a little, yeah. But I can't let them know it. I can't let them win."

He grunted in reply.

She settled her gaze on him once more, raised a finely arched eyebrow. "What?"

"I don't like you being exposed that way." If it were up to him he'd whisk her out of the city, far away from this mess until it was over. He wanted to wrap her up in his arms and promise to protect her from everything, but he couldn't.

And to be fair, had he been in her position he wouldn't run either. While he admired her dedication, it drove him crazy that her life was in danger now.

"Can't you have someone bring you your files, so you can work from here for a few days? At least until they can figure out if this really was *el Santo* and figure out who he is so they can arrest him?" Which he and his team would happily carry out personally, under cover of darkness, and drag the asshole out of whatever hole he was hiding in.

"What makes you think it might not have been him?"

"How many times do you think he's warned someone like that?" He gave her a pointed look.

"No idea. What I do know is that he's trying to intimidate me, hoping to make me back off the case or maybe disrupt it. Not going to happen."

"I think you should think about this more." It scared him to death to think of what could have happened tonight. A world without Marisol in it was just unthinkable. And for her to die by violence… No. "Either work from here or take some time off," he urged, trying to get her to see reason.

He understood her point about not being intimidated,

but her job wasn't worth her life. An ironic thought, since he put his life on the line every day he put on his uniform, but this was Marisol he was talking about.

She visibly bristled. Her spine stiffened. She lifted her chin, her eyes narrowing on him slightly. "Once again," she began in an edgy tone, "I'm not your responsibility. I'm a big girl and I can take care of myself, no matter what you think. And you wouldn't run from this if *el Santo* threatened you either."

She had him there, dammit.

Needing to touch her, he reached out and cupped the side of her face with one hand, determined to get through to her. "I know you can, kitt'n. I just want you safe, that's all."

Either the pet name or the rest of his words disarmed her. She blinked at him in surprise, lost her defensive edge and relaxed her shoulders. Without pulling away she studied him for a long moment, then she frowned in apparent confusion. "Did you call me that because of the tree incident with Hugo?"

"No." He slid closer to her, stopping only when his outer thigh pressed against hers. Turning his hand, he trailed a fingertip down her cheek. She was so damn soft. "It's because you always land on your feet."

And because I want to stroke you all over until you purr.

He didn't say it aloud because he knew if he pushed too hard too soon, he risked alienating her for good.

Her pupils dilated slightly as she stared up at him, her gaze trailing down to his lips. "Oh…"

His heart rate kicked up a notch in response. Okay, maybe it wasn't too soon. All he could think about was kissing her. "Yeah, *oh*."

Marisol sat up straighter. Their gazes locked.

Then she took him completely off guard by curving her hand around the back of his neck and pulling his mouth to hers.

Marisol felt the instant of shock that froze him the moment their lips touched. He went rigid, his entire body stilling in surprise. But only for a second. A hot thrill shot through her when he slid his hand into the back of her hair and slanted his mouth across hers.

Her fingers tightened on the back of his neck, her free hand blindly reaching out to grip his shoulder. His hard, muscled shoulder that flexed beneath her palm when he shifted his arm.

He held her steady as he teased her lips, brushing tender kisses across them, sucking lightly. Making her wait, driving her insane. Her breasts felt tight and swollen and a steady throb pulsed between her legs. She shifted restlessly on the couch, wanting more, wanting closer, deeper, harder.

Pushing to her knees, she pressed her breasts to his chest. Immediately he locked one steely arm around her back, a soft growl issuing from his throat. His tongue touched the corner of her mouth. She turned her head, parted her lips and flicked her tongue against his.

Pleasure hummed through her, thick and sweet. She'd always known he'd kiss like this. Commanding. Skilled. So erotic her head was already spinning.

She rubbed her breasts against his chest in a sinuous motion that only made her nipples throb more. His tongue delved into her mouth to stroke and tease, stealing her breath, flooding her with heat and need.

Ethan made a low sound and ripped his mouth away, turning his face to press his nose against the side of her neck. Marisol arched and froze, the feel of his stubble and the warmth of his breath across her suddenly violently sensitive skin lighting her on fire. She wanted his hands all over her bare body, right this instant. And she wanted his mouth on her again.

"Whoa," he breathed against her neck, the tension in his shoulders and his roughened breathing telling her he was just as affected as her. His hands held her locked to him. "Whoa."

Wait, whoa as in *holy cow that was amazing*? Or whoa as in *stop, why did you just do that*?

An instant of uncertainty hit her. She might not have a lot of experience with men, but she didn't think she'd misread things that badly.

Ethan pulled in a deep breath, kept his face pressed tight to her neck for another moment as he exhaled. The warm rush of air against her sensitive skin was like adding accelerant to a fire. She shivered, bit her lip.

Raising his head, he searched her eyes, their faces only inches apart. Seizing her chance, Marisol took his face in both hands and leaned in for another kiss, covering his lips with hers. He made a negative sound and started to pull back but she tightened her grip and followed, sucking on the tempting curve of his full lower lip.

A husky chuckle escaped him before he eased his mouth away and stared down at her, his golden brown eyes darker now because his pupils were dilated. "Are you sure this is a good idea?" he murmured. His tone was curious and his arms were still tight around her, giving her hope that she hadn't made a total fool of herself. Because he'd definitely kissed her back, so she wasn't sure why he'd stopped.

She didn't see the point in lying. "Because I've wanted to since I was fourteen and I couldn't hold out anymore."

Ever since she'd gone to his house with a plate of cookies one night when his parents were out. He'd been nineteen, home on a short leave from the Marine Corps. She'd made it into the foyer before she'd frozen at the soft, sultry female moan floating down from Ethan's bedroom upstairs.

Ohhh, Ethan, that feels so good...

Marisol could still remember how her stomach had plummeted to her toes, followed a moment later by her heart. She'd seen Alysa with him earlier but hadn't realized they were together until that instant. She'd stood there for a good ten agonizing seconds, listening to Ethan's deep murmurs mixing with Alysa's increasingly urgent cries as he drove her to orgasm before turning and fleeing back to her house.

Worse, Alysa had been friends with Ynez and the next night Marisol had been forced to listen to Alysa regale her unforgettable evening with Ethan. She'd been pea green with envy, had avoided Ethan the rest of his leave because she just couldn't bear to face him after that.

But now he was here, it was just the two of them, and he wanted her. The rush of exhilaration almost made her dizzy.

A sexy, almost smug smile curved his gorgeous mouth. "I was planning to kiss you, but you beat me to it."

"You were taking too long."

He huffed out a laugh and shifted his grip, one hand coming up to play with the hair at her nape, the possessive touch sending tingles down her spine. Then his expression turned serious. "You've been through a lot today."

She immediately shook her head, already knowing where this was going. "My head is totally clear. I kissed you because I wanted to, not because I was trying to avoid thinking about what happened tonight." Although yeah, forgetting that for a while was a nice side benefit.

He didn't answer for a moment. "I'll be leaving Miami as soon as this job is done. We'll be sent back to Quantico."

And she had to stay here in Miami. "How long do you have here?"

"A few days more, maybe a week." He searched her eyes. "So given all that, you need to spell out exactly what it is you want from me."

He was warning her that he wasn't offering anything beyond that. And she wasn't worried about ruining their friendship, if that's what he meant. They were both adults and they lived a thousand miles apart. By the time they saw each other again either months or years down the road, any awkwardness will have faded.

"I want you to stop talking and kiss me some more," she said, leaning up to try and steal a kiss.

His lips quirked in a hint of a smile as he evaded her. "Soli, for real. Don't make me guess."

Oh, she loved it when he called her by the short form of her name. Although the way he'd said kitt'n earlier in that deep, tender tone had made her belly flutter. She wouldn't mind him calling her that some more. With effort, she dragged her gaze from his lips, still shiny from her kisses. "What do you want me to say?"

He seemed to weigh his response for a moment. "Carmela mentioned that you might not be very…experienced."

Carm had told her brother she was a virgin? Marisol felt a blush creeping into her cheeks but refused to be embarrassed. "So?"

His fingers stroked across the back of her scalp, the caress almost drugging. She could only imagine how good it would feel to have his fingers stroking all over her naked body. "Is it true? You've never slept with anyone?"

Well, for God's sake. Talk about blunt. "It's true. Is that a problem?"

He grinned at the tart edge to her tone. "No, but it makes things more complicated that way."

"It doesn't have to." This was another reason why she hadn't wanted him to know. In her experience, her being a virgin either freaked guys out or it made them want to be her first just for the power trip of it. Ethan's reaction was neither of those things, but it was equally annoying.

For once she wanted to stop thinking and just feel, experience all the things she'd been missing. Because she trusted him and because no one would ever measure up to him. If a fling was all she could have with him, well, she could live with that.

"Well, it does." He eased his upper body farther away from her but left his hands where they were. "Why have you never slept with anyone?" He said it as though he couldn't fathom how such a thing was possible.

This was not at all how things had played out in her fantasies about Ethan. In her fantasies he'd just completely taken over, driven her to dizzying heights of pleasure. Instead he wanted to talk.

She shrugged. "A lot of different reasons. My Catholic upbringing, for one. Then Ynez getting pregnant in high school, that was a big motivating factor for me to avoid having sex. Then I was busy with school, with work. But mostly, I guess I'm just picky. I wasn't willing to settle."

Not for anyone but you. She didn't dare say the words aloud because she already felt vulnerable enough.

He gave a slow nod and ran that golden brown gaze down to her mouth before meeting her eyes once again. The latent heat there made her breath catch. "Okay. Then you need to be real clear with me about what you're looking for here."

She didn't know how much more she wanted, she just knew she was still throbbing all over and she'd wanted Ethan forever. Now that he was here and she knew he wanted her in return, it opened up a whole world of possibilities previously closed to her. "I don't know how far I want to go," she answered honestly. "I just know I want more."

He shook his head. "And what if you get so caught up in what we're doing that we cross a line you weren't ready to cross?"

She snorted. "I'm a virgin. Not an idiot."

His low chuckle stroked over her entire body like a lazy caress. The kind her body was begging for. Of all the things she'd envisioned with Ethan, it wasn't for him to make her all hot and bothered then leave her wanting. "I'm just saying, it—"

His phone buzzed. He dropped his hands, his expression all business as he pulled the phone out and checked the message. "Shit, I gotta go." He jumped to his feet, paused to look down at her. "I was going to offer to stay the night—here on the couch," he added hastily, "but I don't know when I'll... Shit." He dragged a hand through his hair, clearly agitated about having to leave her.

She stood and set a hand on his forearm. "It's okay. I'll be fine."

He nodded once, his jaw flexing under that ruggedly sexy stubble he had. "It'll be a late night. I'll call you in the morning, okay?"

"Sure." She followed him to the door, suddenly feeling off balance. She'd laid a part of herself bare to him and now he was leaving. For work, and an op she knew was important enough to call him here all the way from Virginia, but still, a strange hollow sensation opened up in her chest.

At the door he paused and cupped the back of her head in one big hand. "I'll come see you as soon as I can." Then he covered her lips with his.

The kiss was different than the last one, more possessive, a kind of vow. He was far from done with her, no matter what reservations he'd voiced earlier, and it sent anticipation curling through her veins.

She slipped her hand around the nape of his neck, parted her lips for him. He groaned, slid his tongue inside for a taste that left her a little breathless, then raised his head. "Lock up tight."

"I will."

He unlocked the door, stepped outside. On his way to a dangerous op entailing God knew what. A sudden frisson of fear gripped her.

"Ethan."

He paused there in the semi-darkness broken only by the streetlamp down the sidewalk, looked back at her.

"Be careful."

A slow, sexy smile curved his mouth. "I will, baby."

Baby, she thought with a smile as he climbed into his truck. She liked it when he called her that too.

Chapter Ten

Deep in the shadows of the greenway that ran behind the split-level house he was targeting, Bautista stretched out onto his stomach in the undergrowth and used the binocular feature on his night vision goggles. The house was located at the end of a private street in a pricey, gated community in south Miami. It had the best security money could buy and 24/7 surveillance.

None of it was enough to protect the man inside it.

It had taken two days for him to check out the tips he'd been given and track Garcia here. Alvarez's enforcer had rung up quite the body count over the past few months, evading enemies and law enforcement at every turn. But Bautista had resources they didn't. And now he was going to end him.

The hum of insects and the croak of frogs in the nearby creek acted as a backdrop and helped cover the tiny sounds he made as he pulled the components of his custom-made sniper rifle from his backpack.

He assembled them in less than a minute without looking, the motions automatic, ingrained from countless hours of drilling and training over the years. Setting the stock of the rifle against his shoulder, he peered through the high-powered scope.

He was a hundred percent certain Garcia was here. Now all he had to do was wait for him to make a mistake.

The forest suddenly went eerily silent.

Bautista lifted his head a fraction and held his breath. A heartbeat later, a slight noise pierced the quiet.

His blood went icy cold. He knew that sound. The distinctive punch of a round striking glass.

Someone had just taken a shot at his target.

He waited there, frozen in position for several long moments. The cicadas and frogs started up again, growing in volume, then went silent a few seconds later. He didn't hear anyone moving in the greenway but he caught a faint blur of movement in his peripheral.

Turning his head, he held his position while he scanned the underbrush. A fern off in the distance moved slightly and he caught a glimpse of what could have been a leg disappearing behind a tree.

He wasn't alone.

His heart rate kicked up slightly and his hands tensed around his weapon. He used his skills to focus on his surroundings, filtering out the natural sounds. No one had ever snuck up on him before, and no one was getting the drop on him tonight.

A full minute passed before he allowed himself to breathe a little easier. But he waited there without moving for another five. Nothing disturbed the insects in the area, their steady hum assuring him no one was moving around.

At least not close by. The shooter could be waiting at a distance though, scanning through his scope.

Moving slowly enough to avoid detection if anyone was using a scope, Bautista focused his attention on the target house once again. The kitchen light was still on downstairs, the blinds pulled down halfway. Both windows and the sliding glass door leading into it were still intact.

When he deemed it safe to move, he inched his way to the left, in the direction where he'd seen the disturbance in the undergrowth. There was no way the shooter could know he was here tonight. The only person who knew about the hit was Perez, and he would never sell Bautista out.

It took him nearly fifteen minutes to creep his way to a point where he could see around the far corner of the house. As soon as he focused on the window leading into the den, he saw it.

A single bullet hole in the floor-to-ceiling window, the glass spider-webbing around it.

There was no light on but as with the kitchen the blinds had been pulled halfway down. And when Bautista peered through his NVGs, he clearly saw the male body lying on the floor, unmoving.

Garcia.

His face was turned toward Bautista, his eyes partially open and the front of his shirt and the floor around him was covered with a dark stain. Dead as a fucking stone, from a single sniper shot to center mass. Not done by an amateur.

An unknown player was involved in the game and he didn't like it. He needed to know everyone involved because it was too dangerous otherwise. Once he got clear he would contact Perez and inform him. He didn't think anyone had been able to follow him or had seen him, but he couldn't be positive.

Whoever the shooter was, he was well trained. And that meant Bautista needed to get the hell out of here, in case he was being targeted too.

It had been a long, long time—years—since the back of his neck had tingled like this while on a sniper mission. The last time it had happened was while he was in the jungle in Colombia, hunting a drug runner who'd made the fatal error of trying to fuck with Perez's teenage daughter after meeting her in Miami.

The asshole had actually threatened to kidnap and torture her, so Bautista had been dispatched to take him out. He had, but that night someone had been hunting him. He never found out who it was, but he'd learned never to ignore his gut. And right now his gut was screaming at him that he was in danger.

He used every evasion trick he'd learned in the military as he made his way to the edge of the greenway, placing his feet carefully, his special boots leaving no clear footprints behind. The other side opened up into a park but he'd be exposed for at least ten seconds as he ran to the edge of the strip of trees bordering the opposite side.

The seconds ticked past as he waited there, poised and ready. There was no one around, not surprising given how late it was, and he didn't see any movement. Finally, he burst from behind a thick stand of trees and raced for the thin line of trees lining the quiet street marking the edge of the next posh subdivision.

No one fired. He made it across, hunkered down in the shadows cast by the trees and took his bearings once more, sliding off his NVGs because of the streetlamps on the other side of the road.

His gaze landed on a partial footprint in the soft earth just before it gave way to the strip of grass that bordered the sidewalk. It was fresh, he could tell from the crispness of it. And when he investigated further, he found another close by.

Definitely boot prints. Several sizes smaller than his. The shooter was small, quick. Possibly even female.

He scanned the street on the far side of the greenway, found it empty. Whoever the shooter was, he was long gone. Bautista filed all the information away for later and quickly changed clothes, stowed his weapon and gear.

Wearing a dark gray hoodie, running shorts and

tennis shoes, he slung his backpack over one shoulder and stepped out onto the sidewalk.

He made it to his rental vehicle parked two blocks away without incident, and he carefully checked it over for tracking or explosive devices or signs of tampering before climbing behind the wheel. Only when he was certain no one had planted anything did he turn the ignition.

He hooked up his hands-free device to make the call to Perez, then paused. The warning tingle at his nape was gone, but he knew someone had come close to seeing him tonight.

And if they'd somehow followed him or had watched him without knowing—he might have said it was impossible, but he'd learned nothing ever was—then he had something else to worry about.

Julia.

He'd never had to worry about anyone but himself before in this game, until now. She'd gotten under his skin. If someone was good enough to get a lock on his location tonight then they could know about her. They were supposed to go out tomorrow night but now it might not be safe for her. Or for him.

Going with his gut, he took out a burner phone and called her. Thankfully she answered on the second ring, sounding wide awake. "Hey, it's me," he said.

"Miguel?"

His heart beat faster at the sound of her voice. "Yeah."

"What number are you calling me from? It came up as unavailable."

"Did it?" He hoped his attempt at playing dumb was convincing. By now he was pretty good at it. "I just called to see if we were still on for tomorrow night."

"Of course. But you wouldn't call me this late to ask me that. Is everything okay?"

"Yeah. What about you?"

When she hesitated, his hand tightened around the steering wheel. "I'm okay."

She was lying. He knew her well enough to know when she sounded stressed, and she definitely did. "What's wrong?" he demanded. He didn't care about the danger to himself, if something was wrong he'd go straight to her place right now, make sure she was safe.

She made an indecisive sound and he pressed. "Julia. What's the matter?"

"I don't know. I just feel kind of unsettled, I guess."

Nuh uh. She was hiding something. "Tell me."

"I can't prove anything, but I feel like someone's been watching me lately."

His hand tightened around the steering wheel. *Dammit.* "What do you mean?"

"It's...nothing specific I can point to. Just a feeling. Like earlier tonight when I was out."

He did not like this. "Are you at home right now?" he asked, making a sharp right to take a short cut to the highway. From here he could be at her place in under ten minutes.

"Yes, why?"

"I'm coming over. I'll check your place out for you, make sure everything's secure."

"Don't be silly. It's almost midnight." She sighed. "Look, it's fine. I've got everything locked up tight and the alarm's on. And I know I don't look it, but trust me when I tell you, I can hold my own if anyone tried to get inside."

That last bit took him by surprise, but he didn't comment. "I should come look around. We'll both feel better."

"You're so sweet, but no. I've had a long day and I just want to go to bed. I need my beauty sleep so I can look my best for you tomorrow."

"You look beautiful every time I see you."

A soft laugh came over the line, easing the tension in his shoulders, loosening the tightness in his chest. It felt good to care about someone again, and be cared about in return. Until her he hadn't realized how lonely he'd become. "Flattery goes a long way with me."

"It's not flattery if it's the truth."

"I can't wait until tomorrow night." He could hear the smile in her voice.

She didn't want to put him out by asking him to come over. He wasn't going to argue about it, but he was going over to make sure her place was secure. He'd stop by, take a look around and ensure everything was as it should be, without her ever knowing. "Me neither. But I'll text you a number you can reach me at if you need anything."

"I will. Have a good night."

"You too." *And I'll make sure you're safe*.

He drove directly to her place, a detached townhouse in a middle-class neighborhood not far from the care home where his *abuela* was. When he pulled up her street he noticed immediately that her bedroom light upstairs was on, muted by the blinds she'd drawn to cover the window, but her truck was missing.

Her garage was too small for her to park in, it was basically a storage unit, and both times when he'd come by before—when he'd first been checking her out, unbeknownst to her—the black Ram had been parked in the spot directly out front. She always combat parked, he'd noticed, reversing into her spot rather than going in hood-first. Made getting away in a hurry a lot easier. Though he doubted she did it for that reason.

In case she'd parked elsewhere he circled her complex, but still didn't see her truck. Maybe it was in the shop or something, or she'd lent it to a friend.

He got out of his vehicle and walked back to her unit to start his inspection of the exterior, his favorite pistol tucked into the holster at the small of his back. He'd check it all out and once he was satisfied that everything was secure, he'd leave.

It took all of ten minutes to complete what he wanted to do. There were no signs of any tampering and he didn't notice anything suspicious. In the shadows across the street he peered up at the warm glow in her bedroom window. She was safe and warm up there, probably reading a book while tucked into her bed.

The thought brought him a surprising measure of peace and satisfaction. *Sleep tight, angel,* he sent to her.

When he turned back around he caught the red glow of a pair of taillights just as they disappeared around the corner at the far end of the road that ran in front of the complex. From this distance he couldn't be sure, but he thought he'd seen a Ram's head symbol on the back of the tailgate.

****

When Tuck tapped him on the shoulder to signal that everyone was in place, Ethan blew the charges he'd placed on the exterior security door. The solid locks and hinges blew apart.

Evers slammed a breaching tool against the ruined door, sending it flying inward, gaining them entry into the house where Alvarez was reported to be. Tuck and Bauer immediately tossed gas canisters into the room then moved into position on either side of the doorway. Shouts from inside started up as smoke filled the room.

Ethan moved into the room behind Bauer, MP-5 to his shoulder, gas mask protecting his eyes, nose and mouth from the burn of the gas. Infrared scans had shown three men in this room prior to the breach. There were four more elsewhere in the house, likely in the in-ground basement or the bunker beneath it.

One of them was Perez. All the intel they had indicated that he wouldn't surrender willingly.

"FBI! Get down on the ground!" Tuck shouted as the team stormed in.

With the help of his NVGs Ethan immediately picked out the three tangos, two standing at the far right corner and the other to the left. Both men on the right reached for their weapons. Tuck and Vance fired, hitting them both as Bauer and Ethan swung to confront the man on the left. He turned to run.

"Freeze!" Bauer roared.

The guy did, stuck both hands in the air. Bauer held his position while Ethan approached. "On the ground, now," he ordered. "Facedown." The red dot of his laser sight lit up the center of the man's chest.

Ethan kept his gaze locked on the man's hands as the guy reluctantly got to his knees then laid down on his belly with his arms stretched out. Knowing Bauer had his six, Ethan slung his weapon and straddled the man's waist, quickly securing the prisoner's hands behind his back before tying his feet as well. "How many others," he demanded.

Rather than answer the man twisted around and tried to spit in Ethan's face. Ethan leaned to the side at the last second to avoid it and shoved the guy's bound hands higher up between his shoulder blades. A raw cry of pain followed, then a string of Spanish curses.

Ethan maintained the pressure, inflicting enough pain without doing much damage to the prisoner's shoulder joint. "How many," he growled back in the same language. He could see Tuck and the others stacked up at the door leading down to the basement.

The guy started babbling, his voice strained as he tried to wriggle into a more comfortable position. Ethan didn't let up, kept interrogating him. When the man had told him what he wanted to know, Ethan turned to Tuck.

"He says four. Down in the bunker. Perez is there."

He climbed to his feet, dragging the prisoner with him. After handing him off to another agent, Ethan crossed the room to stand behind Blackwell, last in line of the seven-man team.

This was the most dangerous part of the op. Alvarez and the others would be heavily armed and knew they were coming. In the few minutes it had taken to secure this room, their target and his henchmen would have had plenty of time to fortify their position.

As expected, the reinforced door leading to the basement was dead bolted shut. Evers placed more charges. He blew the door and Tuck began clearing the stairwell. He raised his right fist, signaling for them to halt. As the others shifted aside, Ethan saw why.

A tripwire was strung across the stairs at knee level. They stepped over it carefully, followed their team leader's movements as they moved down the stairs.

At the bottom they fanned out into two teams to clear the basement. Vance found another tripwire beneath the rug hiding the steel trapdoor leading to the underground bunker.

Ethan trained his weapon on the door while Tuck and Vance worked to dismantle the wire, attached to the pin of a frag grenade. Crude, but effective, if they hadn't seen it.

Who knew what other surprises waited for them on the other side of that trapdoor.

When all was ready, Tuck gave the signal. They used a grappling tool to yank the trapdoor open. Everyone stayed back and got low.

Sure as hell, the moment the door cleared the opening, gunfire erupted from inside it.

A round whizzed past Ethan's head, close enough that he heard the high-pitched whine as it passed by.

Motherfucker...

Schroder was closest to the opening. He tossed a gas canister in and Tuck lobbed in a flashbang, then another for good measure. The firing slowed immediately, grew sporadic. Tuck and Schroder both took aim at the opening.

One of them fired. Someone below bellowed in pain. A moment later Tuck stepped back. "Someone's coming up," he said, his voice clear through the earpiece Ethan wore.

A man's head and shoulders appeared in the opening. He was coughing, scrubbing blindly at his face. Schroder kicked out at the man's hand, knocking the pistol out of his grip.

Bauer lunged over, grabbed the guy by the wrist and hauled him out of the hole like he weighed no more than a sack of flour, and dumped him on the concrete floor. Tuck was still standing over the trapdoor, weapon trained on it.

When the man on the floor turned his head, Ethan realized it was their primary target, the lieutenant, Alvarez, and ran over to help secure him. Not that Bauer couldn't handle the guy by himself, but it sped the process up and they needed everyone on their weapons right now.

Alvarez was wearing a ballistic vest. Ethan yanked the flex cuffs tight around the man's wrists at the small of his back, was just going for his ankles when Tuck's warning shout made his scalp prickle.

"Grenade!"

He turned his head in time to see it hit the floor near him, bounce over to the far wall. He dropped the tango's feet, shifted his weight to dive away, when Bauer reached down. Bauer grabbed Ethan with one big hand and wrenched him off his feet.

They landed on the floor together, Bauer's chest hitting Ethan's shoulder as they rolled toward the opposite wall. The grenade exploded, the force of it rattling Ethan's ears, pounding through his whole body. Something hit him in the back, between his shoulder blades.

Ears ringing, he struggled to his hands and knees. Bauer was rolling away from him. Ethan immediately turned to his teammate, grabbed him. *Shit that was close.* He didn't feel any pain but he knew damn well he'd been hit. Had to be the adrenaline masking it.

"You okay?" he demanded, locking a hand on Bauer's shoulder.

He couldn't hear anything over the ringing in his ears, but he could read Bauer's lips as he responded. "Yeah." Bauer checked him over the same way. "I'm good. You?"

"Fine." How was that possible? His heart was pounding, his breathing erratic. He glanced back at the others. Vance was hauling someone else out of the trapdoor. Tuck and Blackwell had two other men already on their bellies, hands secured behind them.

All four tangos here accounted for and secured.

His gaze strayed to Alvarez, still near the corner of the room. His eyes were open but there were fist-sized holes all over him from the fragments the grenade had thrown out.

Sucked for Marisol and everyone involved in the prosecution for Fuentes's trial who'd wanted Alvarez's confession and subsequent testimony they'd been hoping for, but at least his drug and weapon running days were over. And they might be able to get vital information from Alvarez's lackeys.

"Clear," Tuck called out, and Ethan could hear him a bit easier now that the ringing was fading.

Ethan took a deep breath, ordered himself to calm down. *You're good. You're good. Just a close call.*

He got to his feet, his legs a little unsteady. Tuck and Blackwell headed down into the bunker while Vance kept watch from above.

Schroder came up to Ethan. "You okay, man?"

He nodded. "Yep." Hell of a lot better than Alvarez.

Their medic asked Bauer the same thing, got a terse reply, then went over to check Alvarez. He set his fingers beneath the man's jaw, looked up at Ethan. "Dead." Not a surprise.

Good. Fucking prick almost killed me.

And then, unbidden, an image of Marisol's face came to mind. The fact that he was thinking of her at all right now surprised him.

But he could see her so clearly. The way her eyes glowed when she smiled. The smoldering desire in them when they'd kissed tonight. He could have died a minute ago, without ever getting the chance to explore the connection between them.

Shelving everything for later, he worked with the others to secure the rest of the house. Down in the bunker they found discarded gasmasks, body armor, a stockpile of automatic weapons, and a safe holding half a million in cash.

Once he was topside again, Ethan exited the house and pulled off his gasmask. He headed straight down the driveway, now crowded with FBI and DEA agents, and sucked in deep breaths of the cool night air.

The shakes had him now. Little vibrations ripping through all his muscles. The more he fought them, the worse they got, so he let them run their course, glad for the privacy of the darkness.

His teammates followed him out to the street, didn't say anything as they gathered around their two vehicles. Ethan set his weapon into the back of one and kept walking. He had to keep moving, had to burn off the haze of shock and adrenaline playing havoc with his system.

Holy fuck, he'd almost died in there. Would have, if Bauer hadn't wrenched him away when he had.

Vance eyed him as he made another pass of the SUV. Then his gaze landed on Ethan's back and his eyes widened. "Whoa. Hold up, man."

Ethan stopped. "What?"

"Just stay still." Vance set a hand on Ethan's shoulder, ran his hand over the back of his Kevlar vest. "Holy shit, dude." He ripped the Velcro fasteners free. Ethan pulled the thing off and flipped it around, stunned to see the fist-sized hole in the center of the back plate.

His stomach clenched. He swallowed, took in the visual evidence of just how close he'd come to meeting his maker tonight. He'd had a near miss before, back in his days in the Corps on a mission in Afghanistan. Since then he'd been lucky. They all knew the risks of the job, but it was still a sobering thing, to be faced with your mortality like that.

Bauer whistled and came over to examine the vest. "That's gnarly, man."

Gnarly. Yeah. Ethan clapped a hand to the big guy's shoulder. "Thanks, man."

Bauer shrugged. "No worries, brother."

The others all gathered around to inspect the vest. Tuck made an impressed sound. "That one's definitely going in our museum." They had a collection of things they'd saved from previous ops and training missions back at headquarters in Quantico. Little mementos of their work together. Ethan didn't really want to see the vest again, let alone every time he went into the office.

"First round's on Cruzie," Schroder announced, slapping Ethan on the back. He hid a wince as his friend's hand hit the bruise forming where the fragment had nearly torn through the vest.

"Only one round for you guys," Ethan said, breathing a little easier now with his teammates around him. "But I'm buying Bauer a freaking truckload of beer as soon as I get home."

On the way back to base they were all quiet. Ethan rode in the back with Vance, Tuck driving and Blackwell in the shotgun seat. They all knew how shaken he was and were giving him the space to deal with it the best way he knew how. So he thought about Marisol.

He needed to see her.

The thought was loud in his head, impossible to ignore.

He wanted to touch her, kiss her, drink her in. Wanted to feel her arms around him, her silken skin against his. The desire was overwhelming, and not something he intended to fight. He could see himself having a real relationship with her, if she was willing.

As soon as the debriefing and paperwork were done, he was heading out to see her.

Chapter Eleven

S upervisory Special Agent Matt DeLuca's eyes snapped open at the whir of the mechanism in his hotel room lock turning.

He rolled to his side in the darkness, automatically reaching for the pistol he'd placed on the bedside table. His hand closed around the grip just as the door cracked open to reveal a slender silhouette backlit by the hallway lights.

He'd know the shape of that lithe female body anywhere.

He released the pistol, a smile curving his mouth as his reached up to switch on the bedside lamp, flooding the room with warm light.

Briar closed the door behind her and gave him a sultry smile, a small duffel in one hand and a garment bag draped over one shoulder. "Hey."

"You made it," he said, rolling out of the bed and stalking toward her completely naked.

It had been almost three weeks since they'd last seen each other. With their work schedules, too often they ended up like ships passing in the night. He'd texted her earlier tonight but she hadn't responded. After a while he'd managed to fall asleep but a niggling doubt had kept waking him. Seeing her in person helped dispel the feeling, but didn't erase it completely.

"Hmmm," she replied, her dark gaze raking over the length of his body appreciatively. "Surprise."

"Best surprise I've had in a long time." When he reached her she dropped her bags and twined her arms around his neck, pressing full length against him. Matt crushed her to him. He buried his face in the curve of her throat and breathed her in, detecting the earthy scents of grass, soil and fresh air on her skin. Wherever she'd been, she'd definitely worked outside tonight.

Being concealed in a hide, camouflaged by elements taken from the surrounding foliage and operating under cover of darkness, was a sniper's realm. And Briar was just as much an expert at all those things as he was.

Blocking that thought for now, he slid his hands into the fall of her thick, cool hair. He cupped the back of her head in a possessive grip and brought his mouth down on hers. The kiss was an expression of pure hunger, a stamp of possession. It'd been too long since he'd touched her, tasted her.

You're mine.

Briar made a soft sound of pleasure in the back of her throat that shot straight to his groin. She opened to him, her hands moving to his shoulders then she hopped up to wind her legs around his waist. He caught her, locked an arm around her hips to hold her in place as he slid his tongue along hers.

She tasted like heaven, the sleek, supple feel of her body going to his head. Every time he touched her he always craved more. She was a stark contrast of strength and femininity that he found mesmerizing. He couldn't get enough of her.

With their mouths still fused, tongues twining, he spun and walked back to the bed then lowered her to the sheet. He stretched out on top of her. Immediately she arched into him, rolling her hips against his throbbing erection.

Matt groaned into her mouth and stroked his cock over her covered mound once, twice, teasing them both with the promise of more before breaking the kiss. He wanted her so much he ached, but he needed answers first. And if he kissed her again before asking what he needed to, he'd wind up drowning in her and lose the ability to think at all. She had that much power over him.

Staring down at her, noting with satisfaction the flush of arousal across the bronzed skin of her cheekbones and the desire blazing in her eyes, he marveled once again that this woman was his. They'd only been living together for a few months but he knew she was the one he wanted to spend the rest of his life with. After his first wife died he'd been certain he'd never be able to fall in love again. Then Briar had burst into his life and proved him wrong.

"When did you get into Miami?" he murmured, sweeping his thumbs across her temples. He knew she'd been operating in Florida for the past week, but not where or what exactly she'd been up to.

She tightened her legs around his waist, gently ran her nails over his scalp in the way she knew gave him shivers. "Been here for a few days already. Just couldn't get away until now."

He didn't comment on that part, because her new job as a contract agent for the NSA demanded she keep certain details about operations from him. He had to keep things from her too sometimes. But now the suspicion in his gut had taken root and wouldn't let go.

After the intel he'd received on Garcia an hour ago from Agent Lammers, and since then confirmed by Celida through Tuck, Matt had to wonder. Briar was as deadly as she was beautiful. She definitely had the skillset for tonight's hit. And he'd promised his boss he'd ask.

"Where were you tonight?"

She stilled and gazed up at him with a slightly wary expression, searched his eyes. He usually didn't question her about her work, and never while they were in bed, but this was important. His guys had already had a close call tonight, Cruz especially, and the Garcia thing made Matt uneasy. If there were more assassins in the area targeting the same people the HRT was, he wanted to know.

"On a job," she answered.

"What kind of job?" Her security clearance was even higher than his, due to the nature of the ops she pulled. Sometimes on the books, but just as often not. And while he understood that there were things she couldn't share about what she did, he didn't think she'd keep something as important as this from him.

Her expression turned shuttered, the same one he'd seen when he'd first tracked her down in that snowy Colorado forest seven months ago. "Recon. Why?"

"Just recon?"

She frowned at him. "Yes. Matt, what's going on?" Clearly annoyed, she pushed at his shoulder but he wouldn't let her up. He liked the feel of her beneath him, and he could look directly into her face this way.

"There was a hit tonight," he said evenly, watching her expression. He read people well, but with her, not always, even after living together for the past six months. In some ways she was still as much of a mystery to him as ever.

It was probably messed up, but he found that air of intrigue sexy as fuck. Before her, he'd never met a woman who could hold her own with him, tactically speaking. Briar definitely could. She challenged him, kept him sharp. It made their chemistry burn so hot it was off the charts.

"A big one," he added quietly.

She stopped pushing, held his gaze. "Who?"

"Garcia." Alvarez's enforcer. Matt was concerned about other assassins who might be in the area.

The frown deepened. "Had to be *el Santo.*"

Matt shook his head. "Investigators found him dead in the office of the house he'd just rented two days ago. Single shot to center mass, fired from the greenway behind the house. They got two partial boot prints from the area where the shooter set up, but nothing else. Men's size six-and-a-half." Or a women's eight. Her shoe size.

Surprise flashed in her dark eyes for a second, then she shook her head. "Wasn't me. I was with Alex all night doing recon, you can call him if you want to check my alibi." There was a definite defensive edge to her voice on the last bit, and he didn't blame her for it.

Matt knew Rycroft would just vouch for her either way though. But as he searched her eyes, the tension in his gut eased. She was telling the truth and it relieved him. "No. I believe you. Know of anyone else who might be working in the area?" She had connections he didn't. Former...colleagues who were less than orthodox.

"Haven't heard anything."

"Let me know if you do."

"I will, and tomorrow I'll see what I can find out." She turned her head and pushed his shoulder again, trying to sit up, her expression remote.

Matt wouldn't let her go. "I had to ask, honey," he murmured against her temple.

She huffed out a breath. Apparently she wasn't too annoyed with him because she relaxed against the mattress and peered up at him once more.

He leaned down to kiss the bridge of her nose, let his libido take over. She felt so goddamn good, he couldn't wait to slide his tongue between her legs, listen to her moan and beg before he sank his cock inside her. When they'd first gotten together she'd been a little on the shy side when it came to sex, but within a few weeks she'd learned to trust him and her body and had quickly shed her inhibitions.

Now she was anything but shy about letting him know what turned her on or what she wanted in bed, and it was insanely hot.

"Thank you," he murmured against the tip of her nose, pausing to press a tender kiss there. For all her badass skills, she was still so precious and delicate to him.

"You're welcome." She relaxed beneath him, the hand on his shoulder gliding up his neck to rub at the back of his scalp again. When he let out a throaty groan and flexed his hips against her, she grinned. "Anything else you wanna clear up before we get to the good part of this reunion?"

He was hard as a club at the thought of plunging into her slick heat. "Nope."

"Good. And how long do I have you all to myself? Because I have very specific plans in mind that I've been thinking about for a week now." She tightened her thighs around his waist and rolled her pelvis against him, bringing him to full, aching life in the span of a single heartbeat.

He couldn't wait to find out what she had in mind. "Breakfast meeting with the boys at seven in Tuck's room. I'm all yours until then."

Her eyes gleamed with pure female satisfaction. "Perfect. Now stop talking, commander, and get me naked," she whispered, and pulled his mouth to hers for a deep, intimate kiss.

****

Marisol picked her new phone up from her desk and checked the screen. Since being escorted into the building this morning at nine, she'd only stopped once to check for messages and it was dinnertime already. She'd missed another call from her mom, one from Ynez, and one from Ethan. Her conscience pricked at her.

He'd texted earlier that he'd come by and see her before she left, but she'd answered saying she wasn't sure what time she'd be leaving. In all honesty, she didn't know what to say to him.

That kiss last night had scorched her, left her edgy and unfulfilled and kept her up way longer than she'd expected, given how exhausted she was. Well, that and she'd also been worried about him. She knew he'd been called in for some kind of op, knew what sort of men they were likely targeting and the dangers that entailed.

They'd crossed a line last night. Sure, to him it was probably just a kiss, but to her it was more. For her it was having the man she'd always wanted standing right in front of her, and needing more. It felt like that kiss had branded her in some way. She might have slept with him last night if he'd stayed.

The realization had been eye-opening, but after mulling it over for a few hours, she knew it was true. What she felt for him wasn't just lust, and it wasn't going away.

Not exactly a surprise, though she wasn't sure she was comfortable with it. Falling for Ethan when he lived so far away had heartbreak written all over it, but she couldn't stop, couldn't shut her feelings off.

She called her mom first, in part to stave off a full-blown panic amongst her family, but also to stall and give her time to think about what she'd say to Ethan. She had to play it cool, not let him know how much that kiss had meant to her.

Her mom answered immediately, as though she'd been poised next to the phone, waiting for the call. And, knowing her, she just might have been. Marisol explained the bare essentials of the threat she'd received last night, reassured her mother that she was okay.

"No, I'm not coming to stay with you," she said

firmly when her mother demanded she move back in. "I appreciate the offer, but it's not safe for any of us. We're all better off with me at the safe house until they have a suspect in custody."

"Well then I'll come stay with you," her mother declared.

Marisol blew out a breath, the beginnings of a headache settling into the base of her skull. "No, Mom. I've got U.S. Marshals guarding me twenty-four seven. I told you, it's—" She broke off when a brisk knock sounded at the door.

Before she could answer, it swung open to reveal Ethan standing there. Something inside her jolted at the sight of him. Her heartbeat quickened as she stared back at him, noting the intent, focused way he watched her.

"Mom, I gotta go," she said when Ethan slipped inside and closed the door behind him. The room instantly felt half the size with him in it. "I'll call you later, okay? Love you. Bye." She hung up and set her phone down on the desk. "I was just returning the calls I'd missed earlier," she explained, hating that she was babbling but unable to stop. "Yours was next."

He didn't move from the doorway. He stood with his back to it, his hand poised on the knob. His stillness told her something was off.

She swept her gaze over him, her pulse increasing. "What's wrong?"

"Are you expecting anyone else to come see you in the next while?"

His eyes were too intense. She knew in her gut something bad had happened. "No, it's just me and Frank holding down the fort tonight. Why? What's wrong?"

Instead of answering he reached back and twisted the dead bolt. The sound of it sliding into place seemed overly loud in the quiet room. Her heart drummed faster, her hands tightening on the arms of her chair. "Are you all right?" He seemed unhurt, at least physically, but something was definitely wrong. "Are the guys okay?"

He nodded once, a muscle flexing in his jaw. "Had a close call last night."

She withheld a gasp. "Oh my God. Were you—" She half rose out of her seat, stopped short when he took a step toward her. His face was set, his gaze locked on hers. Marisol couldn't look away. Couldn't move.

She finally sat back down as he reached the desk, that intent look on his face sending an electric tingle up her spine. Part warning, part arousal. He looked…hungry was the only word she could think of to describe it.

"Are you hurt?" she managed, feeling vulnerable and delicate all of a sudden with him standing so close and looking at her like a starving man would eye a perfectly cooked filet.

He didn't stop at the desk. He rounded it, grabbed the arms of her chair and pushed it back from beneath the desk, stepped over to stand inches from the toes of her lipstick red pumps. "I don't want to talk about it." His voice was rough, a little unsteady.

Okay… Marisol blinked up at him, caught her breath when he bent to capture her face in his hands. Her heart fluttered wildly. He was inches away from her. And he smelled incredible.

For a heart-stopping moment he peered deep into her eyes, then spoke. "I had a wakeup call last night during an op. Afterward, all I could think about was you. All I've been thinking about for the last sixteen hours, is you. Because I wanted to do *this*."

Without giving her a chance to move he covered her lips with his and took complete possession of her mouth.

Chapter Twelve

*O*h my God...

Marisol gasped and grabbed hold of his shoulders as desire exploded inside her. His tongue delved into her mouth to stroke along hers, tasting her. She tightened her grip, felt the tension in him when the muscles beneath her fingers bunched.

Heat roared through her, obliterating thought and reason.

She didn't care about the consequences of her actions, that she'd be hurt when he left town, she wanted him. She didn't know what had happened on the op but it had to have been bad to shake him so much. She could have lost him last night and she wasn't going to waste another opportunity to show him what he meant to her.

Ethan shifted his grip on her face, one hand sliding into the back of her hair, holding her still as he plunged his tongue deeper into her mouth. Dominant. Raw male hunger, because he wanted *her*. Her entire body pulsed with arousal.

Ethan broke the kiss. He trailed the fingers of his free hand down the side of her neck, down to the open V of her blouse, then lower.

Marisol held her breath, her nipples already hard and aching against the cups of her bra. His eyes flashed down to them as his fingers crept lower, gently brushing against the underside of one breast. She sucked in a breath, arched her back, wanting more.

Leaving his hand in place, he lifted his gaze and searched her eyes. She stared right back, lost in those blazing, golden brown depths.

"Do I make you ache, kitt'n?" His thumb dragged gently across one straining nipple.

She made an incoherent sound of pleasure and grabbed his wrist to hold him there. Conflict warred inside her. Her body was screaming for relief but her mind was shouting that she was crazy. If anyone found out what they were doing in here it would ruin her reputation at work.

He leaned in to nibble at the corner of her jaw, right beneath her ear, his lips warm against her wildly fluttering pulse point. "Do I?"

Oh, dammit, she couldn't think straight with his mouth on her. The lock on her door was solid. Only Frank and her security team were up here, and they likely wouldn't disturb her, so if she wanted to do this, now was the perfect time.

"Yes," she whispered, needing him too badly to bother denying it. She could be embarrassed about it all she wanted later. Right now she wanted him and he clearly needed her.

He hummed softly in satisfaction, flicked his tongue across her pulse point before sucking lightly. She squirmed in her seat, his grip on her hair holding her in place. The firm display of command was unbelievably exciting, something she'd fantasized about him for forever.

"Want me to make it better?" he added in a beguiling

whisper.

Logic finally pierced through the fog of lust clouding her brain. She tensed a little as his meaning sank in. Sex, here? Her first time, in her office while her boss was just down the hall and federal marshals were on patrol? "I don't think…"

"Don't think," he encouraged. He moved his thumb again, turned his head to capture her tiny gasp with his mouth as he caressed her sensitive nipple. Back and forth, back and forth in a maddening glide that made it hard to breathe. "It's just you and me here and I need to touch you. Let me touch you."

Marisol hesitated. She'd just warned herself against this not five minutes before he'd shown up and already she was wavering. He made her weak. His touch, his nearness and the need she sensed in him, robbed her of the ability to think clearly.

The door's locked and no one's coming in, a voice in her head whispered. *You want him. This might be your only chance.*

There was no way she was walking away from it.

She wasn't sure if he had full-on sex in mind, but even that she was suddenly on board with. Ethan was a lot more experienced than the men she'd dated. She trusted him and he'd be gentle with her. Even if this turned out to be a one-time thing, she could deal with that. Couldn't she?

Her thoughts scattered again when he sank to his knees before her. Pressing his torso forward he pushed her thighs apart the few inches her pencil skirt would allow. Heat flooded between her legs at the raw, possessive move.

"I want you to think of me every time you walk into this office," he said, his voice a seductive rumble against the edge of her mouth. "And every time you sit in this chair, I want to you to remember what I did to you in it."

Her toes curled in her sexy red pumps. She shivered at the erotic promise in his voice, was pretty sure she managed a faint nod. *Yes. Yes, yes, yes…*

It was enough.

His hand shifted, his long fingers moving to pluck the top button of her cream silk blouse. He pressed a tender kiss to her lips, watched her face as he slid the first button free. Then the next.

Marisol made no move to stop him. There was something so decadent about this situation. Being hidden behind her locked door, Ethan on his knees before her, undressing her while she reclined in her plush leather chair.

Her heart knocked against her ribs as he undid the blouse and peeled the two halves apart, exposing her pale pink lace bra. He made a hungry sound of approval and hooked a finger into the top of each delicate cup, peeled the fabric down and tucked it beneath her breasts. The rolled-down lace pushed her breasts up even more, her nipples hard, begging for his attention.

"So damn gorgeous, Soli." Ethan looped an arm around her to set a big hand between her shoulder blades and pulled, arching her back more, pushing her breasts toward his waiting mouth. With a low sound of wanting, he bent and tongued one straining peak.

Marisol bit back a moan and grabbed his head with both hands, holding him close. Her eyes slid closed as he took her into his mouth and sucked, the pleasure streaking through her like fire. She was panting, so wet already, the hot throb between her legs sharpening with every luscious stroke of his tongue.

"Ethan," she whispered, her voice unsteady. It was a good thing she was sitting down because her legs were wobbly as hell.

The hand cupping her other breast caressed down her ribs, followed the curve of her waist and hip and ran down her leg. Before she realized what he was doing, he grabbed her ankle and slid off first one red pump, then the other. He set them aside then skimmed his hands up the back of her bare calves, over her knees to the tops of her thighs.

Her belly muscles clenched, her core throbbing, needing his touch. His mouth switched to the other nipple now. Marisol dug her fingers harder into his head.

Don't stop. Don't stop, she begged silently.

Sucking at her gently, Ethan gripped the hem of her skirt and began inching it upward. She didn't stop him, didn't want to.

When he had it bunched up around her hips he reached down for her ankles. She had only a second to tense before he bent her legs and propped her feet up on his broad shoulders. Releasing her captive nipple with a soft pop, he slipped his hands up her inner thighs.

The moment his fingertips brushed over her mound she sucked in a breath. Her thigh muscles tensed. Eyes smoldering, Ethan looked up at her, eased his fingers under the stretchy sides of her matching lace thong and began sliding them down her thighs. Automatically she started to close her knees.

He set his hands on the insides of her knees, holding her open, and pulled them to her ankles, quickly gliding them over her feet and dropping them out of view. Then he leaned back to survey his handiwork. She flushed at the feeling of exposure, she couldn't help it. It was bright in here and no one had ever done to her what she suspected he was going to…

Her heart pounded as he pressed her knees farther apart and turned his head to press a slow, lingering kiss to her left inner thigh. Tingles scattered up her skin like sparks.

Oh God, oh God, she didn't know if she could take this. Ethan, on his knees in front of her at her desk, his head between her legs. She was breathless, dizzy.

Those big hands shifted around to grip the outside of her thighs and he glanced up at her, his lips still pressed to her inner thigh, just inches from where she was dying for him.

"Hold on tight," he warned in an intimate whisper, then bent to kiss the aching flesh between her legs.

Soli clapped a hand over her mouth to stifle her cry of mingled shock and pleasure. Her hips lifted automatically, pressing her core against his mouth. Ethan groaned and closed his eyes, sliding his tongue through her sensitive folds and up to circle her swollen clit.

A high-pitched whimper shot out of her. The hand on his head curled into a fist, bunching around his hair. But he didn't seem to have any intention of stopping. His tongue stroked and caressed her exquisitely sensitive bud, then slid down and plunged inside her.

The move was so raw, so intensely sexual, this time she couldn't contain her reaction.

She slapped the hand covering her mouth onto the armrest of the chair and bowed against his mouth, needing something to anchor her. Ethan firmed his grip around her thighs and licked upward once more, settled his lips around her clit and sucked gently.

"Ethan," she quavered, not sure whether she was begging for more or begging for mercy. She let go of the armrest to grab hold of his shoulder, digging her fingers into his muscle.

He made a low sound of reassurance and released one thigh to slide his hand between her legs. A moment later she felt pressure as he carefully slid a finger into her.

Yes, she willed him, fisting his hair. *More*.

Sucking gently, he withdrew his finger and added a second. He pushed in slowly, watching her face now, and touched a spot inside her that simultaneously eased the terrible ache as it increased it at the same time.

She bit back a strangled moan and held onto him for dear life. The pleasure was incredible, growing, coiling tight beneath his mouth. She was so primed, already beginning the climb to release. Her breathing was erratic, her thighs and belly quivering as her body tightened more, more, a spring pulled until it was about to snap.

He stroked his fingers inside her, rubbing with firm pressure while his lips and tongue caressed her most sensitive spot pushed her even higher. She rolled her hips against his mouth, so close to the edge now.

Through glazed eyes she drank in the sight of him that way, mouth pressed between her legs, fingers buried inside her, his tongue doing wicked, wicked things she'd only ever dreamed about.

Suddenly the pleasure intensified. The orgasm crested for a moment, then finally burst free, sending her flying. Her body arched. She was dimly aware of him cupping a hand over her mouth to quiet the cries of release she couldn't contain. Right now she didn't care who heard her. Ethan had just gone down on her in her office, made her come with his mouth, and it was even better than her hottest fantasies had ever been.

As the waves finally began to ebb she all but collapsed back into her chair, breathing like she'd just run a half marathon, all her muscles quivering. Ethan sucked on her one last time and at last lifted his head. He licked his lips, all shiny from her, and slowly eased his fingers from her body.

She groaned, let her head drop back as she caught her breath. The man had definitely perfected his technique when it came to pleasing a woman.

It made Marisol wonder what he could do with the rest of his body.

A light shiver rippled through her at the thought. She looked down at Ethan, still between her thighs, her feet propped on his broad shoulders. God, that was hot.

His lashes dipped as he turned his head and pressed a lingering kiss to the inside of one ankle, then the other. Then he retrieved her panties from wherever he'd put them and slid them back over her feet.

The move snapped her back to reality. Feeling shy all of a sudden, she hastily slipped the cups of her bra back in place and snapped her knees together.

Her hands weren't quite steady as she grabbed her panties and shimmied them back into place, then pulled her skirt back down to her knees. She could feel how wet she was, felt her face go hot at what she'd just allowed Ethan to do to her.

Now what? Did she thank him, or...?

He smoothed a hand up the back of her calf in a gentle caress, squeezed once before releasing her and pushing to his feet. Grimacing, he slid a hand into the waistband of his jeans.

Her eyes locked on the sizeable bulge straining the denim as he adjusted himself. Immediately she imagined what it would be like to unzip him, push him back to sit on her desk and treating him to the same pleasure he'd just given her. More heat flooded her body.

A low, sensual chuckle brought her gaze up to his face. His cheekbones were flushed and his eyes were molten with desire. "Keep looking at me like that and neither of us will be leaving your office for a long time."

Was that supposed to be some kind of a threat? Because she definitely wanted more of him. Like, *right* now.

She leaned forward, reaching for his waistband, but he caught her hands and tugged her from her chair. Releasing her, he cupped her face between her hands and kissed her.

She could taste herself on his lips. Rather than turning her off, it did the opposite because it reminded her of what he'd just done and how willingly he'd given her pleasure. The orgasm had taken the edge off but she still wanted more.

Everything he had to give her, in case it was all she ever got.

Ethan sucked lightly at her lower lip before lifting his head, his eyes glowing with desire. "Rain check. If you're still up for more once you're back at the safe house, I'm game. But I want you to have time to think about it."

A smile spread across her face. "That's really sweet, to give me that."

He eased his thumb across her mouth. "With you, yeah. Because you matter to me. I don't want you having any regrets later."

His words reinforced that he was still thinking of this as a one-time thing. Or at least, that's what she thought he meant, and she wasn't going to ask.

She kissed his thumb, parted her lips to catch it between her front teeth and let her tongue play gently. A thrill zinged through her at the way his nostrils flared, the way his gaze went all intent and smoky as he focused on her mouth.

Even though there was no future for them she still wanted him, at least once. "I won't regret it. Because you matter to me too." And so she wanted him to be her first.

Ethan let his hand drop. His expression became shuttered, all business, like he'd flipped a switch. "Text me when you're ready to leave. Let me know if you want me to come over."

"I want you to."

"You sure about that?"

"Yes." She was absolutely certain she wanted Ethan with her tonight. She'd waited long enough for him already.

Chapter Thirteen

Bautista climbed out of his truck at two minutes to eight and walked up Julia's front walkway. After circling her complex twice to make sure no one had followed him, and not noting anyone suspicious outside, he'd decided to park in her driveway next to her truck where she'd backed it into its usual spot.

He ran a hand down the front of his shirt, something almost like nervous butterflies humming in his stomach. He'd worn black dress pants and a deep blue button-down dress shirt, had even stopped to pick up the bouquet of fresh flowers now clutched in his hand.

It was weird, but his pulse beat faster as he approached the front door. He couldn't remember the last time he'd looked forward to something with this much excitement and anticipation.

Over the past few hours he'd considered canceling a couple of times, but something had always held him back. As stressed as he was about last night's op and still having no leads as to who the shooter had been, he couldn't blow off an opportunity to spend time alone with Julia.

He had another op scheduled for tomorrow, couldn't

be sure when he'd get the chance to be with her next. In his line of work, he'd learned to live life one day at a time. Last night had been a pointed reminder that he might not come back from the next job.

Julia opened the door before he'd reached the front step and for a moment he stopped in his tracks. She was dressed in a formfitting black dress that cut low in the front, giving him a perfect view of her cleavage. The hem stopped several inches above her knees, revealing part of her toned thighs, and the sexy leopard print heels gave him vivid ideas.

He'd love to have her gorgeous thighs wrapped around his neck as she rode his tongue, and after, those sexy heels digging into his ass as he plunged into her.

Yanking himself out of those thoughts, he smiled at her, the buzz of anticipation growing stronger in his belly. "Hey."

"Hey yourself. You're very punctual. I like that in a man." Her pale blue gaze stroked over him in a bold caress, lingering on his chest and crotch for a moment before sliding back to his face. "Mmm, you sure clean up nice," she said when he reached the front step. She slid her arms around his back to hug him.

He had only an instant to absorb how amazing she felt, breathe in her subtle, sweet scent before she pulled back. Giving him an inviting smile, she stepped back and beckoned him inside. "For me?" she asked, looking at the flowers.

"Yeah." He handed them over, stuck his hands in his pockets and tried not to stare as she lowered her face to the brightly colored blooms and inhaled. She was so damn pretty. So vividly alive, while he felt half dead inside.

Until he was around her. Then, something unexpected and magical happened. He didn't understand it, couldn't figure it out, but it was there nonetheless. All he knew was, he wanted to experience more of it.

Lowering the flowers, Julia cast him a sultry smile, her lips painted a deep, glossy red that screamed pure, raw sex. "So, what did you have in mind for tonight?"

"There's a place I want to take you to, for dinner. If you're hungry." A quiet, classy place by the water he sometimes went to when he was in town. It was owned by one of his most trusted contacts. He never needed a reservation. They'd fit him into the private room upstairs and they'd be undisturbed except for their server all night. And if they were going, he should get her to his truck right now.

Because based on that sensual look she'd just given him, if he didn't get them out of here soon, he doubted they'd be leaving her townhouse at all tonight.

Julia eyed him with that pale, smoldering gaze, lingered on his chest and shoulders again for a second before answering. "Oh, I'm definitely hungry. Do you have anywhere important to be tomorrow morning?"

Her question made it clear she was hoping he spent the night. As much as he wanted that, he wasn't sure it was a good idea. He thought again of the truck he'd seen turning the corner up the street last night, wondered if she was being honest with him. Whether he could really trust her.

But then he reminded himself that he was a cynical, paranoid bastard and let it go. He'd vetted her carefully long before ever considering asking her out. She was clean, no threat to him that he could tell.

But he was a huge threat to her, and she didn't realize it. It made his conscience squirm. "Have a work thing I've got to leave early for."

"How early?"

"Before dawn."

Disappointment showed in her eyes. "In town?"

"No. Down in the Keys." Key West, to be exact, but he wasn't going to tell her that.

He trusted her, to a point, but if anything happened, the less she knew about him and his activities, the better. For her own safety, so his enemies couldn't target her or use her to get to him. If things somehow progressed between them he'd reevaluate that policy later.

"Oh." There was a wealth of disappointment in that one word response, and it surprised him. She didn't know him. Not the real him, and he felt bad for duping her. But he couldn't very well tell her he was a private assassin for one of Fuentes's strongest lieutenants.

"Well then," she said when he didn't respond. "We'd better make the most of the time we've got."

Her words hit him square in the heart. His work was dangerous. The unidentified shooter was still out there, might be targeting him. He knew he was a selfish asshole for coming here, possibly exposing her to the danger.

And yet…he couldn't stay away. He'd lived in the darkness for too long. At this point she was the only light in his life. His way forward. She was strong but soft, smart and sweet, and for whatever reason, she cared about him. That was enough for now, even though he longed for more.

Needing to touch her, he lifted a hand, reached out to stroke a lock of her shiny chocolate-brown hair behind her ear. Her breathing hitched. Her eyes flashed up to his, her pupils dilating. His heartbeat sped up in reaction.

"I'm not the man you think I am," he admitted quietly into the silent room, feeling like he needed to be at least that honest with her, give her this last out. A final chance to save herself, turn him away before it was too late.

Because if she invited him to her bed tonight, there was no way he could let her go. He wanted out of the darkness he'd been trapped in, wanted to be with her, but he also wanted to protect her. And he knew he couldn't have it both ways.

Even though the kindest thing would be to walk away, he just didn't have the strength. Not with her.

Understanding filled her gaze and she leaned into his touch, a soft smile on her face. "Yes you are." She set the flowers down on a small table next to the door, raised an arm to twine it around his neck as she stepped into him, pressing that sweet body full length to his.

He went rock hard in his dress slacks, automatically slid his hands around her waist.

"You're exactly the man I think you are. I admire you more than you'll ever know."

The snick of the deadbolt sounded as she locked the door, then a digital beeping as she set the alarm. The act of her locking them in together made fire burst to life deep in his gut.

"And whether it makes sense or not, I'm crazy about the man standing in front of me," she finished, her seductive whisper pouring accelerant on the fire raging inside him.

When she slipped her other arm around his neck and stood on tiptoe to kiss him, his control snapped.

One hand cupping the back of her head, he curved his other arm around her ass and hoisted her off the floor, turning to pin her against the wall with his body. She gave a hungry mewl and eagerly met the bold stroke of his tongue, her long legs coming to wrap around his waist, hands sliding up to grip his hair. He could feel her need, the urgency driving her, and it fueled his own.

They weren't going to dinner. Weren't going anywhere but her bed, and he wasn't leaving it until morning.

It was the best damn thing that had happened to him in recent memory.

He spun them around, his arms locked around her. He would give as much as he got, show her what she meant to him, the softer side that only a handful of people had ever seen.

He'd give her pleasure, not pain.

Then come morning, he'd climb into his truck and head to Key West for his next kill. But until then, he had hours to explore this woman who'd managed to tangle him into knots and he was looking forward to every second of it.

Keeping their mouths fused together, he headed for the stairs that led to her bedroom.

****

Marisol shut down her computer with a sense of satisfaction and leaned back to stretch her arms over her head. It was after nine and she'd made enough headway to call it a night and be able to put her feet up for the rest of the night. With Ethan.

As if on cue, her phone buzzed. Sure enough, she found a text from him. *Thinking about you. I loved making you purr for me this afternoon, kitt'n.*

Oh, she'd more than purred. If he hadn't had the sense to cover her mouth at the end, Frank would have heard her ecstatic cries all the way down in his office.

She flushed at the reminder of what Ethan had done to her in here just a few short hours ago. Then she smiled to herself. He'd done exactly what he'd set out to do. She'd never be able to set foot in her office again or sit in this chair without remembering it.

I'm done with work, will be heading to house soon, she typed. *You coming over?*

Is that a trick question? he responded a moment later.

She grinned. *So that's a yes?*

Absolutely. See you there.

Marisol bit her lip as anticipation built inside her. She couldn't *wait*.

With any luck she'd get there a while before he did so she could take a shower and freshen up. She'd cleaned up a bit in the ladies' room earlier but she wanted a proper shower. Tonight was going to be one of the most important nights of her life and she wanted to be comfortable and confident when it happened.

Filled with excitement about the coming evening, she gathered her purse and some important files she'd need for the trip to Key West in the morning. When she opened her door she saw Frank coming out of his office down the hall.

"You outta here?" her boss called out.

"Yes. Meet you in the morning for the thing, at the place with the guy," she said in her best Jersey/Mafia accent. The marshals assigned to her would drive her to a location to meet Frank, then accompany them to Key West for extra security. She was glad to have them coming along, it made her feel that much safer given everything that had happened lately.

He chuckled. "Yeah, see you then."

"Don't work too much longer. And you should probably take your wife out for a late dinner tonight, before she gets fed up with you and leaves you for a younger man who's not a workaholic."

"Nah, already bought her a diamond bracelet as a preemptive strike on the weekend. I'm covered."

Marisol shook her head. "I'd never be bought off so easily."

"I pity the man who sets his sights on you," he teased.

Marisol smiled. "He'd have to be pretty special. You know I don't settle."

"I know, and that's one of the reasons I like you so much. Have a good night."

She waved goodnight and started down the hall, a secret smile on her face. Ethan was far more than special.

A delicious thrill curled through her at the thought of seeing him tonight. She couldn't wait to get him alone, take off his shirt and explore all the hard muscles she'd felt beneath her hands today, touch him, taste him.

As long as what she and Ethan did together was her decision and it felt right, then it wasn't settling. Even if it turned out to be a brief affair, as long as it was meaningful to both of them she could deal with that. It would hurt when he went back to Virginia, but better to have the experience with him than not at all.

She hastened her steps toward the elevator. One of the marshals assigned to her was waiting in the lounge. He stood, tossed aside the magazine he'd been reading when she approached. "Ready to go?"

"All set," she answered. He tapped his earpiece and relayed the message to the other two men on her detail. They stepped into the elevator and rode down to the lobby together.

When the doors opened he stopped her at the corner where she had to turn to head to the front entrance. "Fisher's just bringing the vehicle around. We'll wait here another few seconds."

Marisol stayed where she was and waited for him to give the all clear. He led the way, rounding the corner into the main lobby. One of the other marshals was waiting near the front door. Marisol was partway there when a shout came from outside.

The marshal in front of her stopped, whipped an arm out to stop her. She backed up a step, a jolt of alarm hitting her.

A loud pop sounded from outside, then something smashed through the front glass door. A female intern near the entrance let out a shriek and ducked under her desk.

Gunshot.

Automatically she dropped to the floor. The marshal

did the same next to her and quickly rolled her beneath him. Her purse and files scattered on the granite tile.

She lay on her belly with the man's weight squashing her, barely daring to breathe. Turning her head, her gaze sought the front door and she saw the hole punched through the middle of it, the glass spider-webbing outward.

Her mouth went dry, her muscles turned rigid.

Suddenly the marshal lifted off her, grabbed her beneath the arms and hauled her upright. Her heels clattered to the floor as he half dragged, half pushed her back around the corner near the elevator. He flattened her up against the wall, his body between her and whoever had taken that shot.

Out in the lobby people were shouting. The marshal was speaking to someone via his earpiece. She swallowed and stayed still, willing her heart back down her throat. Had *el Santo* just targeted her? As far as she knew, he'd never missed a target before. If that bullet had been meant for her, she was lucky to still be breathing.

A strange weakness set in, sapping her leg muscles of strength. She locked her knees, refused to give into it. If she was still in danger she needed to keep a clear head and be able to run.

A commotion broke out near the front entrance as more security rushed to the scene. The marshal's body relaxed slightly and he eased away from her. Marisol drew in a deep breath and found her voice. "What's going on?"

"Security took down the shooter."

El Santo? They got him? Her heart drummed in her ears as she waited. The stairwell door shoved open and the marshal whirled, weapon in hand. Frank froze in the doorway, raised both his hands. "What the hell's going on?"

"Someone just took a shot through the front door,"

Marisol told him as the marshal lowered his weapon, her voice surprisingly shaky. "Security just took someone into custody."

Frank muttered a curse. "Is the building secure?" he asked the marshal, who nodded. "Wait here until I know what's going on." He headed for the entry.

It took nearly twenty minutes for Frank to come back. He was scowling, his expression black. "Not *el Santo*," he told them. "Just a fucking punk gangbanger I put away four years ago for possession and dealing. He got out on parole this week. Tonight he went and got high and decided to come down and even the score with me. When he couldn't get into the building because of the extra security, he decided to take a shot through the door instead to make a statement."

He ran a hand through his hair, shook his head in disgust. "I'm just glad nobody got hurt."

Marisol let out a deep breath as relief flooded her. Frank's gaze shot to the marshal. "You taking her out of here now?"

"Yes. As soon as my team gets in position and verifies that the building is secure. We'll be going out the back this time."

Frank nodded and looked her way. "I think you're right. I do need to take Dianne to dinner tonight."

Marisol gave him a stiff smile and nodded. Even though she hadn't been the target this time, she was still a little rattled. Right now she wanted Ethan. Once she felt his arms around her she'd know she was truly safe, and not until.

Chapter Fourteen

The same marshal from the night before let Ethan into the back door of the safe house.

"How is she?" Ethan demanded when he stepped inside. He'd only found out about the shooting from the marshal who'd stopped him when he'd started up the driveway. It made him angry that she hadn't called him yet again. What was it going to take to make her reach out to him?

"Fine. She's upstairs taking a shower. Said you'd be by." The guy eyed him. "You staying for a while?"

"For a few hours, yeah." He didn't elaborate because he didn't want anyone knowing his and Marisol's business, and also because he wasn't sure how long he had.

There was a chance he could get called back in for another op if they received more intel in the coming hours. They were gunning for Perez next, the lieutenant protected by *el Santo*. If a critical piece of intel came in, they'd have to move fast on it. Perez had proven impossible to corner thus far.

The marshal nodded. "My guys are watching the

house and the neighborhood. Since you're HRT and on her approved list of visitors, I can give you some privacy. I'll be in my vehicle if you need me."

Ethan locked the door behind him and set the alarm to stay mode. When he turned back around he heard light footsteps coming down the carpeted stairs.

Marisol appeared at the bottom of them, dressed in a pair of tights and a long, snug top that hugged her lean curves and ended at mid-thigh. Her long hair hung in damp waves around her shoulders.

A delighted smile lit her face when she saw him. "Hey, you're here already." She started toward him.

He met her halfway and grabbed hold of her shoulders, ignoring her gasp as he dragged her into his arms and hugged her tight. "Why didn't you call me and tell me what happened?"

She returned the embrace, snuggling her cheek into the curve of his shoulder. "Because no one was hurt and they captured the guy. I wasn't the intended target and I knew you were coming over anyway so I was going to tell you when you got here. I didn't want to worry you."

Didn't want to worry him? He made a gruff sound, pressed his face into her hair that smelled all soapy clean. "Anything at all scary happens to you or around you, I want to know about it. Asap." The thought of anything happening to her made him crazy with the need to protect her.

"Okay, I promise," she soothed, running a hand up and down his spine. "But I'm fine. Really."

He let out a breath, eased his grip a little but didn't let her go. Knowing bullets had been fired anywhere near her scared him. "You sure?" She didn't seem rattled at all, but this latest event had to have frightened her.

"At the time, yes. But once I knew they had the shooter in custody and that I wasn't the target, I felt better. The marshals acted fast. I had good protection. Now that you're here, though, I feel *way* better." She wriggled in closer, sighed.

Ethan closed his eyes and took a moment to savor this. She was safe and warm in his arms and seemed content to be there. She was letting him in more and more, and for that he was grateful. Made things harder though. He already knew it was going to be tough to leave her when they pulled out of Miami within the next week. He'd been gearing up to end things between them when he returned to Virginia, make the break nice and clean, but he knew it wasn't going to happen.

There was no way he could simply walk away from his feelings for her. He couldn't remember the last time he'd been this into a woman, and the connection between him and Marisol was strengthened by their history together. He wanted more time with her after he left, to see if they could make a relationship work. The distance would be hard but they could make it work if they were both willing to try.

"Just glad you're okay," he murmured into her hair. His entire body buzzed with awareness. The way she'd allowed him to strip her barriers away in her office this afternoon had left him in a constant state of arousal. Every time he thought of how she'd reacted when he'd settled his mouth between her legs, he got hard.

And he'd thought about it a *lot* over the past few hours they'd been apart.

Marisol nuzzled his chest with her cheek, the trusting, intimate gesture making his heart squeeze even as it flooded him with arousal. "I missed you this afternoon," she murmured.

"You did?"

She hummed in affirmation. "I was distracted the rest of the day." She tilted her face up to nibble at his jaw, her hands wandering from his back to his shoulders, then down his chest.

He loved it, loved everything about what she was doing, but given how turned on he already was, he felt the need to slow things down. Once clothes started coming off, things could get out of hand in a hurry.

He curved his hands around her waist and pressed a tender kiss to her forehead. "Hey. We don't need to do anything else tonight." Yeah, he wanted inside her, but if not, he'd be content to just crawl into bed beside her and hold her flush against his body for a few hours. Savor her warmth and listen to her even breaths as she slept, trusting him to take care of her.

She paused, leaned back an inch or two to look him in the eye. "But I want to."

Her sea green eyes were bright with desire and anticipation. He still needed to be sure she wanted more for the right reasons. "You don't owe me anything because of this afternoon," he said quietly.

One side of her mouth turned up. "I know. I've been dying to get my hands all over you, and yours all over me, ever since you and Alysa got together that once."

The mention of the name surprised him so much that he laughed. "What?"

She broke eye contact to stare at his chest. "I uh, may have...heard you guys."

His smile faded. "You heard us?" As he recalled it, they'd been up in his room while he had the house to himself that night.

"Yeah." She cleared her throat. "I came over to say hi. You didn't hear me knock. The door was unlocked, so I went inside and I...yeah."

Now it was his turn to flush. "Wow, that's...okay."

She hummed in agreement and kissed the point of his chin, her pert little breasts pressed to his chest. "And God, I nearly died of jealousy."

Yeah, he had no idea how to even respond to that. And now that he thought about it, Marisol had been conspicuously absent every time he'd seen her mom or sisters for the rest of his leave. "Is that why you avoided me that week?"

"Pretty much, yeah."

Ethan cupped her jaw, bringing her gaze up to his. "I was a nineteen-year-old kid and I barely remember her because she meant nothing to me. You *matter* to me."

She gave him an adoring smile that made him want to devour her. Just eat her up, one bite at a time. "I know."

"Good." Hell, he'd had no idea she was that into him back then. Of course, she'd been way too young for him at the time and he wouldn't have ever dared touch her, not even if he had thought about her that way. Which he hadn't.

But she was all woman now and old enough to decide what she wanted. If it was him, he'd deliver. With all the gentleness and skill she deserved from a lover.

Her *first* lover.

A dark wave of possessiveness rolled over him at the thought. He wanted that right so badly it was all he could do not to pick her up and carry her to the nearest bed right now.

Thankfully his feelings for her curbed the impulse. She wasn't just someone to have a good time with. And she'd never said she wanted full-on sex tonight anyway.

She deserved tenderness, patience, and as much pleasure as he could give her. There were plenty of other ways for them to enjoy themselves while still leaving her technically a virgin if that's what she wanted. It was her call.

He swept his thumb across her cheekbone. "Whatever you want, kitt'n. I'm all yours."

At the endearment her eyes lit up. Her eyes glowed as she smiled at him. "Thank you."

Without another word she took his hand and led him upstairs. Ethan's pulse raced as they hit the top of the stairs. The master bedroom was dark. She flipped on a bedside lamp, illuminating the queen-size bed and the chocolate brown sheets turned down invitingly on it. Still holding his hand, she sat on the edge of it.

He followed her down, his hip touching hers. She was nervous. He could read it in the sudden stiffness in her shoulders, her slight hesitation before she lifted her gaze to his.

He squeezed her hand. "There's no pressure. We do only what you want, and if you say stop, we stop." He didn't want her to be nervous with him or worry that he wouldn't respect her boundaries.

She shook her head. "I'm just...I don't want to disappoint you."

His chest constricted. She had no idea how much she undid him. "Sweetheart, you could never disappoint me, trust me. And I don't want you to do anything you're not comfortable with."

"Okay," she said with a nod, then came up on her knees. Eye level with him, she set her hands on his shoulders, her expression determined. And a lot aroused. "I want to touch you. All of you." The impassioned way she said it hit him hard.

"So touch me," he said, lifting one of her hands to his mouth and pressing a damp, lingering kiss to her palm. "All of me." He was dying for it.

She sucked in a breath when he stroked his tongue over her palm. Setting her free hand on the side of his face, she leaned in to kiss him.

Ethan met her halfway but let her lead, opening to the gentle pressure of her tongue as she sought entrance. She moaned softly and pressed closer, all but crawling into his lap. He set his hands on her waist to keep a few inches of space between their bodies and ordered himself to keep them there, at least for now.

This afternoon in her office he'd taken what he

wanted, what he'd needed. He wanted to give her the same opportunity now. And dear God in heaven, it turned him inside out to know she wanted him so badly. That she trusted him enough to allow him to be her first. The thought of any other man touching her now made his hackles go up.

Marisol's hands wandered down to the hem of his T-shirt and worked the fabric up his torso while she kissed him. He broke the kiss only long enough for him to tear the garment over his head and throw it aside. He had no idea where it landed, and didn't care. Her reaction to seeing his naked chest had him hard all over.

She stared at his torso with a rapt hunger that made his heart thud in his ears. He was already erect and aching, but that look on her face seemed to shrink his skin, tighten it, turning it ultra-sensitive.

A moment later she began exploring his bare skin with her fingertips, trailing them over the muscles in his shoulders, across his pecs. When they moved lower over his abs and she bent to press her mouth to the top of his left pec, his fingers bit into the indent of her waist.

Her soft hands and tongue teased him, drew every muscle in his body taut until he was breathing hard, his erection squashed painfully against his fly. Then her fingers dipped beneath his waistband. His abs contracted and he leaned back, stretching out on the bed to give her better access.

She undid his jeans and worked them over his hips when he lifted them, then slipped her fingers into the top of his boxer briefs and drew them down. Her gaze went straight to his rigid cock and stayed there as she slid to her knees beside the bed. Ethan squeezed his hands into fists to keep from reaching for her, stayed still and let her do as she wanted.

After stripping his pants and underwear off she rose to her knees and set a hand on his belly. The muscles twitched beneath her palm. She flashed him a questioning glance before focusing back on his cock, and he wondered exactly how much—or exactly how little—experience she had. Had she ever touched a naked man before? She must have.

His quads bunched when she curled a soft hand around him. He bit back a groan, couldn't tear his eyes away from her as she gave him an experimental stroke. Her touch was light but he felt it all the way to his toes.

Suddenly it was hard to breathe, as though steel cables were wrapped around his chest. Then she kissed a spot right beneath his navel and he forgot to breathe at all.

He reached out to slide a hand into her hair, the need to touch her overwhelming. She squeezed him gently in her fist, lifted her gaze to his as she trailed her tongue southward, toward the head of his aching erection.

Ethan swallowed and braced himself, waiting for the moment when her mouth touched him. Then her smooth, wet tongue stroked over the ultra-sensitive head. He clenched his back teeth together and held his breath. She swirled her tongue over him again, let her lips part and began to slide him into her mouth.

The sight of her on her knees taking his cock between her lips made something in his brain short out.

He'd had plenty of blowjobs but none of them had ever been this hot. Watching Soli discover what pleased him, watching her explore her own sexuality with the use of his body was the most arousing thing he'd ever witnessed in his entire life.

That primal tide of possessiveness rose inside him again. He wanted to make her his, couldn't stand the thought of another man's hands on her. Hell, just the thought of her doing this to another man made him crazy.

Mine. She's MINE.

Gaining confidence now, she took him deeper between her lips and sucked. He moaned at the exquisite sensation. Those gorgeous, sea-witch eyes gazed up at him, filled with arousal and a wicked glint that told him she loved driving him wild.

He slid his other hand into her hair as well, stroked her scalp gently. Then she sucked him harder and he almost lost it. He threw his head back and dragged in a shaky gasp, let it out on a deep groan as pleasure streaked up his spine, hot and electric.

Marisol sucked him deeper then raised her head until she nearly released him before she plunged back down again. Ethan grabbed fistfuls of her hair now, tried not to pull too hard, but Jesus, her mouth felt so goddamn good.

One of her hands curled around the base of his cock, fisting tight to hold him where she wanted him. Her sultry mouth drove him out of his skull as her free hand smoothed up and down the inside of his right thigh. Almost like she was trying to soothe him.

Sweat broke out across his chest and the base of his spine. The sweet pull of her mouth was too much and yet not enough.

Torture. Beautiful, sensual torture.

She swirled her tongue around him, rubbing over his most sensitive spot and he couldn't help but arch his back. He barely heard the sound of encouragement she gave over the roar of blood in his ears, the pressure in his cock growing with every heartbeat. He was too close, didn't think he could hold on much longer.

"Soli, you're gonna make me come if you don't stop," he warned, his voice ragged, a little desperate.

She slowed but didn't stop, her gaze fastened on his. He shuddered at the sight of her like that, lips all shiny and swollen as they stretched around his aching flesh, her eyes glittering with lust.

For *him*. An image straight out of his wildest fantasies.

But then it occurred to him that this might not only

be the first blowjob she'd given anyone, but that she'd probably never swallowed before, either.

And fuck, but the thought of being the first to come in that hot little mouth almost pushed him over the edge.

The pleasure quadrupled in a sudden rush, a warning tingle rocketing up his spine. He barely had enough control to pull back from the brink before it was too late.

"Baby, stop. Stop for a second," he managed. He grasped her head, gently pulled her away from him, unable to stifle a groan as her mouth released him.

Squeezing his eyes shut he lay there panting for a few moments, hands fisted in her hair while he fought to regain control. When the sensation ebbed enough for him to open his eyes, he looked down to find her watching him, her hand still curled around the base of his cock.

He didn't want to ruin the moment, but he wanted to fulfill her needs as well. He uncurled one hand from her hair, slid his fingers down to stroke over her flushed cheek. "What do *you* want?" he whispered. It was important to him.

She licked her lips and shifted a little. The way she squirmed told him sucking on him had turned her on. That made it even hotter. "I want to make you come."

While he'd kill for the chance to come in her mouth, he sensed she was holding something back. And he didn't want her finishing him off that way if she felt like she owed him from earlier. "What about you though? I wanna make you come again too."

She blushed. Actually blushed even though she'd had his cock in her mouth not ten seconds before. His heart squeezed. She was so fucking sweet.

He rubbed his thumb across her mouth, his abs tightening when she took the tip between her lips and sucked lightly. His cock twitched in her hand, wanting back in her mouth. "Say it," he told her, unwilling to let it go.

"I want you inside me," she whispered back.

Ethan exhaled slowly as triumph roared through his veins. *Yes.* He'd be the first to sink into her tight little body, the first to feel her squeeze around him as she came. It was totally caveman of him to think it but he didn't care.

He would make love to her, ensure her first time was special and that she had at least one orgasm to offset any discomfort she might experience. Make her *his* and his alone. After that, he'd do whatever it took to keep her.

His hand was slightly unsteady when he pulled his thumb free of her mouth, surprising him. And his heart was racing like he'd just run ten miles. "Okay."

A slow smile curved that luscious mouth. "Okay," she agreed.

He held out his hand to her, his entire body pulsing at the thought of burying his cock inside her. "Then come up here and I'll give you what you asked for."

Chapter Fifteen

━━━━━━━━━ ⌒ ━━━━━━━━━

This was it. No going back after this.

Rather than make her nervous, the thought filled Marisol with a heady rush of anticipation. Ethan was finally going to be hers.

Even if only for one night.

She shook the thought away. It didn't matter if she wanted more from him, this is what he was willing to offer. Having him once was better than not having him at all, and she knew he'd not only treat her with care and consideration, but make this an experience she'd never forget. The arousal flooding her body was so intense she felt light-headed.

Her breathing was erratic as she rose and slowly began stripping. With the light on she felt a bit shy but then Ethan sat up to watch, his eyes molten with desire.

He tracked each of her movements, devoured the sight of every bit of skin she exposed to his gaze. When she was naked, she took the hand he held out, feeling a tiny bit nervous now that all the attention wasn't on him anymore.

With one quick move he pulled her down onto the bed and rolled on top of her. She gasped at the sensation of his weight pressing her into the mattress, the heat of his skin on hers.

Common sense intruded for a moment. "I don't have anything..." she began, then trailed off. She hadn't wanted to ask her security team to stop at a store on the way here just so she could buy condoms. And until a minute ago, she'd already made up her mind to be happy with focusing on pleasing Ethan for now.

"I'll take care of it," he answered, dropping three kisses across her upper lip before sucking lightly on her lower one.

Winding her arms around his shoulders, she raised her head and covered his lips with hers. It felt like she was melting as she twined her legs around his, their mouths fused together.

He had most of his weight propped up on his forearms. Then he shifted, sliding a hand into her hair to tilt her head back and give him access to her neck. Her eyes drifted shut, tiny shivers racing across her skin at the feel of his lips and tongue on her flesh.

A soft sigh escaped when one large hand cupped her breast. Her nipple beaded tight in anticipation of his mouth, moving ever closer. She sank her fingers into his hair, squirmed a little as he lowered his head to suck.

Marisol arched her back, her hips moving restlessly. The hand on her breast skidded down over her ribs to her hip, glided across her inner thigh.

Lifting his weight from her he reached down to cup between her legs. The heat and pressure of his hand felt amazing but made the ache worse. She clung to him, tugged him up for another deep kiss as his fingers stroked and teased. One slid into her, testing, then eased out to circle her clit.

Impatient, she reached down to grab his hip, dug her fingers into that taut flesh. He ignored it, seemed in no hurry as he kissed her and stroked her until she was trembling and gasping. The pleasure was rising fast, too fast. She wanted him inside her. Her muscles tightened and she whimpered into his mouth, rolled her hips against his hand.

Ethan pulled his hand away and rolled to grab something from the floor. He came up with a condom packet in his hand and quickly tore it open. Unwilling to be a passive participant, she sat up and wrapped her fingers around the base of his erection. He covered her hand with his, raised it to help him roll the condom down the shaft.

When it was done he pressed her to her back with a hand on her shoulder and reached up to drag a pillow down from the head of the bed. After setting it beneath her hips, he moved in between her open thighs.

She set both hands on his back and pulled him close, expecting him to push into her. Instead he bent to nibble at the sensitive spot beneath her ear, his warm breath raising goose bumps across her skin. He set one hand beside her head, leaned his weight on it, and slid his other one back to tease the swollen flesh between her legs.

This time he pressed two fingers inside her and paused there, his thumb circling her clit and his eyes on her face. The pleasure rose sharp and bright. She pushed it back, held her breath when he withdrew his hand and settled deeper between her legs.

Her fingers dug into the muscles in his back. She felt warmth and pressure at her opening as he eased the tip of his erection inside her.

That golden brown stare stayed locked on hers. Breathless, heart pounding, she couldn't look away. He had her spellbound, her body on the brink of something wonderful. And it wasn't just physical, for either of them. There was no way he could look at her like this and not feel something inside.

His hand shifted between them, one fingertip circling

her clit gently as he watched her. The ache inside her grew, maddening and pleasurable at the same time. She felt more pressure, a slight burn as the heavy stretching increased. Her eyes closed.

Ethan stilled, breathing hard. As his finger continued to stroke her, the burn faded, leaving only that gnawing ache behind along with a heavy fullness that made her nerve endings sizzle.

He was completely buried inside her.

A thrill shivered through her and she opened her eyes. Ethan's face was taut with desire, his nostrils flared. The muscles beneath her fingertips bunched tight as he held himself there, watching her reaction, making sure she wasn't in any pain.

There was no pain, only pleasure now, coiling tight inside her where he was lodged so deep in her body. Her heart swelled and her throat tightened. She'd always dreamed it would be like this with him. He treated her like she mattered, made her feel cherished and adored.

With a soft smile she slid her hands up into his hair and lifted her head to kiss him, giving her hips an experimental rock. She gasped into his mouth as pleasure streaked through her.

Ethan groaned and met the glide of her tongue, still stroking her clit. She rocked her hips again, moaned at the dual sensations. Having him inside her while he caressed her felt incredible. Way better than she'd ever expected.

When she rolled her hips again, seeking more of that delicious friction, he shuddered. It thrilled her to know he was just as affected. Her heart was full to bursting at being able to experience this moment with him.

Shifting his weight, he moved his hips back then surged forward. He hit a spot inside her so sweet that she tore her mouth free of his and squeezed her eyes shut, a cry of wonder tearing from her throat.

He murmured something and slid the fingers of his

free hand into her hair. His lips layered kisses over the corner of her mouth, her jaw.

"Oh," she gasped out. "Ohhh…" *Ethan. Ethan, Ethan*, she chanted in her mind.

His hand tightened in her hair, the sudden increase of pressure causing a pleasurable burn along her scalp. He caught her lower lip between his teeth, bit down gently as he pushed deep once more, his finger still caressing her clit.

A helpless whimper escaped her. She covered his mouth with hers, devouring him as the pleasure gripped tight and wouldn't let go.

Every time he moved inside her it got better, and better, until she was rocking desperately against him. The orgasm was rushing at her now and she was greedy for it. Craved it with every cell in her body.

Tightening her thighs around his hips, she drove up to meet each thrust. Ethan growled into her mouth, the primal sound fueling the desperate need for release. The friction was incredible, driving her higher, higher, until all the pressure inside her snapped free. She drowned in it, clung to him while the waves took her, her cries ringing unchecked off the ceiling.

Her release seemed to trigger something inside him. Ethan pulled his hand from between them and planted it on the other side of her head. He grabbed fistfuls of her hair, holding her in place, slid his tongue into her mouth as he plunged deep into her body.

Little ripples of pleasure rocked her. She wound her arms around his back, let her hands drift over his damp skin and focused on increasing his pleasure.

A low, rough groan rumbled through his chest. The kiss grew wild, desperate, the motion of his hips speeding up. He'd been so gentle before, out of consideration for her, and even now she sensed he was tempering the raw power in his body.

Marisol sighed and sucked at his tongue, luxuriating in the experience. She was utterly relaxed, her body warm and heavy, a lovely heavy feeling stealing through her limbs. Feeling the flex and release of his muscles as she ran her hands over his back was its own thrill.

She absorbed all of it, his spicy, masculine scent, each raw groan that told her how good she was making him feel. Her heart thudded hard as she held him, lifted into his rhythm. She felt him swell inside her, growing even harder.

Suddenly he sucked in a breath and tore his mouth free, his entire body seeming to lock. She gazed up at him, drank in the sight of his agonized expression, his eyes slammed shut, jaw clenched.

He shuddered once, twice, his head falling back a little as his low moan of pleasure filled the room. She could feel him pulsing inside her.

In the quiet she trailed her fingers over his slick shoulders, raised her head to rain soft kisses across his jaw. With a quiet growl he captured her mouth with his. His body relaxed, more of his weight settling back on her.

The kiss was languid now, sweet and intimate, a slow stroke of tongues, a melding of lips. Gradually her heart rate returned to normal. After a minute Ethan pressed a lingering kiss to her mouth and eased back to look at her, his hands framing her face.

"You all right?"

"Mmm, better than all right."

His lips quirked, then he sobered again. "Did it hurt?" he murmured, fingers playing with the hair at her temples.

"Barely at all." She smiled up at him, ran the sole of her foot down the back of his leg, then up again. The sex had been wonderful but she loved this part even more. "It was perfect. Thank you."

He huffed out a laugh and kissed the end of her nose.

"I should be thanking you." He shifted but stilled when she covered a wince as something twinged inside her. "Sore?"

"Maybe a little."

He eased out of her body carefully and she immediately missed the connection, the warmth of his body. "I'll go get you a warm cloth."

Before she could protest he was up and out of the bed. She switched off the lamp and drew the covers up over her breasts, enjoying the sight of his shadowed, naked ass as he walked to the attached bathroom. The man was all gorgeous, controlled power.

The water ran in the sink. A few moments later he came out with a washcloth in his hand and crossed to the bed.

Instead of handing it to her, he pulled the covers back and gently pressed it between her legs as he leaned down to kiss her. She sighed at the soothing warmth, reached up to cradle his face between her hands and rub her thumbs over his bristly cheeks. He was so tender and attentive with her, and even though she knew it wasn't a good idea because a relationship was impossible for them, a seed of hope took root inside her.

She definitely wanted more time with him, whether or not they had sex again. Although based on what he'd just shown her about her body, she couldn't wait to try other things with him.

When the cloth cooled a little he cleaned her gently then took the cloth back to the bathroom. Marisol braced herself for the moment when he got dressed and said something to try and make it less awkward before he left.

But it didn't happen. He came out of the bathroom and slid beside her into the bed, tugging her into the solid wall of his naked body. She rolled into him, hummed in enjoyment as she cuddled close, her cheek resting in the crook of his shoulder. Her eyes drifted closed.

"What time is it?" she whispered drowsily. She felt like she was floating, all her cares and stress gone. Nothing mattered except this moment, being in the shelter of his arms, wrapped around her like a cozy cocoon.

"About midnight." He stroked a warm hand up her spine, settled it on the back of her neck and kneaded the muscles there. She made a purring sound and he chuckled softly. "Tired?"

"Yes, but in a good way. I feel like I don't have a single bone left in my body."

His answering laugh stirred the hair on the top of her head. "That's exactly how you're supposed to feel after sex."

What they'd just done together wasn't sex. As inexperienced as she was, even she knew that. And he had to as well. "Well, it worked."

"I'm glad." He kissed the crown of her head.

For some reason the simple, chaste gesture of affection pierced her. It made no sense, given that they'd just been joined in the most intimate way two people could be, but that kiss made her heart ache.

You knew going in that this was only for one night, she reminded herself. *Enjoy it while it lasts*. He'd warned her he'd be leaving soon and hadn't made any mention of continuing anything beyond that. He'd respected her wishes, now she had to respect his. And yet, she couldn't help but long for more.

Marisol kept her eyes closed and inhaled, breathing him in. She felt so close to him right now, was absolutely dreading the moment when it ended. He hadn't said anything about wanting more than this one night together, even if she knew he cared. And she wasn't going to make things awkward by asking for more than he was willing to give. As far as she could tell, he had no plans to settle down anytime soon.

She didn't either, at least for the next while, though

she'd love to be in a committed relationship someday, provided her partner respected and accepted the rigors of her job. The practical side of her knew it could never work long term anyway. With them so far apart and both of them heavily invested in their jobs, they'd barely see each other even if they did try to make it work.

The thought depressed the hell out of her.

"What time do you have to be up in the morning?" he murmured, his long fingers stroking through her hair now. The caress was gentle, drugging.

"I was planning for five-thirty. Have to be on the road at six."

"Me too, unless I get called in to base before that. Mind if I stay over?"

Surprised but glad that he didn't seem to be in a hurry to leave, she tipped her head back to look into his face, the faint illumination of the bedside clock allowing her to see him. "Not at all." She'd love to spend the night curled up with him in this bed, maybe even go a second round later if she wasn't too sore.

"You need anything before we get some sleep? A hot bath maybe?"

"No, I'm so comfortable I don't ever want to move again." And she was going to memorize the feel of him, so it stayed with her forever. She settled deeper into his embrace, let her fingers drift over the line of his shoulder.

With nothing left to say and small talk way beyond her ability at the moment, a subtle tension took root between them. She kept waiting for him to say something about some kind of a future for them, kept hoping he would. But he didn't. Neither of them said anything for several long minutes.

"Good night," she finally whispered.

"'Night," he answered, and she felt the way his body relaxed when she didn't question him about what was going to happen between them after this.

Closing her eyes, she let herself drift but her mind refused to let go of one thing.

He might not have said the words, but she knew what they'd just shared had affected Ethan as much as it had her. He'd touched her with such care, made love to her rather than simply having sex, and now he was holding her close as though he couldn't bear to let go.

Those things told her there might still be hope for them after all.

There were feelings involved, on both sides, and she wasn't sure where they were going from here. All she knew was, it was going to hurt like a bitch when he left her behind.

****

Bautista's eyes snapped open when the bed shifted and an arm draped across his chest. His entire body went rigid until his brain caught up to the present a second later.
Julia.

He was in her bed, hadn't left it since he'd carried her up the stairs last night. He was on his side facing her and she was tucked against him, her breath warm against his upper chest.

Pulling in a deep breath, he let it out slowly and absorbed the feel of her. He'd been right in guessing the chemistry between them was hot enough to melt steel. Every step of the way last night she'd been right there with him, demanding he give her everything, nothing held back.

He swallowed and carefully set his hand on the small of her back. She shifted and sighed in her sleep but didn't wake up.

Her skin was silky smooth beneath his palm. He could spend hours running his fingers over it, would love to tie her to the bed and tease her for hours until she was begging for him. But the light seeping in around the edges of the blinds told him it was nearly dawn.

Time for him to hit the road down to Key West and start hunting.

He stayed where he was for a few more minutes, milking every last moment he could with her. But even he couldn't hold back time.

Hating to leave her, he gently eased her away from him. She stirred but he leaned over her and tucked the blankets securely around her shoulders. "Go back to sleep. It's early."

"You'll call me later?" she murmured.

"Sure," he lied. He wanted to be able to call, he just wasn't sure if he could. Or whether it would be safe to.

A sleepy smile curved her lips, tempting him to lean down and kiss her again. But if he did that he'd never get on the road.

""Kay," she murmured, pressing a kiss to the back of his hand.

He straightened and stood by the bed, memorized the sight of her curled up there before leaving the room and shutting the door soundlessly behind him. At the front door he paused and reached back for the weapon holstered at the small of his back. It was so early no one else was out wandering around the complex.

Stepping outside, he scanned the area then headed for his truck. After checking it over to make sure no one had tampered with it, he climbed in and started the engine.

As he drove away from her complex, he'd already come to a decision. He'd been thinking about it for a while now, but last night had solidified everything. He knew what he had to do.

He waited until he'd hit the highway to ensure no one was following him, then dialed Perez.

"You on your way to Key West?" his lieutenant asked, not a hint of grogginess in his voice despite the early hour.

"Yes." He took a breath, released it, and said what he needed to. "But after this job, I want out."

A shocked silence filled the line for a few tense seconds. "What?" he said with a startled laugh.

"You heard me. After this, I'm out."

Another pause. "You're not joking."

"No."

"What brought this on? Are you all right?"

Once again, he was going with his gut. He was done with this game, wanted out once and for all. Sever all ties to his old life. "I'm fine. It's just…time."

"Where will you go?"

The Caymans, maybe, or some other non-extradition country. He had enough money saved up to move his *abuela* there quietly, maintain a comfortable lifestyle off the grid. He wouldn't tell anyone where he planned to go though, not even Perez. "I don't know."

"What will you do?" The older man sounded bewildered.

"Not sure." He trusted Perez and knew he'd never betray him. It was why he'd made this call before the job was over.

But he also knew he didn't want to live like this anymore. Living in the shadows, killing for money. Even if he normally eliminated targets he considered to be evil, one day he'd still have to answer for his crimes.

And there were others. Innocents he had no choice but to eliminate. Like Marisol, whom he was watching closely.

If she compromised this last job or his cover, he'd have no choice but to silence her forever. Those stains on his soul would never come clean. Before his final judgment came, he had a lot of moral ground to make up. He wanted to wipe the slate clean, start over.

And hopefully one day, be with the woman who'd

stolen his heart.

"Well shit, I don't know what to say. I'll be sorry to lose you," Perez said finally. "But I understand why you'd want that, and you know I wish you the best."

"I appreciate that."

His boss cleared his throat. "You'll contact me once it's done then?"

"Yes." He disconnected and drove in silence, mentally listing the steps he needed to enact an exfil plan from his current life. He already had the bones of one in place, an emergency strategy to fall back on if he'd ever been compromised. It needed fleshing out immediately.

By tonight when this last job was over, he had to have a final plan in place. And once he enacted it, he had to somehow convince Julia to take a huge chance and come with him. Because after last night, going through the rest of his life without her was unthinkable.

Chapter Sixteen

Marisol crossed her legs again, aware of a slight soreness between them as she settled more comfortably against the backrest of the padded deck chair.

The witness they were here to interview, Nick Clancy, sat across from her with his lawyer. Frank was seated to her right, and Agent Lammers beside him. They were outside on Clancy's back patio in his upscale, newly renovated house in Key West's historic district.

She had to admit, this was the most gorgeous setting she'd ever conducted an interview in. All around the immaculately kept crystal blue pool, a veritable oasis of lush plants and flowers enclosed the backyard, giving them total privacy.

The house itself had to have cost him a mint, but with the improvements he'd put into it—he'd listed them all during a tour when they'd first arrived—she was betting it was now worth double what he'd paid for it.

Which begged the question, how did an ex-con who'd formerly been stripped of his assets and material wealth afford such a home after being out of prison for only the past two years?

Since getting out of jail he'd supposedly taken a million dollar nest egg that belonged to his live-in partner of two years, and somehow managed to turn it into five times that much. Hence the FBI and IRS investigating all his offshore accounts and scrutinizing his investments.

Little wonder they were analyzing his finances with the forensic accounting equivalent of a high-powered microscope. If they found anything the slightest bit shady, he'd wind up back inside a cell.

"Like I already told the cops and the FBI," Clancy began, his tone adamant, "the only dealings I've ever had with Fuentes were some investment opportunities a few years ago. All that information's on record. He approached me about buying into several of them and I helped him with the initial purchases, wire transfers, things like that. Again, all on record previously. It wasn't until later that I realized who he was."

"But you didn't come forward to the authorities with your concerns. They came to you after you'd been flagged in their systems, after you'd not only taken on Fuentes as a client, but many of his associates as well. And in your previous statements to the FBI concerning this upcoming case, you said you didn't come forward before your arrest out of fear for your safety," Marisol added.

Clancy set his coffee mug on the glass-topped table and gave her a get-real look. "With good reason. The man's ruthless, and so are his lieutenants. Anyone gets on the wrong side of their radar, and *boom*. They put an enforcer on your ass and you're dead by nightfall."

"And yet you're suddenly willing to testify against him now, if it helps you avoid jail time."

So far investigators had been able to scrape together enough evidence to prove he'd been operating in the gray to black end of the scale of the tax code over the past couple years. This time they had enough to prove several counts of minor tax evasion and a few other things that, combined with his previous conviction and sentence, would land him back in jail. The U.S. Attorney's Office was counting on the promise of immunity being enough leverage to get him to cut a deal and testify against Fuentes.

Unfortunately, with most of the witnesses involved with this case, force was the only thing they understood and respected. Clancy, though to the rest of the world he appeared like a successful white businessman, was no different.

"He's behind bars and he won't be getting out," Clancy replied with a shrug. "I helped him a long time ago without knowing all the facts and I've already served my time. He's got no reason to target me now. Everything I have to say about our business dealings, I've already said before in court. If my testimony will clear my record sooner, then yeah, I'll do it." He sighed, settled back against his seat. "I've put a good chunk of my newly acquired net worth into my home here. It's all I've got left."

Yeah, her heart bled for him. So terrible, to only have a couple million dollars to your name. She withheld a snort of derision. The price tag on this place was worth ten times any of the houses on the street she'd grown up on.

"I just want to settle down here and live my life without a cloud of suspicion following me everywhere."

Marisol eyed him. *Well then maybe you should make sure you earn money through legitimate means and pay your damn taxes like the rest of us have to.*

"And that's a good possibility, providing the investigation of your finances doesn't turn up anything more than what they already have on you," Lammers said from the end of the table.

Clancy inclined his head. "Understood."

Marisol shared a look with Frank. Clancy had been a

high-powered investment banker in New York before going on his own to open up a private company, when he'd first dealt with Fuentes a few years back.

He'd laundered more than a hundred million dollars for Fuentes, buying up real estate and using the sale of the properties to make a profit that all looked legitimate from the outside.

He'd also helped set up various charities and shell companies that paid Fuentes's "employees" black salaries—salaries paid strictly in cash that were nearly impossible to trace—and committed thousands of cases of "smurfing", whereby Clancy had broken up large sums of cash into smaller deposits to avoid detection.

In short, he'd helped Fuentes hide a shitload of dirty money and helped him make more money from it, then helped a large group of people involved in Fuentes's network do the same. Clancy had been compensated well for his work and the increased risks, making a handsome commission with each transaction, and receiving lavish bonuses in cash.

But even he couldn't launder the funds well enough to escape detection and the long arm of the law had finally caught up with him. The only reason he'd received this deal from the U.S. Attorney's Office was because of his cooperation with the Fuentes case.

So far, whatever the investigators had turned up on Clancy's finances hadn't been enough to warrant pulling the plug on the deal Marisol and Frank were here to deliver. Not when compared to the opportunity to put Fuentes away for life or get the death penalty.

The government was willing to overlook a little tax evasion in that case. She just wanted the papers signed and the ink dry before something happened to change that.

Frank reached into his briefcase and pulled out three copies of the document they'd brought. "This is the agreement we sent to you and your lawyer previously," he said, sliding the copies across the table toward Clancy and his lawyer. "We've made the changes requested, and nothing else has been altered."

Clancy removed a fancy, tortoise shell pen from his shirt pocket and uncapped it. An old-fashioned fountain pen, Marisol noticed. The man had expensive taste, even in his choice of writing utensils.

He scanned the document while his lawyer quickly reviewed one of the copies. A few minutes later the lawyer nodded his consent, and Clancy signed all three copies. Frank and Marisol signed them all as well, and Lammers witnessed them.

Frank collected them and placed them back in his briefcase. "All right, now that that's taken care of, we need to go over the particulars of your part in the trial."

Clancy nodded, seemed far more at ease now that the main order of business was taken care of. Probably because he knew the investigators would turn up something in his financial dealings over the past two years that would have made the deal he'd just signed impossible.

"We'll be calling you to the stand early on, to establish a framework for the kind of money Fuentes was pulling in at the time you knew him, and to discuss what you knew of his business ventures and revenue streams. We're also going to be questioning you about people involved in his network. Specifically, his lieutenants. And to a lesser extent, their enforcers."

Clancy's face paled at the announcement. "I already told the Feds I don't know any of them personally."

"But you know about them. Their names, details about their finances and business dealings," Frank said calmly.

He shook his head. "Not enough to help your case against them if you're planning to put them on trial."

Marisol noticed Clancy's forehead and upper lip

grow shiny with perspiration, and it wasn't because of the heat or humidity. He was sitting in the shade, had looked cool as an ice cube until the mention of the lieutenants and enforcers. "Let us be the judge of that," she told him.

Clancy's gaze cut to her, and his pale green eyes turned cold. "I'm not interested in getting killed just to save myself another year or two in the clink."

She raised a brow. "Yet you're willing to testify against Fuentes."

He snorted. "He won't come after me, but those guys would if they thought I was involved with trying to hunt them down. No thanks."

Marisol folded her arms. "If you withhold anything under oath, you'll be in contempt of court. That will also land you in jail."

"If you can prove I'm withholding something, maybe." He shook his head, his lips twisting into a thin line as he glanced first at his lawyer, then back at her. "I agreed to testify against Fuentes," he said, thumping his index finger against the tabletop, "and that's what I promised to provide with my signature on those documents. No more, no less. You put me on that stand and start questioning me about guys like that, whom I've never met, and you might as well paint a bull's eye on the middle of my chest when I walk out of that courthouse."

"And I'm not ever going into WITSEC," he added in a scornful tone. "Not after that shit show with the witnesses for the Qureshi trial up in D.C. a couple months ago."

Marisol held his gaze, refused to be the first to look away.

"We're not looking to endanger your life, Nick," Frank said.

Clancy finally broke eye contact with her, turning that angry gaze on her boss instead. She didn't like him, didn't trust him. But sometimes that's just the way things went in her job. Clancy and several other witnesses like him were a means to an end. As long as they helped her team get a guilty verdict in the Fuentes case, that was the most important thing.

It pissed her off that scum like this would walk while others went to jail, but she knew it had to be done. Justice wasn't nearly as black and white as she'd first thought upon entering law school.

"Can we get back to the preparations for the trial?" Clancy's lawyer asked. "I've got another meeting at noon."

Frank's mouth twitched in a semblance of a smile and he darted a look at Marisol. Clancy's lawyer apparently didn't like him any more than they did. "Yes," he answered. "Let's do that."

It took nearly another hour to review everything and wrap up the meeting. Two of the three marshals assigned to her detail were waiting in the foyer when they reached it. After checking with their teammate outside in one of the two SUVs they'd driven down in, the team leader exited the house.

Frank followed him, then Marisol and Lammers, the second marshal bringing up the rear. They were on alert not just because of her, but because there was concern that Clancy might be a potential target as well. The sooner Marisol got back to Miami, the better. Ethan had promised to come see her again tonight and she was looking forward to that.

"Clancy's just as charming as always, I see," Lammers commented dryly on the way to the waiting vehicles.

"Yeah, he's a real peach, I can't wait to sit down with him again," Marisol replied, her high heels clicking on the expensive mosaic tile set into the driveway. Had to have cost a fortune. Who the hell paid for craftsmanship like this and then just drove over it with their vehicle? She shook her head.

The lead marshal opened the rear passenger door for her while Frank slid into the front passenger seat. She passed the front bumper, smiled at the marshal and ducked her head to slide into the backseat. Suddenly the marshal grunted and slumped to the ground, his back resting against the side of the vehicle.

She jerked her head around to stare at him, her startled gaze landing on the bright red stain blooming at the base of his throat.

"Oh my God," she blurted and dropped her briefcase. She reached for him, going to her knees on the mosaic tile. Someone had shot him but she hadn't heard anything and his bullet-proof vest began well below where the bullet had struck. Lammers rushed toward her.

"Anderson's down," the second marshal snapped into his comm. He planted himself in front of them with his weapon drawn as Lammers crouched next to her, scanning for the shooter.

Not knowing what else to do, Marisol pressed her hands over the wound in the other man's throat. It was pure reflex, driven by the instinct to help. He was still breathing but not well. Wet gasps gurgled from his throat, his hands fumbling to push hers out of the way.

She didn't let go. "Just stay still. We're getting help." She could hear Frank already on his phone to 911, requesting an ambulance.

"Get in the vehicle," Lammers ordered her, stripping out of his shirt. He wadded it up and pressed against the wound, then checked the wounded man's pulse. "Get in, *now*." With one hand on the wound he pivoted on his haunches, weapon in hand, scanning the foliage where the shot had to have originated from.

Marisol pushed up and started to lean into the backseat of the SUV.

"He's conscious, still breathing," Frank told the

dispatcher, and popped open his door.

The second marshal cried out and fell just as a round slammed into the side of the SUV, inches from Marisol's head. She jumped and cried out, instinctively ducking.

Lammers and the downed marshal both returned fire in the direction the shots had come from.

"Move," Lammers barked at her. He whirled around and shoved her toward the hood of the vehicle. Frank jumped out of the front passenger seat and rounded the hood before ducking down, using the front end as cover.

Her heart was in her throat. Before she could take another step the remaining marshal burst out of the other SUV, weapon up, and fired into the bushes. She scrambled to gain her footing as Lammers propelled her toward Frank, kicked off her shoes and lurched to keep up with him. The agent fired twice more, the shots sharp and loud, making her flinch.

At the front right fender he jerked and fell to his knees, a bullet hole in the center of his lower back.

A scream broke from her throat.

She dove around the front of the hood. Flat on her belly, she crawled back to grab fistfuls of Lammers's shirt and lugged him behind cover.

The front door of the house opened and Clancy stood there, body shielded by the door, his eyes widening when he took in the carnage. "What the hell's going on out—" His words cut off when a round smacked into his throat, dropping him where he stood.

Marisol screamed, immediately bit down on her lips to stifle it. The shooter was picking them off, one at a time despite Lammers and the second marshal having fired back, and hitting them where the vests couldn't protect them. The third marshal was moving behind the front end of his SUV now, returning fire.

Another bullet punched through the front end of the SUV, so close she flinched and ducked. Heart pounding, she slapped a hand over the wound in Lammers's back. He was facedown, struggling to get up.

Blood poured from the wound and when she looked down at his face, her stomach lurched to see him struggling futilely to turn over. His spine. The shot had paralyzed him.

"Frank!" she yelled. He was behind her somewhere and she needed help.

"The shooter's to our right, Soli, we've gotta run! Run *now*!"

"Lammers is wounded bad," she cried, twisting her head around to look at Frank. His face was ashen and glistening with sweat, his eyes wide with fear. "We have to help him." The FBI agent slumped to the ground, groaned.

Her hands shook as she applied pressure to the wound. The blood was warm and sticky, the metallic scent of it mixing with her terror, turning her stomach.

Frank had called 911, but how long would it take for the cops and ambulance to get here? She grabbed for Lammers's pistol, raised it and curled her finger around the trigger.

There was no target. She couldn't see anyone in the bushes, but she knew he could see her.

The remaining marshal fired twice in rapid succession then cried out and fell, a hand to the base of his throat. Fear turned to full-blown panic, burning in Marisol's chest. Her entire security team was down, either dead or dying, and the shooter was still out there.

"Go!" Frank roared at her. He darted out from behind the SUV, running blindly for the thick hedges on the far side of the driveway.

Marisol stared after him helplessly. Her entire body shook. Lammers groaned again and tried to get up, his hand reaching for his pistol.

I can't just leave Lammers.

She darted another glance at the hedges. Frank was gone but it wasn't safe for her to move now. Even if she could get into the SUV she'd be a sitting duck and she wasn't sure if it was bullet resistant or not so she wasn't taking the chance. Dammit, she was too far away from the hedges, she'd be exposed if she—

Running footsteps behind her.

Heart in her throat, she whipped her head around in time to see a masked figure dressed all in back explode out of the lush foliage where Frank had just disappeared to the left of the driveway.

A scream trapped in her lungs as he came at her. She released Lammers, rolled to her knees and surged to her feet, her only thought escape.

Another round impacted the hood of the vehicle, plowed into the tile near her right foot. Shards of broken tile flew out. A hot kiss of pain flared up the back of her calf but she kept going, terror driving her as she ran for the house, her only remaining refuge.

Strong hands caught her shoulders before she'd even made it two steps.

She drew in a breath to scream, twisted in his iron hold as he grabbed her. His grip was too strong, she couldn't escape. Holding her over his shoulder he took three running strides then dove over the row of hedges.

Sticks and foliage scraped across her face and arms as they sailed through the air and landed in the dirt. The air exploded from her lungs. Before she could even understand what was happening the man rolled them behind cover, turned her over and brought a hand down over her nose and mouth.

"*Be still*," he hissed.

Marisol thrashed her head back and forth, fighting for air, for freedom, but it was no use. A hot prick stabbed her in the side of the shoulder. A heartbeat later her muscles turned weak.

A needle. He'd just drugged her with something.

No! She tried to knock the syringe aside but couldn't lift her arm. It was like she was paralyzed, her body refusing to obey her.

The man got up, rolled her to her back. He set an arm around her ribs to raise her upward and she caught a glimpse of his face when he pulled the black ski mask off.

Her heart careened in her chest, disbelief and betrayal slicing deep.

Miguel?

It made no sense. Why would he hurt her?

Then she was weightless, rising into the air, and powerless to stop it. Everything spun around her, a strange roaring filling her ears.

Shouts echoed in the distance behind her but she couldn't even cry out as Miguel carried her deeper into the foliage. Fighting to keep her eyes open, she managed to get one more look at his face just before the darkness took her.

Chapter Seventeen

E than checked his harness one last time then slid from the rooftop over the side of the exterior wall. For this exercise they were using an abandoned industrial building in South Miami. Bracing the soles of his boots on the thick concrete, he leaned his weight back and held still with his brake hand on the rope beneath him. To his left, Schroder mirrored his movements.

"Three and four in position," he said quietly into his comm, the weight of his rifle resting against his chest.

"Stand by." Tuck's voice was just as soft. Their team leader was on the ground floor in another part of the building with members of the DEA FAST team, seven stories down. Bauer, Evers and Vance were on the eighth floor already, twenty yards down the hall east from the target apartment.

In this training scenario the tangos had the far west side of the building locked down, so while Bauer and the others closed in from one side, Ethan and Schroder were going to infiltrate via an open window of an abandoned unit on the opposite side of the target apartment. Blackwell had already rappelled down to secure it while

Ethan and Schroder had provided security from above.

Weight distributed in the harness, Ethan stayed still, his breathing even as he awaited the command.

"Bravo team, go."

At Tuck's order, Ethan and Schroder both shoved away from the wall. They rappelled fast, hopping their way down the side of the building. They slipped inside the open window, where Blackwell was waiting for them. Together the three of them made their way out into the hallway, avoiding detection by the tangos at the far west end, as well as the ones barricaded in the apartment between them and Bauer's squad.

After checking to make sure the hallway was empty, they eased toward the tangos' apartment in the dimness. The lights were out, all the electricity turned off by the drug dealers currently holding captives in the apartment.

Ethan pulled down his NVGs and switched them on. He and the others headed for the target, their boots silent on the thin, worn carpet. They stopped twenty yards away from the apartment, on the opposite side of the door from Bauer's team.

"Bravo team in position," Ethan murmured.

"Alpha team ready. No movement on this floor," Bauer confirmed from inside.

"Roger," Tuck answered. "Hang tight."

Everyone held their positions while they waited for the signal.

"Green light," Tuck said a minute later.

Ethan signaled to the guys behind him to follow and started for the door. Bauer closed the gap between them on the other side. He and Ethan paused there while the former SEAL set the breaching charge on the lock.

Ethan leaned back when he gave the signal. When the charge blew, Bauer sent the door flying inward with a single, powerful kick and Ethan tossed in two flashbangs. It took only moments for them to infiltrate and lock down the place. They "arrested" the three hostage takers and freed the four FAST team members posing as hostages for this practice run.

On the way out they took the stairs down to the bottom of the building. Once they exited and handed over their charges, Ethan and the others took off their helmets and walked toward where Tuck and the other DEA members were waiting. His team leader met them partway, his expression way too serious considering the training op was over.

"DeLuca sent a message," Tuck told him. "Wants you and Vance to call him ASAP."

Ethan blinked. Tuck's expression held no traces of alarm, but the guy had been former Delta so he was impossible to read if he didn't want to be. "What about?"

"Didn't say. You two take five. Make the call in the command center and meet up with us when you're done."

Ethan shared a questioning glance with Vance, and headed for the street. The converted motorhome that served as a mobile command unit sat at the curb. Three DEA agents were inside it, but left to give him and Vance some privacy while Ethan made the call. DeLuca answered on the second ring.

"Hey, it's Cruz. I've got Vance with me. What's up?"

His commander sighed in a way that signaled bad news, and Ethan's stomach tightened. He knew that sound, could easily picture DeLuca dragging a hand through his hair. "There's no easy way for me to say this, so I'm just gonna say it."

The warning wasn't even close to anything he'd been expecting on this call. Ethan gripped the cell tighter. "What's wrong?" Vance was watching him closely. It worried the hell out of Ethan that DeLuca had requested his closest buddy on the team be present while he received whatever news their commander had for him.

"I got word twenty minutes ago about an incident that went down in Key West this morning."

Ethan's spine jerked taut, all his muscles locking. There was only one reason why DeLuca would be calling about that. "Marisol," he rasped out. "Is she okay?" Vance's eyes were locked on him but all Ethan was aware of was the pounding of his heart as he awaited DeLuca's answer.

"She's missing."

His stomach twisted hard. "Missing?" he echoed.

"A shooter attacked her security team at their interview this morning. The guy they interviewed is dead, along with two U.S. Marshals. Another is wounded, and so is Agent Lammers. They're both in surgery right now. Her boss got away, said he saw some guy come out of the trees and grab Marisol."

"She's been kidnapped." His voice sounded dull even to his own ears, the reality hard to grasp.

"Yes."

Ethan let out a shaky breath and closed his eyes. He felt like he might puke. "But she's alive?"

"We don't know. But since everyone else is dead or wounded and was left on scene, there's no reason to take her unless the kidnapper wanted her alive."

All Ethan heard was the *we don't know* part. He dragged a hand through his hair, gripped the back of his neck and swallowed. Was she even alive? The thought of someone killing her made him fucking ill. Helpless.

He couldn't handle her being taken from him this way, couldn't imagine the world without her in it. She was such a bright light. To have that extinguished, snuffed out in such a heinous way, was unthinkable.

DeLuca must have known he was losing it internally because his voice took on a snap of command. "Listen to me. Our agents are doing everything they can to find her. I'll meet you guys at the Miami field office in fifteen minutes. Have Vance drive you there. We'll get an update and go from there."

Shaken to the core, Ethan mumbled some sort of a response and ended the call. Vance clapped a big hand on his shoulder, turned him to face the door. "Let's go."

"Marisol," he began. "She's—"

"I overheard everything," Vance replied, his voice flat. "Come on."

Ethan barely remembered getting into their rental. Vance got them to the Miami office as fast as he could and together they met DeLuca outside the doors.

Their commander studied Ethan's face for a moment, his expression determined. "I'll help in whatever way I can."

Throat too tight to speak, Ethan nodded his thanks and headed inside. DeLuca took them straight to the agent in charge of the investigation. The man ran through everything they knew about the attack and Marisol's disappearance to this point.

All evidence from Key West pointed to one shooter, still on the loose, and nobody had identified the man who'd taken Marisol. They knew there were two men on scene because the shots had come from one direction and the man had come from another when he took Marisol. It was presumed they were working together though.

Next Ethan relayed everything he knew about Marisol's situation. Where she'd been heading this morning, the recent threats, everything and anything he could think of that might be useful.

Which amounted to a handful of shit. She'd already been attacked and kidnapped. He was praying they wanted to use her for ransom and not torture.

When he was done detailing everything he fell silent, his heart pounding hard against his sternum. "Have you informed her family yet?" he asked the lead agent.

"No, but we'll have to shortly."

"You want me to do it?" He'd rather be gutshot than deliver that news to Marisol's mother and sisters, but maybe it would soften the blow if they heard it from him and knew he was with the investigative team right now.

"That might be best."

Ethan nodded, forced out a slow breath to quell the rolling of his stomach. "I need some privacy." He wanted to throw something, put his fist through the wall, but he couldn't. There was no outlet for the violent mix of emotion roiling inside him.

Someone showed him to a private office down the hall. He closed the door and sank into a chair in front of the desk, a knot the size of a boulder lodged in his throat as he immediately flashed back to the leather chair behind her desk at her office, and what he'd done to her there. Now she was gone.

No, he ordered himself. She had to be alive. Had to be okay. He thought of how incredible it had been to make love to her last night, the way she'd given herself to him. Then this morning when she'd smiled up at him and kissed him goodbye before climbing into the vehicle with her security detail.

"Call me when you get back," he'd told her before putting her into the back passenger seat of the SUV. "Hopefully I'll be off work then and I can bring you some dinner."

"A dinner date?" she'd asked with a grin.

"Yeah." He'd tucked a lock of hair behind her ear, leaned in to kiss her.

She'd kissed him back, slow and hot and sweet, then flashed him a secret smile that got his blood pumping about getting her alone again later. "See you tonight."

His throat tightened as the memory faded. His kitt'n. Was she scared right now? In pain and praying that he was coming for her? It gutted him.

He pulled out his phone and dialed her mother. It was

one of the toughest calls he'd ever made. Mrs. Lorenzo screamed, the heart-wrenching sound making the hair on his nape stand on end.

He did what he could to calm her, let her know he was staying on top of the investigation and that a team of FBI agents would be coming to talk with her. All the while he prayed they'd get a solid lead that would allow him and his teammates to go after her.

When he ended the call he felt…numb. Inside and out.

Vance knocked once and poked his head into the room, his face tense. "You need to see this."

Ethan jumped up and rushed back to the office where the lead investigator was.

"This just came in," the agent said, easing aside so Ethan could see the computer screen on his desk. "CCTV footage from a camera near the harbor in South Miami." He played the footage, showing a big guy carrying a giant duffel on his back. The kind sport fishermen might transport a large catch in. But that was no marlin in there.

Marisol.

His entire body went rigid. Was she still alive? Ethan gripped the edge of the desk, forced himself to breathe. *No.* They were going to get her back, alive and in one piece. He had to stay positive, focus on finding her.

"Here's the best shot we could get of his face. It's not the greatest, but we were able to enhance it some." He tapped a few keys and pulled up an image.

Ethan sucked in a breath and pushed up from the desk as recognition slammed into him. "Miguel Salvador," he blurted, hardly able to believe it.

The agent jerked his head around to stare at Ethan. "You know him?"

Jaw tight, he nodded. "He's from our old neighborhood. Soli and I knew him when we were kids. She said she saw him the other night, out in front of her mom's place." What the fuck? Had he been following her even then? What the *fuck* had that asshole done to her? Ethan's hands curled into fists, a helpless rage flooding him.

The agent waved at someone from his team, snapped his fingers to get their attention. Everyone crammed into the room stared at him as he spoke to Ethan. "Miguel Salvador," he repeated, and two people instantly rushed from the room, presumably to search the name.

"What do you know about him?"

"He's in his late twenties. Served in the military for a while. I heard SF." His stomach dropped. The guy was deadly. Not good news for Marisol.

"What else?"

Ethan blew out a breath, his mind spinning. "His mom died of an overdose when he was a kid, and he was taken in by his maternal grandmother. She suffered permanent brain damage during an attack in a home invasion years ago and was institutionalized, but he always visited her. She's probably still at a facility here in Miami." Miguel had been a quiet, shy kid, and while he'd never been friendly with Ethan, he'd always been kind to Soli. What the hell had led him to do this?

"What's her name?"

"Flora Bautista—" He stopped, the words cut off by an invisible knife as it hit him. The bits and pieces of intel he knew rolled around in his brain, all the edges coming together like pieces of a puzzle.

The answer he came up with didn't seem possible, and yet his gut screamed that it was true.

"No," he breathed, leaning forward to stare at the screen. "No fucking *way*." His blood iced up, fear for Soli screaming through his system.

"What?" DeLuca demanded, pushing closer to peer at the screen. "What is it?"

Ethan pushed up again, feeling dizzy. "Bautista. It's

a surname relating to John the Baptist." He turned toward DeLuca, saw that his commander was frowning. Oh, Jesus, what if he was right? "He was a saint," he continued, his pulse thudding hard and fast.

"*El Santo*," DeLuca muttered, looking as stunned as Ethan felt.

A split second of taut silence filled the room as everyone absorbed the gravity of it. Then the lead investigator leveled an urgent look at his assistant.

"Get me everything you have on *el Santo*, and everything you can find on Miguel Salvador and Miguel Bautista. Military and employment records, tax returns, everything. I want to know every place he's been seen the last five years and find out where his grandmother is. Somebody there might recognize him. Let's move."

The other agents all shot out of the office in a flurry of movement. Ethan envied them. They had a task to complete, a purpose, something to occupy their time. All he had was a gut full of anxiety and a red-hot coal burning a hole beneath his sternum. His chest was so tight he could barely breathe.

If Miguel was in fact *el Santo* and he had Soli, her odds of survival weren't good to begin with. And those odds declined with every passing minute. Ethan clung to the small sliver of hope that Miguel had to have taken her for a reason. Why kill her now, after going to all that trouble when he could have killed her back in Key West?

Vance stepped up beside him and laid a hand on his shoulder. "I'll wait here with you, man."

"Me too," DeLuca added. "I've already called Celida, maybe she can help with something on her end."

Ethan nodded but didn't respond. He was totally preoccupied with what had happened to Marisol, with what might be happening at that very moment, and the odds of her surviving abduction by the Fuentes cartel's deadliest enforcer.

Every twisted, fucked-up thing he knew about the state of *el Santo's* victims came back to haunt him.

He remembered every picture he'd seen of their blood-soaked, dismembered bodies, the pieces scattered in the swamp to await the gators. The halo symbol carved into their skin, done while they were still alive.

His stomach pitched. He swallowed repeatedly to battle the wave of nausea that gripped him. He shook it off, ordered himself to get his shit together. His lady needed him.

A female agent suddenly appeared in the doorway, her expression urgent. "Just got an anonymous message from a burner phone stating that both *el Santo* and another enforcer named Villa are both near a marina not far from here. Surveillance video caught a picture of a guy matching Miguel's description carrying that heavy bag again. He stashed it on a boat, then left."

Ethan surged to his feet, needing to move, get there right fucking *now*. "What marina? What boat?" he demanded.

DeLuca was already on his phone. He must have already discussed authority protocol with the Special Agent In Charge, because in the background Ethan heard his commander say Tuck's name and start explaining the situation. It meant if a rescue op or takedown was involved, the HRT would be deployed.

Adrenaline rocketed through Ethan's veins. He wanted to get moving, go after Marisol and then take out that fucker Miguel and whoever the shooter had been this morning.

The female agent told them what they needed. Ethan looked at DeLuca, who was still on the phone, relaying the fresh intel to Tuck. "Get the boys ready, bring the DEA guys in too just in case. I want everyone at that marina within the next fifteen minutes, with two boat crews ready to go."

Ethan didn't wait to hear more. They were going after Marisol, possibly both *el Santo* and Villa as well in the process. He didn't care about bringing the enforcers down, he only cared about getting Marisol back. She had to be okay. *Had* to be. He couldn't handle the thought of losing her, of how empty his life would be without her.

He started for the door.

"Cruzie, wait."

He halted and looked at DeLuca over his shoulder. Trepidation gripped him when he took in his commander's grim expression. His heart thudded as he realized what was about to happen. Oh God, no, he couldn't be benched. Not when Marisol needed him.

"You know the rules here. And you know it's not personal."

Ethan shook his head, pushing aside the blast of panic. DeLuca pulling him wasn't personal, it was protocol. His commander had final say over who participated on an op, and because he knew Ethan was emotionally invested in Marisol, for safety reasons he could pull him. His teammates' lives depended on every one of them having a clear head on an op.

He searched for the most logical argument he could muster, needing to prove his head was on straight. "We don't have time to replace me on the team, even if you used one of the DEA guys. Her life's at stake. She means something to me, yeah, but I won't let it affect my judgment or performance out there. You *know* me, you know I'm solid and you also know we can't waste time talking about this."

A hot ball of anxiety pushed up from his diaphragm. If he was sidelined on this one he'd go out of his fucking mind.

DeLuca sighed and took off his Chargers ball cap to run a hand over the top of his head, then tugged it back on. "Don't make me regret it. If you can't stay detached on this one, you need to pull yourself before someone gets hurt."

Ethan nodded, his lungs finally opening up again. Without waiting another second he rushed for the door with Vance and DeLuca right behind him.

****

A bitter, metallic taste coated her mouth.

Marisol struggled to surface from the heavy weight pulling her under. She forced her eyes open, could only pull her lids apart a fraction of an inch as her brain rebooted. But it was enough.

She was tied hand and foot to a post beneath a table in a small room. The salty scent to the air and the slight rocking motion told her she was on a boat of some sort. It took monumental effort to twist her head enough to look at her hands. Duct tape.

Now that she was becoming more alert, adrenaline flooded her bloodstream. The shootings. Miguel. He'd taken her. Why? And why leave her here?

She wasn't waiting around for him to come back so she could ask him.

Struggling into a sitting position, she yanked at the tape holding her wrists to the metal post holding the table up. She leaned forward to see if she could use her teeth on the tape but she couldn't quite reach. The tape rubbed her wrists raw but she didn't care, just kept pulling in short jerks.

Bit by bit it loosened. Heartened by the sound of the adhesive tearing away little by little, she wrenched harder, biting down on her lip as her skin burned.

One more hard jerk and some of the tape gave way. It took some maneuvering but she managed to twist her hands back and forth until she finally slipped one free. Her fingers shook as she ripped at the tape holding her other hand captive. Once both were free she began working on the tape binding her ankles together.

On shaky legs she stood, throwing a hand out to catch herself on the tabletop while she gained her balance. The small cabin spun for a moment. She closed her eyes, breathed through her mouth until the dizziness passed.

Then she heard it.

Light footsteps on the topside deck.

Shit!

Her gaze darted desperately around the cabin, searching for a weapon of some sort. She might not have any hand-to-hand training but she would defend herself. If Miguel or anyone else came through that hatch, she would attack them. Anything to gain her freedom.

She spotted a long handle of some kind tucked beneath the bulkhead on the left hand side of the cabin, and rushed for it. An oar.

The footsteps came closer. Whoever it was stood directly over the hatch now.

Marisol grabbed the oar. Her fingers wrapped around the long handle and curled tight. Raising it over one shoulder, she braced her feet in a wide stance and held the weapon in a white-knuckled grip, waiting for whoever was up there to come down.

The hatch popped open.

Marisol held her breath, the slamming of her heart making her dizzy.

Two booted feet appeared, followed by slender legs encased in skin tight black. Then curvy hips, a slender waist.

A woman? The thought confused her but she held fast, waiting to strike. She was too far away to hit her with the oar.

Rather than walking down the remaining steps, the woman leapt and landed in an agile crouch on the floor. Momentarily thrown off by the move, Marisol stood there, frozen. That single move told her this woman had training.

The woman had deep brown hair and ice blue eyes. Eyes that swept over her from head to toe and back again. Then she smiled as though in approval.

Marisol suppressed a shiver. "Get out of my way," she growled, prepared to bash the woman's head in to get away.

Rather than look surprised or amused by her threat, the woman cocked her head. "I'm here to help you."

"Bullshit."

"It's true." The woman straightened, even that movement lithe, like she was coiled to spring. Marisol gripped the oar tighter. "You're in deep already. You're gonna need a hand getting out of this. That's why I'm here."

She shook her head, refusing to believe it. Did she look stupid? "You're here to kill me."

"No, I'm here to help."

"Are you working with Miguel?" There was no way around her. The only way to the ladder and her escape was to go through her. She'd only get one good swing in, had to make it count.

"Not exactly."

The answer made her fear spike higher. "I'm not going to make it easy for you."

The woman made an impatient sound in her throat. "If *el Santo* had wanted you dead, he'd have killed you already."

"What?" she demanded. Miguel was *el Santo*? It couldn't be. She swallowed, tried and failed to suppress a shiver.

The woman nodded, her expression sober. "He warned you with that phone message, and then I warned you with the fake bomb on your car. Look, I know you have no reason to trust me, but if you want to live, you've got no choice."

Marisol tightened her mouth and shook her head. The woman was trying to trick her.

"Call me Julia. And I know your security team was targeted by another one of Fuentes's lieutenant's enforcers just over an hour ago."

The blood rushed in her ears. "How do you know that?" *She's in on it, that's how.*

Julia shrugged. "Because that other enforcer was my target. And *el Santo's*, too. But instead of staying to take him out, Miguel chose to grab you and get you to safety instead." She cocked an eyebrow. "That's pretty telling, don't you think?"

None of this made sense. Her head was pounding, her stomach swirling. *Out. Have to get out.*

"Put the oar down, Marisol. We don't have time for this." Her voice was even but held a warning edge, signaling she was running out of patience.

Marisol couldn't back down. She'd fight for her life. *Now or never.* Baring her teeth, she swung the weapon at Julia's head with all her might.

And hit nothing but air.

She stumbled with the momentum of her swing, found herself dumped on her ass as Julia calmly knocked the oar from her hands and tossed it aside. Marisol rolled to her knees, her heart plummeting at how easily she'd been disarmed, and braced herself for the coming attack.

It didn't come.

Julia gave her a cool stare. "I'm not going to hurt you. But we can't stay here. He's hunting us."

"Who?" she made herself ask.

"Villa. The other enforcer. He was sent to kill Clancy, you and your boss this morning."

"Frank," she whispered.

"He's alive. He went straight to the police. Which is exactly what you've got to do." She started toward her.

Marisol scrambled back but Julia merely grasped her hand and pulled her to her feet. Once Marisol was standing, the other woman took her by the upper arms and stared into her eyes.

"Listen to me very carefully. I'm going to get you off the boat and out of the marina. There's a bank on the corner across the street. Go straight there, don't stop, and go right to the first security agent you see. Stay away from the windows and doors. Call 911 and tell them what happened. You're the only one who can clear Miguel's name. Right now they think he's the one who killed your team and that he's holding you for ransom. They're wrong." Her grip tightened. "You have to tell them the truth. Understand? But right now we've got to get you away from this boat before he finds us."

Not sure if she believed it, Marisol had no choice but to agree if she wanted a shot at getting away. "Okay," she managed.

Julia nodded once and released her. "I'm going up the steps first. Stay right behind me and don't make any noise. Follow exactly where I go. Got it?" She pulled a black pistol from the back of her waistband.

Marisol's eyes widened. But when Julia didn't point it at her, instead turning to the stairs, she took a hesitant step forward. Was this a trick? A ploy to earn her trust just enough to lure her up to the deck and then kill her? But that made no sense. Way easier to kill her here, and keep her body out of sight.

Swallowing hard, Marisol forced back her fear and followed Julia up the steps. The other woman paused at the top, scanning the deck and whatever lay beyond it.

Julia motioned with her hand to follow and eased out of the hatch. Marisol hurried after her, her bare feet silent on the fiberglass and giving her good traction.

She squinted at the harsh Florida sun beating down on her and followed Julia across the narrow deck toward the dock. She copied the woman's movements as closely as she could, her heart thudding in her ears. If this wasn't a trick, was Villa here? Did he have them in his sights right now?

Julia set her hand on the dock, pushed up to make the short jump onto the dock—

Wood exploded inches from where her head had just been.

Marisol instinctively ducked at the same time Julia bit out a curse and leaped back onto the boat, yanking the rope free of the mooring with one quick move. She grabbed Marisol by the arm and wrenched her toward the hatch. "Get down and stay there," she ordered.

Marisol flattened herself onto her belly and slid inside the hatch as Julia flew past her to the controls. Another round punched through the side of the boat just behind her. She hugged the railing on either side of the steps and hung there, frozen, her heart racing as raw terror washed through her.

"Don't move until I tell you," Julia yelled down. From her position at the top of the steps Marisol could see her fiddling with some wiring. A few moments later the inboard engine roared to life.

The boat lurched to the left as it shot away from the dock, sending Marisol careening into the wall. She caught herself with her feet, barely preventing her body from slamming into it, and steadied herself as Julia suddenly opened up the throttle.

Marisol held on tight as they raced away from the dock, crushing her last hope of escaping on dry land. Her jaw tightened as she climbed to her knees. She was a fighter, she would find a way out of this. There was no way she'd just sit here and cower.

Her gaze measured the largest window on the port side of the cabin. She might be able to squeeze through it. She wasn't the greatest swimmer so the idea of plunging into the water was terrifying, but it beat the hell out of being shot to death by the crazy assassin chasing them.

She stood up and grasped the window frame to pry it open. The second the boat slowed enough, she was jumping into the water.

Chapter Eighteen

When he saw the footage unfolding on the small monitor he was holding, Bautista did a double take.

From his position in the back corner of an upstairs patio of a café a block away from the marina, he had a two-hundred-seventy degree view of the streets below. And with the electronic eyes in his hand, he could see much more than that. He'd wirelessly connected to a closed-circuit security camera on the exterior of the bank across from the marina before leaving to track his target.

Villa was somewhere nearby. Bautista had lost him when he'd stowed Marisol in the empty boat just over twenty minutes ago.

But he was close. The tingling at the back of his neck confirmed it. He'd wait another few minutes to see if Villa came sniffing around the marina, but if he didn't, Bautista would begin the hunt all over again. He pushed back the frustration eating at him.

The other enforcer should have been long dead by now. Would have died a few hours ago in Key West, if Bautista hadn't had a sudden attack of conscience and made the decision to rescue Marisol rather than take Villa out.

He wasn't even sure why he'd taken the risk. All he knew was that when he'd seen her scramble around the hood of that SUV as the bullets flew and she'd tried to stem the bleeding on the FBI agent's wound, something inside him had compelled him to act. Maybe it was because he knew her personally, or because she'd always been nice to him back in the old neighborhood.

Didn't matter now. He'd loaded her unconscious body into the trunk of his rental and headed for the mainland. With the cops en route and Villa moving out of the Keys, Bautista had headed back to Miami, knowing the other enforcer would do the same.

Hell, though. The angle from his hiding position near Clancy's place had been perfect, and the added confusion with the firefight between Villa and the security team had given him the ideal chance to close in and make the kill.

His damn conscience better not have cost him Villa, he thought in irritation. His entire future hinged on fulfilling this last obligation to Perez and making a clean getaway.

He tightened the resolution of the image on screen as the female who'd pulled up on a motorbike at the end of the dock a moment ago parked and swung a long leg over the seat to stand beside it. She wore a black leather jacket, black formfitting pants, boots and gloves. He couldn't see her face because of her helmet.

She turned her head, looked around for a moment then walked down the length of the dock. All he could see was the back of her when she pulled the helmet off, revealing dark brown hair secured at the nape of her neck in a ponytail that reached the top of her shoulder blades.

Something inside him stilled. With her hair color and figure she reminded him so much of…

His gaze snagged on the slight bulge beneath the

back of her leather jacket as the unknown female continued to the end of the dock. It was subtle, only someone with training would have noticed it. But she was definitely armed.

And she was headed directly for the boat where he'd left Marisol. He'd left her there because with Villa on his tail he hadn't had time to wait for her to wake up and explain everything.

Who are you and what are you up to, lady?

He waited, watching every move she made. She hopped onto the deck of the boat and went directly to the hatch. Cursing under his breath, he held his position, waiting to see what she'd do. He couldn't go after Marisol without exposing himself to Villa.

The woman emerged from the hatch a few minutes later. Finally she turned her head toward him. Bautista caught his breath, his stomach twisting into a hard knot.

Julia.

Denial punched him hard in the solar plexus, his mind refusing to acknowledge what he was seeing. She must have followed him to Key West today, then here. Maybe by placing a tracking device on his truck without him noticing.

Dammit, he hadn't checked it this morning. But why would she do that? And for her to be going directly to the boat now, she must have seen him put Marisol there earlier.

He didn't know how long she'd been following him or how much she'd seen, but if she was here then she knew he wasn't who he seemed. And she'd probably already called the cops too. So why was she here, going after Marisol alone?

Anger and pain collided inside him, constricting his lungs. He'd trusted her. Had believed she cared about him. But she obviously wasn't the woman he'd thought he'd known. She'd betrayed him and now—

His phone buzzed in his pocket. Keeping an eye on Julia as she emerged through the hatch, he checked the display. Surprise flashed through him when he saw a text from her. His gaze darted back to the handheld surveillance device and sure enough, he could see a cell in her hand.

Villa close. I'll take care of Marisol. Watch your six.

Confusion hit him. He glanced back at his monitor, trying to figure out what the hell was going on.

His mind grappled for answers, and each one of them was as bad as the last. Her warning had to be a ploy. She had to be trying to lure him into a trap, an undercover agent of some sort. Hell, maybe she was even working with Villa himself and had been all along.

He was such a fucking idiot. *How could you have let yourself fall for her?*

A cold, bitter void opened up in his chest. He flashed back to last night, picturing the way she'd smiled up at him in the aftermath of her second orgasm. They'd been lying tangled up together in the rumpled bedding that had come free of the mattress as they'd rolled and grappled.

With that serene smile in place she'd stroked her hands over his back and shoulders so gently, trailed her fingertips across his face as the sweat cooled on their bodies. She'd gazed into his eyes and touched him like he *mattered* to her.

He'd met some gifted actresses in his day but she was truly Oscar level because she'd done the impossible by duping him, the world's biggest cynic.

And holy hell, finding out it was all a lie fucking *hurt*. Hurt more than being shot or blown up by an IED, both of which his body bore the scars of.

It's your own fucking fault. You knew you were never meant to have a happy ending.

Now he had a tough decision to make. If Julia was involved with Villa then she was his enemy too. He swallowed past the thickening in his throat, shoved the pain down deep inside where it could fuel him, drive him.

On screen, Julia—or whatever the hell her name really was—moved cautiously toward the bow. A moment later, Marisol's head appeared in the hatch opening. She followed Julia across the deck toward the dock. But just as Julia set a hand on the wooden surface, wood splinters kicked up less than an inch away. She jerked backward, ducked.

He came halfway out of his seat at that shot, his gaze riveted to the screen. Julia reached out to unmoor the small vessel, her expression stamped with determination.

That shot changed everything.

Villa. Bautista knew it was him. He had Julia in his sights, had just taken a shot at her. A deadly warning, and the only one she'd get.

His heart careened in his chest as the truth hit him like a sledgehammer.

If Villa was targeting her then she *hadn't* betrayed him. He didn't understand how she'd found him or what she was doing here, but at least she hadn't stabbed him in the back. She'd even warned him. Maybe she truly did care for him. The relief flooding him almost made him light-headed.

Then another shot slammed into the deck, missing Julia by inches only because she'd veered at the last second on her way to the helm.

Without thinking he dropped the monitor and grabbed the backpack at his feet. In two seconds he'd vaulted the waist-high iron fence surrounding the patio and was charging toward the dock.

Both those shots had come from east of the bank, from up high. Villa would be on the move now, repositioning to avoid detection. Bautista didn't care that he was exposed, didn't care about the risk to his life at running toward the dock.

Julia was in danger and she needed him. He was going to get to her. Protect her.

His heart hammered against his ribs as he ran, fear for her safety pushing him into harm's way.

****

Her fingers slipped off the window frame as the boat veered to the left.

Marisol gritted her teeth and grabbed at it again, catching her balance and using all the strength in her back and arms to slide the stubborn window open. It gave inch by inch, so slowly she wanted to scream.

Darting a glance out the small window in the rear of the cabin, she saw why Julia was driving flat out away from shore. Another speedboat was coming after them. Had to be that Villa guy.

Heart in her throat, she watched for a few seconds. The boat tailing them was sleeker, had to be faster than theirs because it was slowly gaining on them.

Marisol turned back to the portside window and heaved it open. Even with cool air whipping through it and the hatch, she was sweating.

With one big shove she pushed the window all the way open. She gauged the size of it again. A tight squeeze but she had to try to escape once the boat slowed or stopped. If she sliced up her hips and ass getting through it, oh well.

Julia turned sharply to the right. Marisol braced her weight against the cabin wall and stole another glance outside. The opposite shoreline passed by in a blur. Even if she could get through the window, she could never jump at this speed—she'd kill herself in the attempt.

Forcing out a slow breath, she maintained her grip on the windowsill and divided her attention out the port side and the rear window. Villa was steadily gaining on them.

At this rate he'd overtake them in a matter of minutes.

She flinched and ducked when something cracked off the hull. Her eyes shot out the window set into the back of the cabin, locked on the sliver-dollar-sized hole in the fiberglass near the engine.

"Shit," she whispered, her heart galloping.

Dropping to the floor she pressed her spine tight against the wall, making herself as small a target as possible.

Another shot punched into the rear of the boat, followed seconds later by a third. A loud bang made her jump and the engine made a weird choking sound.

The power cut, dropping the bow of the boat into the water as it plunged to a near halt. Already she smelled smoke. She got to her belly and crawled her way to the steps, grasped the handrail just as Julia called down to her.

"Marisol, get up here, hurry! We've gotta go."

Go? Go where?

Her legs were unsteady as she climbed the steps, halting near the hatch.

Julia was hunkered down low behind the captain's chair, pistol in hand, lips pressed into a thin line. She cut Marisol a glance, the whine of the approaching boat growing louder. "Engine's blown, and we can't stay here." Those ice blue eyes locked on hers. "Can you swim?"

Her stomach lurched and she couldn't help but dart a glance at the murky water. You wanna stay here and get shot, a voice in her head demanded. She forced her gaze back to Julia, made herself nod. "Y-yes."

The other woman nodded once. "Good. Come on." She held out a hand.

Marisol took it, a strange numbness taking hold. She'd already made the decision to jump. Now her body was moving on autopilot.

"Stay low," Julia cautioned, stealing another look to

their stern. "Swim as fast as you can to shore. I'll be right behind—" She trailed off, her gaze stuck on something behind them.

Marisol automatically followed her gaze, saw a second boat fly around a curve in the shoreline, racing toward them.

Before either of them could move, something flashed in the second boat. Villa's craft veered sharply to the side a second later.

Marisol stared at the new boat. "They're shooting at Villa," she blurted, a spurt of hope spiraling through her.

"Yeah. Come on." Julia tugged her to her feet, towed her toward the port side.

Another crack rang out. Marisol stifled a cry and scrambled to the edge of the deck.

The water was so deep she couldn't see the bottom. She'd never been a great swimmer. How far was it to shore? Her stomach contracted, squeezing the air from her lungs.

"Go," Julia barked, shoving a hand against the center of her back.

They were out of time. Marisol said a silent prayer and dove headfirst into the water.

The sudden shock of the cool water hit her like a punch to the solar plexus. What little air she'd had in her lungs escaped in a stream of bubbles. She pushed water away with her arms, kicked hard with her legs.

Her head finally broke the surface. She dragged in a heaving lungful of air, cast a desperate glance around her to get her bearings. Julia was in the water, cutting toward her like a knife, her strokes strong and sure.

The roar of Villa's boat was getting louder, mixing with the rush of blood in her ears. *Go, hurry!*

Heart hammering, she turned toward shore and began a clumsy front crawl, not bothering to even attempt the proper breathing technique she'd never mastered as a kid.

Her arms and legs moved all on their own, her body acting on pure survival instinct. She picked out the nearest spot to exit the water and headed for it, keeping her eyes glued there so she didn't become disoriented.

Julia came up beside her. "Faster! Come on, you can do it. We can't count on Miguel stopping Villa. We've gotta get out."

Miguel was in the other boat? She didn't have the breath to answer.

Heart slamming against her ribs like it was about to burst, Marisol put her head down and swam for all she was worth.

Chapter Nineteen

E than scanned the waterway ahead of him as he raced with his teammates to the Zodiacs waiting for them at the end of the dock. Marisol was out there somewhere, and she needed him.

He locked that thought away, needing to compartmentalize and focus on the op. *El Santo* and Villa were both waiting up ahead for them. To save her he needed to be a hundred percent locked in, have his game face on.

Their boots pounded over the wooden dock as they ran.

The Bureau's Critical Incident Response Group had managed to get the inflatable boats here for them in time for their arrival a few minutes ago. New intel was coming in all the time from agents monitoring satellite footage of the waterway where the boat carrying Marisol was traveling. Eyewitness accounts said two other boats were chasing it, and shots had been fired.

Normally before an op they went over everything carefully before deploying, but this time they couldn't afford to wait. They'd rushed straight here and were doing this on the fly—something that was possible only because of the countless hours they'd spent operating together as a unit. They'd done plenty of maritime ops together in the past and every one of them knew what to do.

Tuck doled out instructions via their comms as they neared the end of the dock. He was getting constant updates from DeLuca and the Special Agent In Charge from the Miami office, who were both in the mobile command unit a half-mile away. Their sniper teams were positioned further north, at the end of the canal, just in case the tangos somehow got past Ethan and the others. The DEA's FAST team was securing the far southern end of the harbor.

El Santo and Villa had nowhere to go. And cornered animals were always the most dangerous.

Ethan jumped into the first rubber-hulled vessel and gripped the rope lining the gunwale near the bow. Tuck, Vance and Bauer climbed in after him, the former SEAL taking the helm. Behind them, Blackwell, Schroder and Evers manned the second Zodiac.

At his place in the bow, Tuck suddenly lifted his head, a hand going to his earpiece. "Copy. Moving to intercept now." He half-turned to address them, the guys in the second boat alerted via their comm units. "Witnesses say both females are currently in the water, making their way toward shore."

Marisol and the unknown woman who'd taken the boat. Ethan's gut tightened. From what he remembered, Marisol wasn't a good swimmer and hated being in the water. Something about a near-drowning when she was a kid.

The urge to race to her clawed at him. It drove him insane to sit here when he knew she was in danger, but the team's safety came first, and they still had two lethal enforcers to take down before they could help Marisol.

"Both of the remaining vessels are still in pursuit.

Satellite images confirm Panther is in the second boat, and Jaguar in the other," he said, using the codenames for Villa and *el Santo*. "Both tangos are wounded. Helo's inbound to give us eyes on target, ETA four minutes. We gotta move fast on this. Let's go." He signaled to Bauer, who started the Zodiac's engine with a throaty growl.

They shot away from the dock and swung to the south, moving to intercept their targets. Ethan and his boat would go after *el Santo* while Schroder and his crew would target Villa. The rival tangos would try to take each other out. Only once both tangos were down could he get to Marisol.

We're coming, Soli. Hang on. Please hang on for me, baby.

He leaned lower against the gunwale, the salty air whipping across his face as Bauer sped them down the canal, Schroder's crew right behind them. The wide waterway was the only way out to the open sea. By heading south they were effectively blocking Villa and *el Santo's* escape route.

They were set on a collision course in a deadly game of chicken. The stakes were life and death and there would only be one winner.

****

Bautista swung his boat around and opened the throttle, racing toward Julia and Marisol, who were both in the water seventy yards ahead of him. And that bastard Villa was in between, headed straight for them, knowing he would follow. If he couldn't stop the other enforcer in time, Villa would kill them both.

Not fucking happening. He wouldn't let Julia die.

He squinted to protect his eyes from the wind as he raced at top speed. Villa was the main threat, but not the only one. The cops and FBI would be here soon, if they weren't already. If they were smart, they'd try to barricade the end of the canal before he and Villa reached it.

Which meant Bautista had only a few minutes more at best to kill Villa, pull the women from the water and get to shore to make his getaway.

He set his jaw. His boat was fast, but not as fast as Villa's. He had the throttle wide open and still wasn't gaining on him. The bow skipped over the relatively smooth water, the shoreline whipping past in a blur. He kept his gaze pinned dead ahead, focused on stopping the assassin currently targeting his woman.

With his feet braced wide apart on the deck, he released the wheel, raised his rifle and took aim. Twenty-five yards ahead of him, Villa glanced back and swerved to the left.

Bautista didn't release his weapon to correct his steering, just followed his target with the muzzle. Villa was crouched low, the engine cover at the stern of the boat giving him some cover. But he couldn't hide entirely.

A cold, deadly rage filled him. *You're mine.*

Bautista slowed his breathing, curled his finger around the trigger, and fired.

Villa jerked his arm in front of him and his boat careened to the right. But he didn't stop.

Reaching down with one hand, Bautista corrected his steering then immediately gripped his rifle and took aim again. Villa's shoulder appeared in his sights. He fired again, and this time he saw the spurt of blood as his bullet struck. Villa's boat swung sharply away to the left, toward shore.

Bautista didn't stop. Couldn't. While likely not fatal, that wound would slow the other enforcer down and make it hard for him to get off a good shot. He shot past where Villa had turned to shore and kept his gaze pinned straight ahead, on the women in the water. Julia was right beside Marisol, who seemed to be struggling.

Then, a few hundred yards beyond them, two Zodiacs appeared around a bend in the canal.

Either the Feds or a local SWAT team. Even though his instincts were screaming at him to get out of there, he couldn't leave Julia to die after how bravely she'd tried to protect him and Marisol. He couldn't live with himself if he lost her.

Gritting his teeth, he sped toward the women, counting down the seconds as he closed the gap. When he was twenty yards away from them, a shot burrowed into the hull near the bow of his boat.

He jerked the wheel to the right, slammed the throttle back to drop his speed and wheeled about in the water, cutting in a tight arc around the women. With the motor on low he aimed straight for them, braving another shot from the Zodiacs.

Both women had their heads up now, watching him. He moved in close, dropped the engine into idle and thrust out a hand to Julia, who was now swimming toward him with sure strokes. He felt the seconds ticking past with every beat of his heart. *Come on, come on…*

His eyes locked on hers, those pale blue depths spearing him. "Take my hand," he shouted, stretching his arm out as far as he could.

She swam three more strokes and swung her arm out of the water, clasping his hand tight. Her fingers were cold, her face pale as he dragged her up and into the boat. She leaned into him, soaked and bleeding from her arm. That bastard Villa would pay with his life for wounding her.

Hugging her into his side, he squeezed her tight as he steered toward Marisol. She was clearly in trouble. He couldn't just let her drown, and Julia would be horrified if he did. Marisol's eyes were wide, her expression panicked.

He bent low, his arm still around Julia. "Come on,"

he called to her urgently, holding out his hand. He could hear the hum of the Zodiacs' engines now, braced himself for the feel of a bullet at any moment. Even wearing Kevlar body armor wouldn't protect him from a head or abdominal shot. And the men coming after him were deadly marksmen.

But he'd made it out of tighter jams than this before, and he was determined to get out of this one too. He had so much to live for now. Every second he waited cost him the chance to escape but Marisol was still too far from shore and he couldn't just leave her. "Grab my hand," he barked, knowing the urgency in his voice would counteract her shock.

She thrashed her way over the last few yards toward him, her movements sluggish and uncoordinated. Whether from the shock of being in the water or exhaustion, he didn't know and didn't care. He just wanted to grab her so he could get the hell out of here.

Finally he was close enough. He grabbed her by the forearm and bodily dragged her out of the water. While she collapsed at his feet he gripped the wheel and hit the throttle again, wheeling the boat back around to face the way he'd come.

"There are cops everywhere," Julia gasped out, chest heaving from the exertion of her swim. She was bleeding pretty bad, cradling her left forearm to her chest. Pinkish-red rivulets ran down her arm and dripped on the deck.

"How bad were you hit?" he demanded. There were a million questions he wanted to ask her, like who she was and who had trained her. Because based on what he'd just seen, she was no simple civilian.

"Just a flesh wound. And the Feds—those are HRT guys back there," she shouted over the noise of the engine as she looked behind them. She looked up at him, her face pinched with worry. "What are you going to do?"

"Take out Villa and get to shore." He had no choice

but to run the gauntlet of the other enforcer, waiting somewhere up ahead, and whatever law enforcement had arrived on scene. With grim determination he sped them southward.

Julia ducked beneath his arm and grabbed the wheel. Her wet hair whipped back from her face by the wind as she shouted at him. "I'll drive, you shoot."

"No," he shouted back, pushing her downward to the deck. "Stay down. It's not safe."

She refused to budge. Her pale eyes drilled into his, and he could see the fear for his safety there. "I'm not who you think I am either," she told him, "and I can handle myself. Now shoot our way out of here and let me drive."

He held her stare for a moment, pride and surprise twining inside him. This woman was incredible. Once this was all over, he was going to learn every last one of her secrets.

With a nod, he relented. She couldn't know how huge that was, for him to relinquish control to someone else in a situation like this. But in spite of all the secrets she'd kept from him, his gut still trusted her. "Keep low," he warned, going to one knee on the deck and putting the stock of his rifle to his shoulder. "He's wounded, but I don't know how bad."

"I see him. Two o'clock, forty yards out."

Searching off the starboard bow he immediately spotted the pale blue speedboat heading their way. Apparently that bullet hadn't taken Villa out of action after all.

"Head left," he called out. He was aware of Marisol crouched behind him, frozen in place as she braced against one of the seats. Her head was turned to look behind them, at the HRT boats approaching. "Get down," he growled at her, and she ducked her head.

Ethan Cruz might be on one of those boats, coming to rescue her. He pushed the thought from his mind. He had to think of himself now, and Julia.

Nothing mattered but taking out Villa so he could be free, and then do everything in his power to get away.

Julia turned the boat to the left, allowing him a better view of Villa. He caught a flash of movement near the helm, automatically aimed and fired.

Villa dropped, but Bautista jerked as a deep, burning pain hit him in the abdomen. Julia cried out and released the wheel, her eyes wide as she reached for him.

Biting back a growl of agony, he struggled to his knees. Bastard had hit him just below the lower edge of his Kevlar.

Julia was next to him, had her hand over his belly. He pushed her away, needing her out of the line of fire in case Villa took another shot. The pain made his vision hazy but he shook his head to clear away the fog and fought through the burn to take aim again.

Villa wasn't moving.

He eased forward to get a better look as they closed in on his boat. Still no movement. Bautista's heart raced. If Villa was dead then he could go to shore and try to disappear. It wasn't too late. He still had a chance—

A round slammed into his back, punching through his ribs just below his armpit. He grunted and slumped forward, losing his grip on his weapon.

"Miguel!" Julia screamed it, the terror in her voice slicing through the haze of agony engulfing him.

He tried to roll over, reached a hand toward his fallen weapon. His lungs burned like they were filled with acid and he couldn't get any air.

Safe. He needed to make sure she was safe.

Gathering his remaining strength, he pushed up onto all fours and curled his hand around his rifle.

****

When Julia dropped to help Miguel, Marisol jumped up and grabbed the wheel.

The reaction was automatic, her body moving all on its own to control the boat before it crashed. Her breathing was erratic, her entire body trembling with cold and shock as she wrapped her hands around the steering wheel.

The wind blasted past her, making the shivers worse. Villa had stopped but she didn't know if he was dead. She darted a glance toward shore. If she jumped now, maybe she could make it to—

Julia whipped out her pistol and aimed dead center at Marisol's chest. "You stop or slow down to let your boyfriend catch up, and I'll kill you."

The threat locked up all her muscles even as the woman's words penetrated the panic clawing at her. Marisol had heard her say the HRT was back there. Was Ethan on one of the boats behind them?

She bit down hard on her back teeth and for a moment thought about kicking the pistol from Julia's grip. Three things stopped her.

She believed the woman would kill her to protect Miguel. Having seen her in action, Marisol knew she had no chance of kicking the gun from Julia's grip. And Villa might still be gunning for them. His boat was closer than the two behind them. Even if she managed to disarm Julia and jumped overboard again, Ethan would never reach her before Villa did.

She faced forward once more. They were going terrifyingly fast up the canal that was becoming more and more crowded by other boats in the distance but she didn't dare slow down.

God, what do I do? "Where am I going?" she shouted over the roar of the engine and the wind in her face.

"Go left, away from Villa," Julia shouted back, her voice edged with desperation. "Just get us to shore so I can get him away from here."

Casting a glance down at them, Marisol's heart lurched. Even wounded as badly as he was, Miguel was still trying to lift his rifle. He was bleeding heavily from both wounds and wasn't listening to Julia's urgent commands for him to stay still.

With her pistol aimed at Marisol, Julia tore off his shirt with her free hand and pressed it against the wound on his stomach. Somehow he raised his rifle, his expression so full of determination and pain that her heart ached for him. He'd saved her from Villa multiple times now, at risk to his own life. She didn't want him to die.

Marisol looked in front of her again. Villa was approaching them from up ahead on the right. She had to evade him somehow. "Hang on," she called out, and turned the wheel to the left.

The boat reacted with the precision she expected from an expensive craft like this. It changed direction and sliced through the water effortlessly in a tight, terrifying arc.

Her heart pounded sickeningly in her throat. If she'd turned the wheel any harder, she would have flipped them and killed them all.

Straightening the wheel, she aimed for a small dock, maybe sixty yards ahead. In her peripheral she glimpsed Villa's boat coming toward them.

Something hit the windscreen, shattering it. She cried out sharply and let go of the wheel as she ducked. An instant later they hit something in the shallower water.

The boat went airborne, coming right out of the water, the bow kicking up like a horse rearing on its hind legs. Marisol flew backward, knocking into Julia and Miguel.

Blindly she threw out a hand to grab something to hold on to. Her fingers closed around the edge of the gunwale but slipped. A moment of terror hit her as she skidded toward the side. Then a hand shot out and locked around her wrist, stopping her from pitching over the side.

She flipped over onto her stomach and saw Julia hauling her back, her face flushed with exertion. She was still bleeding from the wound on her forearm and her hands were slick with blood.

The moment Marisol was safe, Julia lurched to her knees and grabbed for the wheel. She slowed them and turned, narrowly avoiding the end of a dock straight ahead.

Marisol whipped around on her knees and craned her neck to see behind them. The two HRT boats were gaining on them now. A burst of elation and hope swelled in her chest.

Then out of the corner of her eye, she saw Miguel point the muzzle of his rifle behind them.

"*Nooo!*" The word tore out of her in a desperate scream. She grabbed for the barrel of the rifle without thinking, intent on swinging it away from Ethan and the others.

Miguel grunted and lashed out with a foot, catching her in the side with the sole of his boot. She dropped her hands and doubled over, gasping for breath. The next thing she knew, a hard arm clamped around her waist.

Miguel dragged her up against him, her back to his front. He was trembling, his breath coming in shallow bursts. "Don't you fucking move," he rasped in a menacing voice that sent chills down her spine.

Trapped in his hold, Marisol froze and locked her stare on the two boats rapidly approaching as understanding slammed into her. Miguel wasn't going to kill her.

He was using her as a human shield, knowing the HRT would never fire for risk of hitting her.

Chapter Twenty

————— ✑ —————

Ethan's heart stopped beating as Miguel hauled Marisol in front of him as a shield. He was still holding his rifle despite being wounded twice, and Ethan had seen the woman aiming a pistol at Marisol a minute ago.

Rage gathered inside him, pushing to the surface. He fought it back, needing to remain in the zone. Marisol's life and his teammates' relied on him being mentally locked in. He wanted to launch himself at Miguel right now, go right at him, hand to hand, and pound his goddamn face in for what he'd done.

I got you once already, asshole, he thought grimly, staring at Miguel through the sight. *I'll hit you again.*

"Cut to port," Tuck ordered.

Bauer turned them toward Miguel's boat. They shot left while Schroder's boat headed right, toward Villa's vessel. Overhead a helicopter appeared, keeping pace with the boats so it could provide Tuck and everyone back at the command center live images.

Tuck spoke over the comm, his voice calm. "Capture Panther alive if possible," he said, even though they all knew neither of these guys would allow themselves to be taken alive.

"Roger that," Evers responded.

Ethan's hand tightened around the grip of his M4 as he kept looking for a shot. He lay flat against the front of the left gunwale, his left leg bent so that his foot hooked around the safety rope. The stock of his weapon was snugged up tight against his shoulder.

Miguel's boat was still racing away from them but it was well within range. But with Marisol in front of Miguel as a shield, there was no way Ethan or his teammates could fire without risking hitting her.

When their boat had hit something in the water earlier the impact must have damaged the engine because Ethan's boat was steadily gaining on their target. The woman at the wheel was crouched low as she cast a glance behind them. She veered right then left, maintained an evasive serpentine motion that made it hard for them to get a clean shot off.

But as good as the maneuvering was, she had four of the best-trained shooters in the world on her tail, and a former SEAL manning the helm. She wasn't getting away.

He tightened his legs to hold himself steady on the gunwale. Bauer mimicked the other boat's movements effortlessly, bringing them closer and closer. Soon Miguel would have nowhere to go.

"Anyone got a clear shot?" Tuck said into the comm.

"Negative," Ethan muttered, and Vance indicated the same. On their right, Schroder and crew were intercepting Villa's boat. He heard three staccato shots, then nothing but the roar of their own motor.

"Panther is down," Evers reported a moment later. "Doc's working on him but it doesn't look good."

"Copy," Tuck answered, never taking his eyes off Miguel.

Ethan adjusted his aim as the woman steering the boat turned hard to port. The motion caused Miguel to lean over to keep from falling but he had Marisol back in front of him before Ethan could get off a shot.

He saw the muzzle flash, then the splash of the rounds hitting the water a few feet to his left. If he'd resorted to spraying bullets, then Miguel was getting desperate. He knew he was running out of room and that he only had a minute or two more to get to shore and make his escape. Wounded as he was, he wouldn't make it a hundred yards before the agents on shore closed in on him and dropped him where he stood.

Bauer didn't let up on the throttle, just sped straight for them.

Adrenaline pumped hard and fast through Ethan's veins, making his heart race and raising goose bumps all over his body. Fucker was going *down*.

For a split second he shifted his gaze from Miguel to Marisol. Her face was deathly pale, her eyes wide and locked on him. He could feel the fear and hope in that stare, and it ate a hole through the center of his chest.

Hang on, baby. I'm right here.

As though she heard him, her terrified expression morphed into one he'd seen on her face many times before—pure determination.

He had only a second to tense, to think *oh shit, no*, before she reared up and twisted hard. Heart in his throat, Ethan watched helplessly as she knocked Miguel off balance and toppled him over. They hit the deck and knocked the driver's legs out from under her. Marisol bounced and rolled to the edge.

Then Miguel moved and Ethan's training kicked in. He took aim at the spot above where the top of the tango's Kevlar vest would end, and fired.

Miguel jerked and fell flat. The female driver grabbed the throttle and plunged the boat to a sudden stop.

As she knelt next to Miguel, Ethan shifted his gaze to Marisol. She was already climbing to her feet at the port side of the boat. Casting a furtive glance in their direction, she jumped into the water and began paddling for shore.

But at least she was out of the line of fire.

They couldn't stop to help her. They were almost to the other vessel now, had to neutralize Miguel and his female accomplice.

He and Tuck both rose to one knee in preparation to make the jump, weapons aimed at the female and Miguel. Ethan was itching to board the other boat and take Miguel down.

"Hands!" Tuck shouted. "Get them up, *now*!"

The female froze, but Ethan saw the resolve in her face. Resolve to go down fighting. And Miguel's weapon was within her reach.

Not a chance, lady.

It took only another second to reach the boat. The instant they were close enough, Ethan leaped from the bow onto the other vessel's deck, with Tuck right behind him.

Ethan lunged and ripped the woman away from Miguel for Tuck to deal with, his gaze remaining locked on his target.

Miguel was *his*.

He started to swing a knee onto the bastard's throat to pin him down. Suddenly Miguel twisted hard, his empty right hand coming up to swing at Ethan's head.

He ducked and rolled away. But before he could regain his balance, Miguel dove at him. He crashed into Ethan's chest, sending him flying into the dash.

Ethan grunted at the impact. His helmet came off as they twisted on the deck. Miguel reared back and rammed his head into Ethan's, bouncing the back of Ethan's unprotected skull against the deck.

*Mother*fucker!

The blow dazed him for a moment. He might even have blacked out for a second, he wasn't sure, and when he regained his senses he tasted blood in his mouth.

Out of the corner of his eye he saw Tuck reach for him, felt a steely hand wrap around his forearm. He was yelling something but Ethan couldn't hear it over the rush of blood in his ears. Rage overtook him, obliterating everything but the need to attack. To punish.

Miguel was going to fucking pay for what he'd done to Marisol, in blood drawn by Ethan's hands.

Ripping free of Tuck's hold, he slammed his fist into Miguel's jaw even as the deck vibrated with the heavy footsteps of his arriving teammates. Tuck cursed and grabbed for him again, but Ethan barely noticed as he dodged a vicious right hook to the face.

Authoritative voices registered. Vance and Bauer were shouting at him, ordering him to stand down. He knew they were both standing over them with their weapons aimed. But this fucker wouldn't go down without a fight and Ethan was only too glad to give him one.

He landed one last hard jab to Miguel's ribs and suddenly Vance was there, grabbing Miguel's shoulder to wrench him onto his back. Ethan ignored his friend, completely focused on subduing Miguel on his own.

Twisting hard, he used the momentum to swing a leg over the man's waist and landed on top of him. Instantly he came to his knees and plowed a fist into Miguel's face. He heard a crack, elation shooting through him as the other man screamed in fury, then he leaned down and dug an elbow into the bullet wound he'd inflicted just below the base of Miguel's throat.

The man's face blanched, his eyes flaring at the pain Ethan caused. Triumph roared through him. He grabbed Miguel's wrists, pinned them down while Vance and Bauer moved in.

It was over. Guy was down, probably wouldn't live long now, given the amount of blood he'd lost.

Ethan didn't care. He let his teammates take over.

His legs were surprisingly shaky as he pushed to his feet, from the residual adrenaline coursing through him and the waves of dizziness assaulting him. Immediately his gaze shot to the water, searching for Marisol.

Schroder and the others were already there with their boat, had her safely in it.

Ethan sagged, feeling like someone had just unplugged him. He threw out a hand to steady himself on the back of the nearest seat and focused on calming his breathing. He was panting and a little queasy. He'd hit his head harder than he'd realized.

Tuck looked over from where he stood watching Vance work on Miguel. The tango's face was gray and he was barely breathing. "Doc," he called out to Schroder. "Get over here."

Ethan didn't care if the bastard died or not. He turned toward the other boat as it approached, his gaze colliding with Marisol's. And in that moment, the truth hit him like a roundhouse to the gut.

He loved her. And no one was taking her from him ever again.

****

He was dying.

Bautista struggled to suck in air and fought to drag his rifle upward. His only chance of escape was to fight his way past the Feds, and now that was gone. They had him facedown on the deck, his cheek resting in a pool of his own blood, and his hands were cuffed behind him with zip ties.

He would *not* give up. Had to find a way to get out of this.

But he couldn't move his limbs. Could barely twitch his fingers.

The sudden quiet was jarring. Everything around him was a blur. The blood loss left him weak and cold. Even though the brilliant summer sunshine beat down on him it felt like he was encased in ice. Someone rolled him over to his back, tearing a cry of agony from him.

"Miguel. Miguel, look at me."

At the pain in Julia's voice he turned his head and looked up into her face. She was kneeling beside him. There were tears in her eyes. They rolled down her cheeks as she knelt close, her leg touching his head.

Her arms were bound behind her.

They'd fucking cuffed her. Were going to drag her away because of him.

His heart twisted. He was free in a sense, just not the way he'd wanted. Julia was beside him but he had probably mere minutes left to live. It hurt to breathe and his heart beat sluggishly.

His hand twitched as he tried to move it. He wanted to touch her. Couldn't.

"Ma'am, get back," the HRT member holding her bound wrists said in a Southern accent. "It's over."

"Just let me say goodbye, goddammit," she snarled. Bending low, she pressed her cheek to his. The gesture pierced him, the warmth of her skin penetrating some of the ice.

Julia. His sweet Julia. "I'm s…sorry," he rasped out, feeling the last of his strength fading fast.

She shook her head, the tears falling faster now. They landed on his face like raindrops. "Don't. Just be still. They're going to get you help, okay? A medic's coming, he'll help you."

His heart pumped harder, a jolt of adrenaline flashing through him. *Can't stay here. Have to move.*

But he could barely keep his eyelids open.

She pressed her cheek harder to his. "You saved Marisol and me," she said in a choked whisper. "You *saved* us."

Yes. At least Julia was alive. It wasn't much, not when compared to all the lives he'd taken, but it was something. He wondered what God would have to say about the things he'd done.

You're about to find out.

Grief speared through him at the realization, hot and sharp. He didn't want to leave her. He'd wanted to start fresh, had thought he would have time to figure out how to get her to come with him. His whole body shook, the pain in his heart eclipsing the agony of the bullet wounds.

A nearby motor throttled down and a hard male voice called out. "Hold him steady while I get a central line in."

He struggled, a desperate will to survive erupting. They were arresting Julia. He had to protect her.

"No, lie still," Julia begged.

"S-sorry," he slurred. The cold seeped deeper, freezing him from the inside out.

"Hold on," Julia whispered to him as she drew away. In his fading vision he saw her get to her feet.

"Don't you move." The growl came from the left.

He stared up into Julia's face as the deck vibrated with heavy footsteps. His head hit the deck as someone half turned him. Everything was growing fuzzy. His vision was nearly gone but he could still catch snippets of what Julia was saying.

"Help him. You have to help him."

No.

He opened his lips, tried to force the word out. He didn't want them to save him. Not when he'd only wind up behind bars for the rest of his life. He'd rather die here with Julia beside him, be able to look at her as he took his last breath.

Then they'd both be free.

It had been selfish of him to ever want her to leave everything behind to be with him. No matter how careful they would have been or how often he checked over his shoulder, there would always have been a threat hovering over them. She might have acted like an operator today, but if he died here, at least she'd be safe from his enemies.

Strong hands turned him, shoved something against the wound at the top of his chest. The one that had shattered his lung.

He barely felt it when someone pressed down on his abdomen. With a last burst of strength he moved only his eyes, searching out Julia's face.

She was standing near the edge of the boat, crying silently as she stared back at him. The sun streamed through her hair, forming a glowing halo around her head, her pale blue eyes wide and locked on him. Pleading with him to hang on. His angel.

I love you, my angel. I'll always watch over you.

Imprinting that image of her in his mind before the edges of his vision went gray, then dark, he closed his eyes and consciously let go. His heart thudded slower and slower in his ears. Men moved around him, pressing on his chest, checking his pulse.

The last thing he heard was Julia's panicked voice echoing through his mind. He clung to it, determined to take it with him into the black void of death.

"Miguel, *no*! Don't die on me…"

Have to, angel, he thought in the moment before his heart stopped. *It's the only way I can protect you.*

Chapter Twenty-One

Over. It was all over.

Marisol huddled beneath the blanket Schroder had thrown around her shoulders just before he boarded the other boat. Miguel and Julia were both in custody, but from what she could see, she didn't think Miguel was going to survive.

There were too many things going on in her head right now for her to even know how to feel about that. And she wondered just who the hell Julia was, and how she fit into this mess.

Shivering, she kept her gaze pinned on Ethan as he stood and met her gaze. He seemed a bit unsteady, wove on his feet slightly for a second.

She bit down on her lip as a hot wash of tears flooded her eyes. She'd been terrified when he'd launched himself at Miguel like that.

He stepped over the edge of the speedboat into the Zodiac and she dropped the blanket, surging to her feet to reach for him. He caught her and dragged her close, his strong arms crushing her to him. He smelled of blood and sweat but she didn't care.

"Soli," he rasped out. "God, Soli. You all right?"

She couldn't answer. Could only cling and fight not to cry as he held her. Her shoulders shook as the first sobs ripped free.

He murmured something she didn't catch and cradled the back of her head with one big hand, curving his body around hers. Sheltering and protecting her.

Images from earlier flickered through her mind, a movie on fast forward. She squeezed her eyes shut and fought to block them out.

Slowly the heat from his body penetrated through the wall of shock trying to engulf her. Her hands gripped the back of his fatigues, squeezing fistfuls of the fabric. Unbelievable as it seemed, she was alive. They both were.

Ethan pressed his mouth to her cheek. "Baby, are you hurt?"

She shook her head, wouldn't let go. Yes, she hurt all over from what felt like a thousand cuts and scrapes and bruises, but she wasn't injured.

When the tears had slowed she lifted her head to peer up at him. "Are you ok-kay?" She'd seen him hit the deck when he'd been fighting Miguel, had seen the other man head-butt him. Already a bluish bruise was forming around the edges of the lump in the center of his forehead. He could have a concussion.

"Yeah, I'm good, kitt'n. Now that I'm holding you and know for sure you're safe, I'm good."

She set her hands on either side of his face, stared up into those beautiful light brown eyes. "I saw you go down, and him hitting you." She bit her lip as her throat closed up. "I was scared you weren't going to get back up." Even though his teammates had all been there, she'd still been terrified.

His eyes filled with tenderness. "I'm tougher than I look, baby."

She let out a watery laugh. "You look plenty tough to me."

"And you're definitely tougher than you look. Knocking Miguel over and jumping into the water like that, when I know how much you hate being in it."

"Survival reflex."

He kissed her gently then bent to scoop her up into his arms as he sat in the middle of the boat and wrapped the blanket tight around her body. "Whaddya say we get to shore and get you into some dry clothes so you can warm up?"

She nodded against his shoulder, let her eyes close to block out the sight of Julia standing on deck with Tuck holding her bound wrists. She was crying as Miguel likely lay dying in front of her. There was no question she loved him.

Marisol shivered. "Just as long as you don't let me go for long."

His arms tightened fiercely around her. "That's a promise."

She didn't open her eyes when some of his teammates came on board and started the boat up. On shore a mob of people in uniform awaited them.

Marisol huddled under the blanket as Ethan rushed her to a waiting ambulance. Plain-clothes agents were gathered around talking to his teammates while others went to deal with Miguel's body and Julia.

She glanced around for the woman. Didn't see her. "Where's Julia?"

"Julia?"

"The woman with Miguel." Who the hell was she, anyway?

Ethan stopped and scanned the immediate area. "Dunno, but I saw Tuck hand her off to another agent on shore. Must be with one of the EMTs now, getting checked over."

There were at least five ambulances on scene that she could see. Ethan shifted her in his arms and strode for the back of the ambulance. A paramedic helped him settle her onto a stretcher.

Annoyed, she tried to push up. Going to the hospital would mean she'd be stuck there for hours, not including all the time it took to talk to the FBI and local cops about what had happened.

She wasn't hurt worse than some cuts and scrapes and bruises. More than anything she just wanted to talk to whoever she needed to talk to in order to be cleared to go home. Or the safe house, or a hotel. Wherever the hell they would allow her to go, so she could be alone with Ethan for as long as possible.

"No, I'm f-fine," she protested. Just cold. She couldn't seem to warm up, kept shaking despite the blanket and Ethan being next to her.

Ethan flattened a hand on the center of her chest, keeping her pinned to the stretcher. "You're not fine. Not until the doctors say you are."

She opened her mouth to argue but a sudden commotion broke out beyond the ambulance, near the dock. Raised voices reached her, and people began scrambling away from the scene. Frowning, Ethan stood to see what was going on and Marisol sat up.

A few seconds later DeLuca materialized out of the crowd and came rushing toward them, his brows lowered in a tight frown. "Did you guys see the female suspect anywhere in the last two minutes?"

Ethan blinked at him. "Tuck handed her off to—"

"Yeah, I know. *After* that." He looked at Marisol, his stance radiating tension.

She shook her head. "We thought she was with the paramedics."

He pulled off his Chargers ball cap and ran a hand through his slightly thinning-on-top hair. "She was."

Huh?

DeLuca let out a frustrated growl and replaced his

cap. "They must have cut off the flex ties when they started to treat her. An agent found both EMTs and the escorting agent unconscious in the ambulance. No gunshot or other visible wounds, but all three were down for the count. Taser maybe, I dunno. Agent In Charge is securing the perimeter and two teams are already out searching for her."

"What the fuck?" Ethan muttered, turning to look at her.

Marisol's eyes widened. Julia had done that? Who the hell was she? "I could tell she had training, but I never knew…" Wow.

She wrapped her arms around her middle, suddenly having a whole new level of appreciation for just how lucky she was to be alive. If Julia had wanted to kill her, apparently she hadn't even needed a weapon to do it. It was a sobering thought.

DeLuca stepped back from the rear of the ambulance. "She's the AIC's problem now. I've gotta deal with *el Santo* and Villa. You guys get going so they can check you out at the hospital."

Ethan shot him a frown. "I don't need to get checked out."

"And neither do I," she argued, staring at Ethan. He was the one with the fist-sized knot in the middle of his forehead. He needed medical attention more than she did.

Hands on hips, DeLuca divided a stern look between the two of them. "You're both going. Schroder said you both need to get checked over, so that's how it's going to be. Got it?"

For a moment she thought Ethan would argue, but then he sat down on the built-in bench at the side of the ambulance and folded his arms across his chest, scowling at his commander. "Fine," he muttered.

"Hope they find Julia," Marisol called out as DeLuca turned away.

Clearly there'd been a strong emotional link between Julia and Miguel. She would know all kinds of important information about him, maybe about his operations or other enforcers. They needed to interrogate her in detail, it was critical not only for this investigation, but for the Fuentes case.

He stopped and looked back at her over his shoulder. "They'll find her."

But Marisol wasn't so sure about that.

The paramedic who would be riding in the back with them grabbed the rear of the deck, about to jump inside.

"Wait, can you give us another minute?" she asked him. The guy paused in surprise but then nodded and climbed down, shutting the doors to give them privacy.

Ethan stopped sulking and moved in close, taking her hand. "What's up, sweetheart?"

She half turned on the stretcher, swinging her legs over the side to face him. "Need to tell you something."

He nodded, searched her eyes questioningly.

She took a deep breath, and jumped. "I love you."

Surprise flared in his eyes but she ignored it, kept on going.

"I knew it last night but was afraid to say anything because I thought you'd just dismiss it as me being overly romantic about what happened between us. You know, you being my first and everything."

His eyes sparkled with warmth as he smiled and raised her hand to his mouth to press a kiss to her battered knuckles. "Would I have said that?"

She nodded. "You know you would have. But after all this, I'm not wasting another second hiding what I feel for you. I know what I feel. It's not me having rose-colored glasses on, and it's not because I went through something traumatic today. I love you and that's—"

He leaned in to cradle the back of her head and cover her mouth with his. He kissed her hard and slow and then deep, sliding his tongue in to taste her. She shivered and grabbed his shoulders for support while her body melted.

All too soon he pulled away. It shocked her to see his eyes were wet. "Love you back, kitt'n. I should've told you last night but I was too chicken shit to say it. I'm sorry."

Joy and warmth flooded her, a tremulous smile spreading across her face. "You mean it? You're not just saying that because I did?"

He huffed out a laugh that ended in a low, possessive growl she felt all the way to her toes. "No. Bet your fine ass I mean it."

A sharp knock sounded on the rear door, then it swung open. Schroder stood there with a mock scowl on his face. "DeLuca said you guys were both giving him a hard time about going to the hospital, so it's your own fault that I'm now your escort." He hopped in, took a seat next to Ethan and raised his eyebrows in a falsely innocent expression. "Am I interrupting something?"

"A little bit, yeah," Ethan answered, giving him the same look.

"Well, too bad." He took a blood pressure cuff from the hook on the wall and proceeded to take her vitals. Pulling the stethoscope buds from his ears, he smiled at her. "Good news is, you're gonna make it."

She snorted. "Yeah, I know, that's why I don't think this is neces—"

"Shh." He turned to Ethan, reached for his arm as though he meant to take his blood pressure too, but Ethan ripped the cuff away from him and slapped it on the bench beside him. Schroder blinked. "Wow. Someone's cranky."

He settled back against the wall and crossed his arms, looking comfy as could be. "You need your head checked out," he said to Ethan, "and you," he threw her a pointed look, "need to get your core temp back up along with being rehydrated. The sooner we get you both checked out, the sooner you'll be rid of me and you can get back to whatever it was you were doing." Grinning at them, he winked at her as the driver started the engine.

****

Alone in the elevator, Sawyer blew out a hard breath and scrubbed a hand over his face. It had been a long fucking day already and he still had more debriefings and paperwork to do before he could call it a night and crash back at the hotel. They'd been burning the candle at both ends for so many days now that he could easily sleep all night and tomorrow.

The elevator slowed as it reached the lobby. A soft ding sounded and the doors slid open, bringing with it a wave of stale coffee and staler air.

Instantly he fought back a shiver, a visceral reaction to being in a hospital. God, he hated them. Reminded him too much of when he'd lost guys overseas back in his SF days.

In desperate need of coffee, he headed for the cafeteria. He was nearly to the front entrance when the automatic sliding doors whooshed open.

He halted in his tracks when he saw Carmela fly through them, looking uncharacteristically disheveled in a long T-shirt and sweats. Her hair was pulled up into a messy ponytail and she wore no makeup. She glanced left then right, and spotted him.

He opened his mouth to call out to her but closed it when she suddenly tore toward him, sandals slapping on the linoleum floor, her face a mask of stark fear. Whoa, she was terrified.

"Hey." He caught her by the upper arms but she latched onto his shoulders and started firing questions at him.

"What's happened? Where's Ethan? And Marisol?" She scanned his eyes anxiously, her entire body vibrating with tension. "The agents at the Lorenzo's said there'd been a firefight and that they'd both been injured. It was all over the news but no one would tell us anything. Where—"

"Whoa, slow down," he said gently. In her flip-flops the top of her head barely reached his chin. She was gripping his shoulders so hard he could feel the bite of her perfectly French-manicured nails through his shirt. In his fantasies she'd done that to him in the throes of passion, not out of fear. He didn't like seeing her so upset.

Her eyes widened for a split second, then narrowed in outrage. Her nostrils flared and she leaned in to snarl right in his face. "Don't you dare do that 'speak softly and don't make any sudden moves' thing with me. I want to know what the hell happened to my brother."

"No, listen, he's okay." He squeezed her upper arms gently to reinforce his words.

She shook her head, her eyes flashing angrily. "He's *not* okay. If he was okay he wouldn't be here, and they would've told me what happened."

"Just calm down a sec and—"

"No, I won't stop!" Tears flooded her beautiful eyes and the sight gutted him. "Why won't you just tell me what happened? He must be hurt badly, otherwise—"

Out of ideas about how to calm her, he shut her up the only way he knew how—he took her face in his hands and lowered his mouth to hers.

She gave a tiny jerk, her eyes flying wide in surprise. But she didn't pull away and an instant later her mouth softened beneath his. Her eyes fluttered closed.

Sawyer swallowed a groan of pure longing. *God.*

This had disaster written all over it, in huge, bolded red letters. He'd just crossed a line he knew to stay the hell away from. He *knew* the perils of getting involved with her, had already learned them the hard way with his ex. And apparently even that wasn't enough to make him do the right thing and step back.

She smelled delicious, a tropical mix of sweet coconut and tangy lime that went straight to his head. He'd wanted to kiss her for so long and he was still keyed up from the chase earlier, it was all he could do not to devour her. Ethan would fucking kill him for doing this, but Sawyer couldn't help himself. Not now.

He slid his hands into her hair to cradle the back of her head and slanted his mouth over hers. She made a small mewling sound and leaned into him, pressing those soft breasts against his chest while her lips parted. He slid his tongue along her lower lip, felt her shiver before stealing inside the warmth of her mouth.

Just a taste. Not nearly as much as he wanted, but more than he should have taken. God, he'd wanted to do this for so long now.

When he lifted his head a long moment later they were both breathing faster and her eyes were heavy-lidded. But then her gaze cleared and she narrowed her eyes at him in suspicion. "Wait. Did you just kiss me to shut me up?" she asked, sounding completely insulted.

Well partly, yeah, but he wasn't touching that one with a ten-foot pole. That quick taste of her was all he'd ever get. It had been selfish of him to kiss her at all, but it had done the trick. She wasn't crying and on the edge of hysterics anymore.

"No, now listen to me." He slid his fingers through the thick, cool fall of her hair and held her gaze. She was still angry with him, bright flags of color staining her cheeks, but he ignored that for now. "Your brother's okay, and so is Soli. Ethan had to have a routine CT scan to make sure the bump on his head didn't cause any damage, and Soli had some minor cuts that needed to be cleaned up. Mostly they wanted to bring her here to get her hydrated and bring her core temp back up. She got thrown into the water for a bit. That and the shock of everything that happened meant she needed a doctor to check her out, and they both had a lot of questions to answer."

Carmela blinked at him as she absorbed all that, her thick black lashes making the gold-flecked amber of her irises even more startling. "So they're both okay," she repeated, watching him warily. "You're certain."

He nodded. "Yeah."

"Swear on my mother's life that they're both okay."

"I swear."

Her eyes closed and she heaved a sigh of relief as she reached for him. The sweetest pain flared in his chest when she wound her arms around his neck and pressed close to him, seeking the comfort and reassurance he was only too happy to give. He hugged her close, savoring the feel of her.

"Okay now?" he murmured against her hair a minute later. She was so soft, and now he was hard all over. He could hold her forever but right now he was trying his best to keep her from noticing the erection straining against his fly.

She nodded against his shoulder. "Yeah, better. Thanks."

He pressed a kiss to the top of her head and reluctantly released her when she eased back.

She cleared her throat and looked at the floor, seeming suddenly unsure of herself. Or maybe even embarrassed. Her cheeks were still flushed and she wouldn't meet his eyes. "So, can I see them both?"

Unsure what he was supposed to read into her reaction and knowing he shouldn't touch her intimately again, he nodded. "Yeah. But come with me to grab a cup of coffee first."

She shot him an uncertain look, seeming agitated. "I don't know, I'd rather be upstairs in case they need me..."

"They're both talking with investigators right now anyway, and honey, I'm so tired I'm about to drop face first onto this no-wax floor. So come with me while I get some caffeine into my system and then I'll take you up to see them both in a little while."

He caught the flash of sympathy in her eyes, knew he had her. And in that moment he wished he really *did* have her. All of her, whatever she'd give him.

But that could never happen.

"Okay," she relented, but looked away, avoiding his gaze again. A warning buzz started up in his gut. "One quick cup of coffee."

As he led her toward the cafeteria, neither of them broke the unexpectedly brittle silence between them. And Sawyer couldn't shake the awful feeling that he'd ruined everything with that single, forbidden kiss.

Chapter Twenty-Two

E than woke in the semi-darkness when Marisol whispered his name.

"Ethan." She lightly shook him. "Ethan, wake up."

God, again? "I'm still alive," he muttered back, stifling a groan. She'd been waking him up every two hours throughout the night as per the doctor's instructions, just to err on the side of caution since they'd diagnosed him with a mild concussion. As a result they'd barely gotten any sleep.

He rolled to his back, hid a wince at the sudden pounding in his head the change in position caused. It was way better than it had been a few hours ago though.

Marisol reached past him to grab some more painkillers and the bottle of water from his bedside table. The Bureau had put them in a hotel room for the night, where she would stay until they cleared her to go back home. DeLuca had given him until noon to relax, then he and Marisol were both due in to the Miami office for more interviews and debriefings.

Ethan dreaded that. He wished he could make the

entire world go away for her, but in light of how critical the Fuentes case was and two of the cartel's most feared enforcers dying in the op yesterday, they needed whatever intel she could give them. Especially since she was the only one who could answer questions about the mysterious Julia, who appeared to have vanished without a trace.

"Here, it's time for your next dose," she murmured, handing him two pills and the water.

Ethan couldn't help but grin at the way she fussed over him. But what he loved even more was that she was naked, and the way her bare breasts brushed across his arm and chest as she leaned over him. "I'm liking this whole naughty nurse vibe you've got going."

She laughed softly and propped her head on one hand to watch while he took his pills. Her free hand trailed over his shoulder and across his chest, the light caress making his entire body wake up in the best possible way. His cock swelled, pushing against the sheet.

"I bet you do. How are you feeling now though?"

"Better." He swallowed the pills, set the water aside and reached for her, dragging her half on top of him. There was no way she could miss how hard he already was. He wanted inside her in the worst way.

He heard her quick intake of breath, felt the way her hands tightened on his shoulders. But then she pushed up onto her hands, a worried frown on her face as she stared down at him. "I don't think we should do anything until the doctor says you—"

"Soli. I've had my skull knocked a lot harder than this before, I promise you." It had damn near killed him not to taste her all over, make love to her again last night, but by the time they'd arrived at the hotel it had been nearly midnight and she'd been exhausted. She'd needed comforting and some quiet time so they'd kissed for a while then he'd held her while they fell asleep.

Just as he had every two hours after that, each time she'd woken him. "Unless you're too sore?" he asked. She had plenty of bruises and scrapes to show for her ordeal yesterday, including a cut on her calf from where a ricochet had sent something sharp slicing across her skin. He'd already kissed and stroked each mark last night.

"The only real pain I've got right now is an ache in here," she said, placing his palm flat against the center of her chest. "I miss having you inside me. I want to feel that again," she finished with a whisper.

Lust flared instantly, hot and urgent. "Come here, kitt'n."

Cupping her jaw with one hand, he turned them so she was on her back beneath him, and kissed her. She let out a soft moan and twined her limbs around him, arching her back to get as much contact with him as possible. Her lips parted and her tongue touched his softly.

Ethan growled into her mouth and devoured her, his heart racing out of control. Her hands roved almost greedily across his body, putting a match to the hot glow of desire pulsing through him. He cradled her breasts, bent to suck each tight nipple, savoring the way she moaned and squirmed. She rocked against him in a silent plea for contact where she needed it most.

When he cupped a hand between her thighs he found her slick and soft. He groaned around her nipple, sucked at it before sliding two fingers deep into her body, stroking over the sweet spot hidden inside her.

Her fingers dug into his scalp. "Ethan, get inside me."

Ignoring the soft plea, he eased downward, trailing kisses across her stomach, to the soft thatch of hair between her legs. His hands curled around her thighs as he dipped his head and kissed her. Slow, soft, licking kisses that made her writhe, made his cock pound with the need for release as her taste flooded his mouth.

With both hands she pressed his face to her and rubbed against his tongue. On a low groan he took her clit between his lips and sucked, lashing it gently with his tongue. He loved this woman with everything in him and wanted to give her as much pleasure as he could.

Her long, liquid moan of pleasure filled the air. "Please. Please, I need you inside me," she begged.

He fished a condom from his wallet on the nightstand and rolled it on. Grasping one sleek thigh, he lifted it around his waist and settled between her legs. With one thrust he seated himself fully inside her. She cried out and clenched around him, her fingers tightening in his hair.

Raw hunger roared through him. He pulled his hips back then surged deep, watching every expression that crossed her gorgeous face. Then he slipped a hand between them, his thumb seeking the swollen bud at the top of her sex.

She moaned and rolled her hips against him, her motions restless. "Harder," she panted breathlessly. "I need it harder."

Ethan shook his head. She didn't need harder, she needed deeper. A better angle. "C'mere."

Before she could say anything he withdrew and turned her over onto her stomach, then pulled her up onto all fours. Marisol looked back at him over her shoulder, her sea green eyes glazed with desire, the dark curtain of her hair spilling over the pillow.

Settling in behind her, his cock so hard it hurt, he drank in the sight of her like that. Ass up, legs parted, the slick folds of her sex exposed to him. With a low growl he grasped her hips and eased inside her. She gasped at his entry, mewled and curved her back in a way that told him this new angle was working for her.

"Oh, God, *Ethan…*"

He fucking loved that pleading note in her voice. Loved that he was the only man who would ever hear those gorgeous sounds he was pulling from her. Loved *her* and didn't want to ever let her go.

Reaching around her, he cupped her sex, stroked the hard nub of her clit with slick fingertips as he worked her from behind. She was so tight, so wet, every glide of his cock was both torture and heaven.

Her cries took on a desperate edge, the motion of her hips growing restless, almost frantic. He could feel her tightening around his dick, her breathing erratic, muscles quivering as he drove her to the edge.

A powerful tide of possessiveness swamped him. He wanted to mark her, fucking own her, body and soul. She'd almost been taken from him yesterday and the need to imprint himself on her at the most primal level drove him to set his teeth against the edge of her neck. He nipped her, scraped his teeth against the delicate skin and felt her come undone.

She arched, her head falling back as a sob spilled from her lips, followed by a shattered cry that echoed around the room. She shuddered and bucked in his grip, and the ravenous hunger inside him snapped free. His hands dug deeper into the flesh of her hips. He knew he'd likely leave marks and part of him gloried in it.

He drove into her harder, deeper, faster, letting the lust take over. The orgasm built and built and finally burst over him, wrenching a hoarse shout from his throat.

As it faded he curved over her back and buried his damp face in the curve of her neck. His headache was gone. He felt like he was floating.

She bent forward, resting her cheek on the pillow, and sighed softly. "I *love* sex."

A surprised laugh burst out of him.

Her lips curved in a satisfied smile, her eyes still closed. "Wait, did I say that out loud? What I meant to say was, I love the way you *make love* to me."

Chuckling, he kissed his way across her jaw, lingered

over the corner of her mouth so he could taste her smile. "I love *you*."

"Mmm, love you back. Now spoon me while we get some sleep."

She didn't have to tell him twice. Still joined, he turned her onto her side and curled around her. The quiet of the room settled around them. He felt totally at peace, except for one thing.

"How are we going to make this work?" she asked, as if she'd read his mind.

"We both put in effort. And just to be clear, I want exclusivity. No seeing other people." Just the thought of another man putting his hands on her made him go all caveman.

She snorted. "Of course, exclusive. But how are we going to make the long distance thing work? I can't move. My job is here and so is my family. I can't leave either of them."

"I know, and I can't move right now either." He kissed the top of her shoulder, breathing in the scent of shampoo and soap from the shower she'd taken last night. "Lots of people do long distance relationships. And it won't be forever. I've got around twenty months or so left in my contract, but if and when I leave the HRT, I'd always planned to put in a request for a transfer to Miami. It's home."

She nodded, seemed to relax deeper into his embrace. "So we'll just have to make it work in the meantime then. Fly back and forth or meet in between somewhere whenever we can."

"Exactly."

"Okay. Good."

He smiled at the conviction in her voice. Case closed as far as she was concerned. They were both all in, and looking to make it work long term. He'd never felt happier about anything in his life.

Holding her close, his heart full, he tucked her head beneath his chin and let himself drop into a deep sleep.

****

Matt DeLuca stood when Marisol stepped into the boardroom with Cruz right behind her. Cruz was in full protective mode, an arm wrapped securely around her waist as he pulled her into his side, and he shot a warning look at Special Agent In Charge Winter.

"Thanks for coming in," the agent said to Marisol, smiling a little as he pulled out a chair for her.

"No problem." She sat and crossed her legs, shot a quelling look at Cruz and nodded at Matt before settling her bandaged forearm across her stomach.

"How are you feeling?" Matt asked.

"I'm ok—"

"She's sore," Cruz interrupted, "and needs to be back at the hotel resting." He turned another hard look on Winter.

The agent nodded. "We'll make this as quick as we can."

Matt didn't blame Cruz for being protective of her. Matt would be the exact same way with Briar. And speaking of his lady, she should be here any minute. He'd called her in to see if she could help identify the mystery woman.

From what Marisol had said and everything the evidence pointed to, the woman may have been trained by the military or a government agency. If anyone might know about the female unsub, it was Briar.

"We've already reviewed your previous statements about what happened yesterday," Winter said. "I just wanted to question you a bit more about the woman on the boat."

Marisol shrugged, looking tired and worn. "I already

told the other agents everything I know. She said her name was Julia, and she obviously had some kind of training." She narrowed her eyes. "You still haven't found her, or figured out who she is?"

The agent sighed. "No, but we're trying. We just need a few more pieces to put—" He trailed off when a knock sounded on the glass door.

Matt turned to see Briar pushing her way into the room. Pleasure flooded him. "Hey," he said, snagging her hand to tug her close for a quick kiss. Not enough to satisfy either of them, but enough to show everyone in the room that they were together and that he was proud of it.

She gave him a secret smile that promised a lot more than a simple kiss the next time they were alone and faced Marisol. "You must be Cruz's better half."

"Well, I don't know about *better*," Marisol said, rising to take the hand Briar offered.

"I'm Briar. Matt's better half," she said, throwing a grin his way.

Marisol seemed to relax at that. "Nice to meet you."

"We were just going over some details about the woman involved in the boat incident yesterday," Winter told her.

Matt moved in behind her as Briar walked up to the desk where he had a screen displaying footage from a CCTV camera set up on the outside of a bank across the street from the Marina in South Miami. He hadn't had a chance to send her the footage beforehand.

"We know literally nothing except her alias and that she was apparently involved with *el Santo*. For the past several months she's been volunteering at the nursing facility where his grandmother is being kept. None of the staff knew much personal information about her, and what they did know was fake."

Briar nodded and braced a hand on the desk. Matt moved in and curved a hand around her hip, felt the muscles contract under his hand as he leaned in to look over her shoulder. He forced his attention to the screen.

Winter played the footage showing the woman climbing off the bike and heading to the end of the dock. When she turned to face the camera from the boat, it was only a profile shot.

"Not hugely helpful," Winter murmured, "but this is better." He tapped a few more keys and brought up the satellite images they'd taken. "This is her." A few more keystrokes tightened the resolution until her face was clear.

There was something familiar about her that was driving Matt nuts. He recognized her, but couldn't put his finger on how.

"None of the agents on scene saw her leave, and after managing to take out three men, she didn't leave any evidence behind despite the fact that she was wounded in the arm. So far she's managed to evade all law enforcement out looking for her."

When the woman's face came into clear focus, Matt felt the way Briar tensed. It was subtle, but he was so attuned to her now he picked up immediately on the change in her posture, the slight hitch in her breathing. He looked at her sharply. "You recognize her?"

Briar didn't answer, her entire body frozen as she stared at the screen. Then something like affection crossed her face and her lips curved up a fraction.

"Briar?" he prompted.

She turned to face Marisol. "What did she say her name was?"

"Julia."

"What words did she use? Did she say, 'My name is Julia'?"

Marisol frowned. "No… She said, 'Call me Julia.'"

Matt frowned too. What the hell did the wording matter? But he knew better than to question Briar when she had that look on her face.

Briar made a soft humming sound. "And you say she was involved with *el Santo*?"

"Yes," Winter answered. "They met at the nursing home, but only began seeing each other in the past week. But according to what Marisol has told us, she was emotionally invested in him."

Marisol nodded emphatically. "She was. There's no way she was faking that part. She was torn up by seeing him wounded and dying, and I know she would have followed through on her threat and shot me if I'd slowed the boat down."

Briar turned back to the screen and tilted her head. "Interesting," she murmured, and chewed her lower lip for a long moment.

Matt exchanged glances with Winter and Cruz, both of whom looked confused. "Briar," he finally said. "Tell us what you know."

Tossing her long, dark hair over one shoulder, she turned to face them, her arms folded across her chest. The air of authority radiating from her was sexy as fuck but Matt ordered himself not to think about that. "It's Georgia," she finally said.

Matt whipped his head around to stare at the screen. "The hell it is."

"It's her," Briar answered calmly, her voice certain.

Georgia Juliette Randall. He stared at the woman's face, felt a tingle go up his spine as his brain matched the image to the ones from his memory.

A Valkyrie, like Briar.

A deadly female, government-trained assassin. He'd met her in Colorado this past winter, but she'd been blond then. And she'd also been hunting Briar.

Incredulous, he turned to look at Briar as everything clicked into place. And now he knew who had killed Garcia the other night. "Jesus. Why would she be here?"

"Wait, who's Georgia?" Winter demanded. Cruz and Marisol were both watching Briar too.

She glanced at Winter. "Unfortunately, you'll need to up your security clearance before I can answer that."

The agent blinked at her and drew his head back in surprise. "What the hell?" He looked at Matt for confirmation, as if unsure whether he'd just been insulted or not.

Exhaling a hard breath, Matt nodded. "Sorry, but she's right." He rubbed a hand across his mouth as he tried to put the pieces together. "I'll be damned." He shifted his gaze back to Briar as Winter got on his phone to his supervisor and began demanding more info on their investigation.

Taking Briar by the arm, he led her toward the door. "Excuse us a minute," he said to Cruz and Marisol on the way by.

As soon as they were outside and away from anyone's earshot, he turned to face her. "Why do you think she was here in Miami? It wasn't just to take out Garcia."

Briar shook her head. "Revenge."

The single word answer sent a tingle up the back of his neck. "For what?"

"For her former handler's murder."

Frank Holland. "The guy who was murdered right after…" He didn't say Janaia's name. He knew how hard the death of her former CIA handler still was on Briar.

"Yes."

"How is that linked to Garcia or Villa?"

"Last I heard from Trinity, for the past five-plus months Georgia's been tracking two men, on suspicion that they killed her handler. Enforcers like Garcia or Villa could definitely have pulled that kind of job for extra cash, or maybe Frank had been investigating something that put him on Fuentes's hit list. Whatever she found out was enough to put them both on her hit list."

"Okay, but if you're right, how the hell did she get involved with *el Santo*? The Bureau has been hunting him for more than two years now and hasn't been able to track him down once. Yet she managed to not only locate him all on her own, but get involved with him romantically to dupe him into leading her to her target? Am I understanding that theory right?"

She nodded. "I think that's exactly what happened. She obviously found Garcia without much trouble, but she must not have been able to find Villa. So she located *el Santo* instead, knowing he was targeting Villa too. With her skill set and contacts it's not that unlikely. They had a common goal, to kill Villa, so he was probably a means to an end for her. At least, in the beginning. But apparently things changed for her along the way."

"And what about *el Santo*? Let's go with the theory that she was using him to get to Villa. Wouldn't she have to kill him too in the end? To get clear? So how do you explain her helping him yesterday?"

Briar shook her head slowly, a sad smile on her face. "She couldn't do it," she murmured, her voice slightly husky with emotion. "Maybe she followed him to Key West yesterday to get to Villa, but when she'd first tracked *el Santo* down with the intention of using him, she hadn't counted on falling for him. Then she couldn't kill him and walk away. I think she wanted to save him." She put a hand to her chest as if the thought touched her deeply and Matt heard the sadness in her voice that one of her Valkyrie sisters would be grieving the man she'd loved.

He slid a comforting arm around her shoulders. It was a lot to take in. He was having a hard enough time absorbing everything.

Glancing behind him, he saw Winter was off the phone now, and watching them through the glass door. "Okay. Let's go finish this up. He doesn't look too happy." He held the door for her and she stepped past him.

Winter snorted, looking totally bewildered as he mimicked Briar's stance with his arms folded across his chest. He must not have gotten the answers he wanted from his boss. "What is she, some kind of secret government weapon?" he said to Briar.

Pretty much, yeah.

Briar gave him a cool stare, lifted one brow in a gesture Matt knew all too well. "I could tell you, but then I'd have to kill you." Matt bit back a grin and watched the other agent's reaction.

Winter divided a scowl between him and Briar, then turned for the door. "I'm gonna go see about my security clearance," he muttered, and marched out of the room.

"In those pictures she's bleeding. Looks like a gunshot in her left forearm," Briar said, looking at the screen once more. "How badly was she injured?" She turned to Marisol.

"I didn't see her get hit," she answered. "I'm not sure how bad it was, but it didn't slow her down any. She's a friend of yours?"

"Used to be," Briar murmured, her expression a little lost. Matt put his arms around her from behind. Holding her close, knowing she wanted to begin her own investigation using her old connections to make sure Georgia was okay.

"I'm sorry," Marisol said.

Briar inclined her head. "Thanks."

Matt cleared his throat and spoke to Cruz and Marisol. "You guys can go now. Thanks for coming in. Call me if you need anything, okay?"

Cruz nodded. "I will."

"See you at the airport in the morning."

Cruz's expression tightened and he helped Marisol from her chair, clearly not looking forward to leaving Miami, and Marisol, behind. "Yeah."

Matt knew how he felt. He hated the thought of leaving Briar tomorrow too.

Epilogue

Three months later

"**M**arisol!"

Suitcase in hand, she spun away from the airport luggage carousel to ascertain the source of the female voice calling to her. Somehow she managed to cover her surprise when she spotted the woman hurrying toward her with a wide smile stretching her bright red mouth.

Her ride to Ethan's surprise birthday party wore snug black pants and a black fitted velvet dress jacket with a ruffled bustle that looked like it had come straight out of a Victorian catalogue. August in Virginia wasn't as hot and muggy as it was back in Miami, but still, the woman had to be insane to wear that.

Her long hair was jet black except for the electric shock of fuchsia running from the crown on her head and sweeping down to frame her jaw, and her skin was pale. Her eye makeup was dark and dramatic, making the golden color of her irises visible even from where Marisol stood.

"Zoe?" she asked. Ethan had told her Bauer's other

half was unorthodox, but her appearance was still a shock. It was hard to imagine this woman with Bauer, the hardest and most serious member on the team. Must be a case of opposites attract, she decided.

The woman beamed at her. "Yup, in the flesh. It's great to meet you finally," she said as she approached. Before Marisol could reply, Zoe wrapped her up in a tight hug, the spicy and exotic scent of her perfume swirling around them.

Not knowing what else to do, Marisol reached up and patted her back. Zoe was much warmer and friendlier than she'd expected, considering they'd never met.

Zoe eased back, that megawatt smile still in place. The woman was stunning, and given the Victorian-Goth flare she had going, it was little wonder people all around baggage claim were staring at her. "Sorry. I'm a hugger. Ethan didn't warn you?"

Marisol laughed. "No, but it's okay. That was a much warmer welcome than I expected."

Zoe shrugged and grabbed the handle of Marisol's suitcase then turned and walked for the exit, her gait as confident as the rest of her. "When I heard a fellow lawyer was being welcomed into the fold, I couldn't wait to meet you."

She looked nothing like any lawyer Marisol had ever met. "Oh, what kind of law do you practice?"

"I don't anymore. I was a family lawyer for a while but now I write romantic horror full time."

"Really?" Marisol filed that little tidbit away for later. What the heck was romantic horror, anyway? She'd never heard of it.

"Yep, for a while now. I love it. And it suits me better than working at a stuffy law firm anyhow," she added, giving a slight wiggle of her brows. "Congrats on the Fuentes case, by the way. It was awesome. I followed it every day and cheered like crazy when he was convicted on all counts."

Money laundering, drug and weapons trafficking, human trafficking, as well as being an accessory to over a dozen murders. "I liked it even better when he got the death penalty," she said with a smile.

"Yeah." Zoe's eyes lit with the same vengeance Marisol always felt when a criminal like Fuentes got what they deserved. "Sucks that it might not happen for years though."

"True. But I like to think it'll be an added psychological torture, knowing he's going to die by lethal injection."

"I like it. You're definitely my kind of person. Are you starving, by the way? I bet you're starving."

"A little, but I can wait to eat until I get there. I'm so sorry I'm late."

Zoe waved the apology away. "It's not your fault your plane got delayed by three hours." She cast a look at Marisol as they walked at a fast clip toward the doors. "Man, Cruzie's gonna die when he sees you. It's so great you could fly up to surprise him at the party."

"Yes. I'm dying to see him too." Excitement and anticipation fluttered in her stomach. It had been months since he'd left Miami, two days after her ordeal with Miguel and Villa.

He'd flown down to see her twice since then, but only for a day or two at a time, and this was the first time she'd been able to get away. With the flurry of activity in the aftermath of the kidnapping, then the Fuentes case and Ethan busy with training all over the country, they'd had to make do with mostly phone calls and e-mail. She missed him so much she ached.

"I'll bet. And I'll also bet this is the best birthday present he's ever gotten."

Marisol smiled. "Hope so." Actually she had one more surprise to give him, one that she was a little nervous about.

She'd had a lot of time to mull things over during the past few weeks, and she'd come to a decision. The attack and her love for Ethan had changed everything. Her priorities in life weren't the same as they had been a few months ago.

She knew what she wanted; now she was going after it. She just prayed that Ethan wanted the same thing she did.

****

"Hey, birthday boy, you want a fresh beer?" Vance asked him.

"Nah, I'm good." Ethan took a sip of his warmish one, glancing around DeLuca's living room.

Pretty great, that his teammates would throw him a surprise party for his thirtieth.

He knew Briar was still uncomfortable with social gatherings. Nevertheless, there she was, running around helping DeLuca in the kitchen where they were dishing out platter after platter of food for everyone.

Celida and Tuck had brought the cake. The three layer confection had a badge made out of icing on the front of it, with FBI in big bold letters above, and *Female Body Inspector* beneath it. He'd laughed when he'd seen it.

But there was only one female body he was interested in inspecting, and he hadn't had that privilege in over a month-and-a-half. Being apart sucked, and living so far away from each other was even worse.

He'd already checked with DeLuca to see when he could sneak away to Miami again for a few days because he couldn't stand this. He would've flown down to surprise her last night and spend his birthday with her, but this was their only day off.

"You ready for your steak?" Vance asked.

"Yeah, sure." He got up and followed his buddy outside, but Briar shooed him back in, saying as the birthday boy, he would get served.

While Vance stayed to help man the grill, he wandered across the back deck and onto the grass. Sunshine filled the decent-sized backyard. Schroder was sprawled in a deck chair near the back fence, Taya curled up on his lap while they talked with Evers and Rachel.

It was stupid, since these people were like family to him, but today he felt homesick. And...lonely. Seeing most of his teammates happily paired off made him miss Marisol even more.

He spotted Blackwell off to one side of the yard, nursing a beer while he sat on a chair all by himself. Ethan sighed. If he was having a tough time seeing all the happy couples around here, Blackwell had it worse. As usual, his wife was conspicuously absent.

Ethan ambled over and pulled up a chair beside him. "Feels good to have a day off, huh?" he asked, tipping his head back to drain his beer.

"Yeah." Blackwell watched Briar and Vance at the grill while he rolled the beer bottle between his hands. "Bet it feels even better when that day just happens to be your birthday," he said with a grin.

Ethan laughed softly. "Doesn't hurt. Hey, Vance, Evers, Tuck and I are thinking of going dirt biking later for a couple hours. You in?"

Blackwell glanced at him, then looked away. "Maybe. Summer's supposed to be finishing up an investigation today, might be flying home tonight or tomorrow. I kinda want to pick her up at the airport, see if I can get another day or two off to...talk to her. We've uh, got some things to straighten out," he finished, then cleared his throat, clearly feeling awkward.

Ethan leaned forward to set his forearms on his

knees. It was rare for Blackwell to talk about personal stuff with any of them. Ethan might not be a relationship expert, especially when he'd only just fallen in love and his girl lived over a thousand miles away, but he cared about his teammate and didn't like him going through this.

"That's good, man. I'm sure DeLuca would clear you for a couple days. We're due for equipment maintenance early this week anyhow."

Blackwell nodded, still didn't look at him. "I just…I can't go on like this, you know? I need to know, one way or the other. And I won't let her go without a fight."

Ethan nodded. He didn't know, but he could imagine. Hard enough to miss the woman you loved because she lived in the opposite end of the country, but it had to be infinitely worse to miss the wife you shared a life and a home with.

Even though he and Marisol had only been together a couple months, if things between them started to slide for whatever reason, he'd sure as hell fight to hold onto her. "How long you guys been married for now?"

"Six years, but we've been together for almost nine."

A long stretch. While Ethan didn't know Summer well at all, Blackwell sure as hell seemed like he wanted to stay together and work things out. "That's a long time." Too long, to just throw it away without trying. "Whatever happens, we're here for you, man. You know that, right?"

Blackwell looked at him, the corner of his mouth curving upward. "Yeah, I know." He reached out to slap Ethan on the back. "But I didn't come here to be a downer on your birthday, brother."

Ethan scoffed. "You're not a downer, and I appreciate you being here."

His teammate chuckled and brought his beer to his mouth with a muttered, "Don't mention it."

Vance turned around and cupped his hands around

his mouth, his deep voice ripping through the quiet like a freaking foghorn. "Food's up, come and get it while it's hot!"

"Is that the voice you used to call the pigs in back on the farm?" Ethan called out to him.

Vance merely raised an eyebrow. "You know it, baby."

Ethan grimaced. "Don't call me baby, it's creepy."

His buddy gave an exaggerated sigh. "Just gitcha ass over here and get your food so everyone else can eat, will ya?"

Ethan sauntered over, took a good-natured thump on his shoulder from Vance's big fist and picked up a plate. Turning to Briar, he fluttered his lashes. "Please, ma'am, may I have some more?"

Her lips twitched. "All right, but only because I like you."

"And I am so glad about that," he said, bumping her lightly with his elbow. "I'd hate to be on your bad side."

"Just don't do anything to hurt my man, and you'll be fine." Though she smiled as she said it, Ethan heard the steel in her voice and it made him smile.

He loaded his plate with a steak, baked potato and all the fixings before walking across the patio to grab another beer from the cooler on the deck. As he bent down, he noticed everyone watching him. He straightened, frowning, then heard whispered voices behind him, coming from inside.

Turning around, he squinted to see through the shadows in the comparatively dark living room. Zoe sauntered toward him, tucked beneath the shelter of Bauer's arm, a satisfied smile on her face. One that told him something was up.

"I'm back," she told him, as if he couldn't see that for himself. "And I picked up a little something for you while I was out. You can thank me later for that, by the way."

Before Ethan could ask anything, Bauer tugged her aside and Ethan caught sight of the woman standing behind them in the hallway.

His breath caught. "Soli!" He set down his plate, probably spilled everything all over the deck but he didn't care. He rushed for her, a huge smile splitting his face.

She grinned and walked toward him, her dark hair spilling down her back, a turquoise sundress skimming her curves. She lifted her arms toward him a second before he caught her and lifted her off the ground, hugging her so tight that she grunted then laughed.

Her arms wound around his shoulders in reply, her sweet scent wrapping around him. "Happy birthday," she murmured against his ear.

Still hardly able to comprehend that she was here, Ethan lowered her feet to the floor, took her face in his hands and kissed her. And kissed her and kissed her, until whistles and hoots and catcalls reminded him that they had an avid audience watching.

He didn't care who was watching and took his time tasting her, savoring her before lifting his head. "God, it's good to see you."

Her gorgeous ocean green eyes glowed up at him with pure joy that made his heart do a somersault. "You too. Sorry I was late. The plan was for me to be here before you arrived, so I could be part of the initial surprise."

"This is even better. I got two surprises today. But you're a thousand times better than a party," he added in a hushed whisper.

She framed his face between her palms, pressed a kiss to his lips then dropped her heels back to the floor. "You're even better looking than I remembered."

"Yeah?" He leaned in to nuzzle her cheek, let his lips slide across her jawline. "And you look good enough to eat." He raised his head. "How long are you staying for?"

"That depends."

"On?" It wasn't like her to be all evasive.

"Okay, okay," Schroder said from somewhere behind them, "present time's over. Now get out here and eat so the rest of us can get fed."

Ethan linked his hand with hers. "Hungry?"

Her eyes turned heavy-lidded in a way that sent half his blood volume rushing south to between his legs. *"Famished."*

Oh, man, he couldn't freaking wait to get her alone. The thought of taking her home to his place later, laying her down in his bed and making love to her there, had him grinning like an idiot. He couldn't wipe the smile from his face as he stepped onto the deck with her. "Who set this up, anyway?"

"Vance and DeLuca. Then Zoe volunteered to come get me at the airport. We figured it would look less suspicious if she ditched the party all of a sudden, rather than one of the guys."

"Damn, you guys are good."

She flashed him a grin. "I know."

After getting her a plate they sat and ate with the others. Seeing her chat with all his friends, relaxed and happy, filled his heart to bursting.

When they were done Marisol set her empty plate aside and slid into his lap, the soft weight of her pressing against his groin making him bite back a groan. He wrapped both arms around her waist from behind and cradled her to his chest. This was the best birthday ever.

A little while later, the others started making excuses and going inside. Tuck said something about having to get the cake ready and Vance wandered over to start cleaning the grill.

"I guess they wanted to give us some privacy," Marisol murmured to him, amusement in her voice.

"Guess so. Now let me look at you." He turned her toward him, cupped the side of her face in one hand. "God, you're beautiful." He grinned when she blushed. She was so freaking adorable and precious. "I've missed you so damn much."

"I've missed you too." She threaded her hands into his hair, rubbed his head in a way that made him want to growl. "And I can't wait for you to take me home to your place later."

"Oh, kitt'n, the things I want to do to you…" He'd been storing up fantasies for weeks now.

"Looking forward to each and every one of those," she said with a naughty smile. "Vance told me you guys might have some down time over the next few days, depending on how the scheduling works out."

"I sure as hell hope so, now that you're here." He squeezed her to him, loving the feel of her soft curves melding to his body. "I want at least a few solid days with you before you go back home."

She slid a hand down the back of his neck. "Yeah, about that…"

He focused on her eyes. "What?"

She sat up a bit. "I've been doing some thinking."

That didn't sound good. "About?"

"About us. About how much I miss you and how much I hate being so far apart all the time. With our schedules we'll barely ever get to see each other."

An invisible fist tightened around his stomach. "So what are you saying?" He knew it was hard, but there was no help for it right now, and he'd been clear on his stance.

Yes, he loved his job and the guys he worked with, but he was willing to move once he was able. But he couldn't leave until his contract was up, and since her job prevented her from leaving Miami, there was nothing they could do at this point.

Which left them the only option of commuting back

and forth whenever they could.

"Well, I'm saying that I realized something had to give."

He stared at her, his heart pumping fast. He didn't want to jump to conclusions, but given that she'd flown here to surprise him and the way she was broaching this subject, he couldn't help the hope that unfurled inside him. "And?"

She exhaled, curled her hands around the tops of his shoulders. "You've got about a year-and-a-half left on your contract, right?"

"Yeah." He loved being part of the HRT, but he'd give it up for her. Once his four-year minimum term ended he'd transfer to the Miami office so they could be together.

"So I was thinking I could move up here for a while."

His jaw nearly hit the floor. He gripped her waist tighter and stared at her intently, wanting to be sure he'd heard her right. "Are you serious?"

She smiled, nodded. "I packed a really big suitcase, just in case you wanted me to stay a little longer than a few days."

He did, he totally did, but he didn't want her to make that sacrifice if it would make her resentful later on. "What about your job?"

"With the Fuentes case all wrapped up, I started putting out feelers. Frank and a few of my old profs put in a good word for me and provided the last round of interviews goes well, I've got a job with the U.S. Attorney in Alexandria if I want it. It's a bit of a commute for me, but it's doable. And if it allows me to come home to you every night, then I'm all in."

"Really? It's not a step back for you?" She was so driven and career-oriented and she'd landed such an awesome job at such a young age. He didn't want her to give that up.

She nodded. "Not really, and you mean more to me than whatever job I have anyway. I love you, and I can't stand being apart from you anymore."

Ethan was stunned. This felt surreal. He couldn't believe she'd do that for him when he knew exactly how much her life and career back in Miami meant to her.

He blinked against the sting of tears, and when he spoke his voice was rough. "I love you so much."

Smiling at him, Marisol bent to cover his mouth with hers. Ethan crushed her to him and kissed her hard, sliding his tongue inside to taste her. His heart felt like it was about to burst, along with his cock. He wanted to get her naked right now and worship every inch of her body.

Breathless, she pulled back a few seconds later, a dark blush staining her cheeks. Then she laughed. "You make me lose my head," she said, fussing with her hair now that he'd mussed it. "I forgot we were sitting here in the middle of your birthday party."

He dropped his voice to a sensual growl and tugged her closer. "Just wait until you see what I do with you when I get you home," he told her.

With a mysterious smile, she pushed up from his lap and grabbed his hand. "Then let's go let them sing happy birthday to you so we can have some cake and get out of here. I've got one more present for you to unwrap once we get back to your place." She trailed a hand down the V at the front of her dress, her fingers toying suggestively with the flimsy ties holding the two halves together.

"*Our* place," he corrected.

Her smiled widened and she nodded. "Yeah. Our place."

Boom. His heart exploded with pride and happiness. *I'm asking her to marry me tonight.*

He already had the ring, had been planning to wait until the next time he went to Miami to pop the question. But he couldn't wait anymore. She'd given up everything for him, her career, her home and her family. He would give her all of him in return.

She arched a brow at him as they headed toward the back deck. "What's that sly smile all about?"

He shook his head. "Nothing."

Already dying to get her alone so he could get down on one knee and ask her to be his wife, then find out what she had on underneath that wrap dress, Ethan curved a proprietary arm around her and walked back into the house where his second family was waiting for them.

—The End—

Thank you for reading EXPOSED. I really hope you enjoyed it and that you'll consider leaving a review at one of your favorite online retailers. It's a great way to help other readers discover new books.

If you liked EXPOSED and would like to read more, turn the page for a list of my other books. And if you don't want to miss any future releases, please feel free to join my newsletter. Direct link:
http://kayleacross.com/v2/contact/

Complete Booklist

Romantic Suspense
Hostage Rescue Team Series
Marked
Targeted
Hunted
Disavowed
Avenged
Exposed

Titanium Security Series
Ignited
Singed
Burned
Extinguished
Rekindled

Bagram Special Ops Series
Deadly Descent
Tactical Strike
Lethal Pursuit
Danger Close
Collateral Damage

Suspense Series
Out of Her League
Cover of Darkness
No Turning Back
Relentless
Absolution

Paranormal Romance
Empowered Series

Darkest Caress

Historical Romance
The Vacant Chair

Erotic Romance (writing as *Callie Croix*)
Deacon's Touch
Dillon's Claim
No Holds Barred
Touch Me
Let Me In
Covert Seduction

Acknowledgements

Thanks so much to my personal A-Team for helping me get this manuscript ready for publication!

My awesome buddy and crit partner Katie Reus, my beta reader Kim, editor Joan, and proofreader extraordinaire, my fabulous and supportive DH. I love you guys!

About the Author

NY Times and USA Today Bestselling author Kaylea Cross writes edge-of-your-seat military romantic suspense. Her work has won many awards and has been nominated for both the Daphne du Maurier and the National Readers' Choice Awards. A Registered Massage Therapist by trade, Kaylea is also an avid gardener, artist, Civil War buff, Special Ops aficionado, belly dance enthusiast and former nationally-carded softball pitcher. She lives in Vancouver, BC with her husband and family.

You can visit Kaylea at www.kayleacross.com. If you would like to be notified of future releases, please join her newsletter. Direct link:http://kayleacross.com/v2/contact/